Patrick flinched but made no sound.

Once the wound was clean, Catherine poured the ale into the angry flesh. This time, Patrick swore. "What the bloody—?"

"You've been wounded," she answered, mopping the perspiration from her forehead with her lower arm.

"It isn't the first time. What do you think you're doing?"

"I'm trying to kill the poison."

"And me along with it. What's this?" He grabbed the cask from her hand.

"It's ale. I'm using it as medicine."

"Well, you're putting it in the wrong place," he said, raising himself up on one elbow and taking a long swallow.

Catherine would have reprimanded him, but she was so glad to see the light back in his eyes that she swallowed her protest.

Patrick didn't swallow his. "What happened to my clothes?" He was looking down at his half-nude body in disbelief....

Dear Reader,

November brings us another great month of historicals, all by your favorite authors!

Our big book pick this month is the long-awaited reissue of *Pieces of Sky* by Marianne Willman. In this dramatic and emotional novel, Norah O'Shea flees her isolated past for freedom and adventure in the Wild West. But she is not prepared for the harsh reality of the American frontier—or the sensuality of Comanche Indian Scout Sergeant LeBeau.

In *Deception,* Ruth Langan—author of the popular TEXAS and HIGHLAND series—brings us the provocative story of nobleman Shane Driscoll and street urchin Claire Fleetwood who become partners in a royal jest, but wind up in the midst of a deadly conspiracy.

Laurel Ames made her debut as a 1993 March Madness author with *Teller of Tales.* We are delighted to bring you her latest book, *Castaway.* Sea captain Nathan Gaites gets more than he bargained for as the unexpected "heir apparent" of his estranged family, especially when he falls in love with his prickly "cousin" Margaret in this charming tale.

Grieving a lost beau, Catherine Caden makes a desperate attempt to find her true love by seeking the aid of the infamous river pirate Patrick McLendon.

We hope you enjoy these titles, and look for our 1993 historical Christmas short story collection, *Christmas Keepsakes,* with stories by Curtiss Ann Matlock, Marianne Willman and Victoria Pade.

Sincerely,

Tracy Farrell
Senior Editor

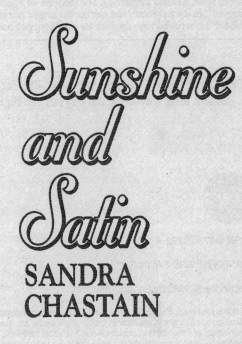

Sunshine and Satin

SANDRA CHASTAIN

Harlequin Books

TORONTO • NEW YORK • LONDON
AMSTERDAM • PARIS • SYDNEY • HAMBURG
STOCKHOLM • ATHENS • TOKYO • MILAN
MADRID • WARSAW • BUDAPEST • AUCKLAND

For Kathe Bray, a dear friend, who, like me, has come a long way since the days of the Signal

ISBN 0-373-28798-4

SUNSHINE AND SATIN

Books by Sandra Chastain

Harlequin Historicals

Jasmine and Silk #156
Sunshine and Satin #198

SANDRA CHASTAIN

started out to be an actress but failed miserably at losing her Southern accent. She switched to journalism, where she failed again because, according to the editor of her college newspaper, she could never tell what, when and why without embellishing the story. In the meantime, she got married, raised three daughters and worked full-time alongside her veterinarian husband in their animal medical clinic in Smyrna, Georgia. Now a devoted historical romance writer, she's happy as a pig in a puddle of Georgia mud, doing what she loves best—spinning tales of passion and adventure for all the perennially young who believe in the magic of love.

The Legend

It is said that in a time long past, a time of great chaos and uncertainty for the Natchez people, there appeared a mysterious messenger from the Great Spirit. He was called the Great Sun.

The Great Sun, proclaimed the absolute ruler of the Natchez, was aided by a powerful female called the White Woman. These representatives of the spirit world set up a new structure of society, creating laws and customs by which the tribe was to live. It was believed that so long as the Great Sun and the White Woman were honored, the Natchez would prevail.

But new chaos came, and the Great Sun and the White Woman were enslaved and taken away, and the Natchez knew that chaos would remain until the Great Sun and the White Woman returned.

Prologue

Calabozo Prison,
New Orleans, March 1793

Patrick McLendon thought he'd experienced heat. He hadn't—not until now.

In this place, even the walls dripped. His clothes, what was left of them, stuck to his lean body as perspiration trickled down his brow and stung his eyes. But the physical discomfort was little more than an annoyance. He'd suffered worse.

It was the anguish of losing his ship and his good name that tore at his soul, of not keeping his promise to Catherine and being unable to tell her why.

Everything had changed. Even he. With his flowing beard and unkempt hair, Catherine wouldn't even want him now. Patrick McLendon was no longer the well-to-do Irish adventurer who'd promised to return to the woman he loved.

Fourteen months earlier, his ship, the *Savannah Lady,* loaded with goods for trade, had been swept off course by a hurricane. He'd sought refuge on a small island and been thrust into the midst of a slave uprising. Frightened plantation owners had commandeered his ship. When Patrick protested leaving his goods behind, they'd imprisoned him in the hold and sailed his ship to New Orleans.

Before reaching the city, they were stopped by the Spanish port official commissioned to collect tariffs from all foreign ships. One plantation owner paid his tariff but resisted paying the additional bribe demanded by the greedy official. When he was later found dead, Patrick, already a prisoner, was falsely blamed for his murder. Captain Lopaz, the military officer on duty, followed his superior's orders and confiscated Patrick's ship.

To make certain they'd covered their larceny the official had Patrick beaten and left for dead in the holding cell where other rebellious slaves were imprisoned. Later, a barely conscious Patrick, and Pharoah, an old slave who'd come to his rescue, were transported to the Spanish hellhole called the Calabozo.

But Patrick hadn't died as they'd planned.

With every day that passed in the squalid cell, his pain and anger festered, growing into a need for revenge so strong that Patrick swore he'd find a way to make the Spanish pay for what he lost to them.

Months later they were joined by a Natchez Indian boy called Jillico, who had been arrested and beaten for accidentally splashing mud on the boots of a prominent New Orleans businessman.

When, at last, members of the boy's tribe managed to signal their presence beyond the prison, Jillico had found a broken piece of metal and made a small crack in the wall through which they could communicate.

Nightly, for months thereafter, the prisoners dug at the mortar between the bricks with the broken sliver of an old manacle while they learned each other's language. Time passed in a haze of heat, damp and darkness.

But time didn't matter. Freedom did.

Freedom, and revenge.

"Shhh..." Jillico's hand touched Patrick's, bringing tonight's digging to a stop. Only the sound of raspy breathing and the constant plop of moisture falling from the wattle-and-sand ceiling could be heard.

Moments later the hand slipped away and Patrick returned to his task. So dark was their prison and so seldom were they allowed out of their cells that they were in little danger of discovery from the drunken jailers, who normally ventured into the cells below only once a day to bring tepid water and the thin gruel they called food. Nevertheless, discovery would have meant instant death.

The last block would be removed tonight. On the other side of the cubicle, Pharaoh, too weak now to help with the escape, waited in the fetid darkness.

"Are you sure they'll be outside?" Patrick whispered.

"Yes. Hurry now."

The block was removed from its place and stacked on the spongy ground beyond the wall. The call of a night bird sounded from deep inside the dark swamp.

"The signal," the slim youth said. He stepped outside, stopped and waited. The eerie sound came again. Jillico turned back. "Come, quickly."

But Patrick paused. He couldn't leave Pharaoh.

Jillico looked over his shoulder, understood Patrick's dilemma and held out his hand to the old man. "Come with us, my friend. I will take you to heaven."

Patrick helped Pharaoh to his feet and Jillico guided him out the opening and into the murky night. They might have made it without incident if the slave hadn't fallen and cried out.

"Who goes there?"

The prison guard on the platform above started down the stairway, his pistol drawn. Too late now to escape detection. Patrick planted himself between Jillico and the guard. He didn't see the second guard, the one whose bayonet sliced through his damp clothes into his shoulder. Neither did Patrick see the dark-skinned men who dropped from the moss-hung cypress trees overhead and made quick work of the Spanish jailers, then assisted the prisoners into the small boats that slid through the brackish waters of the bayoulike shadows.

Only Patrick's hatred for his Spanish captors kept him alive, that and the memory of another body of water and the laughter of a young woman with hazel eyes who'd begged him to love her. He hovered between the dark netherworld of what he recognized as hell and a consciousness that was too filled with pain to be welcome.

Yet even in his shadow world of half life, Patrick felt the memory of Catherine's bright spirit, felt it and struggled to reach the sunshine of her smile.

And then one morning he felt the return of warmth.

Patrick opened his eyes and closed them just as quickly. A second try confirmed his first impression. He was lying on a pink satin bed, draped with filmy pink hangings. His body was absolutely nude, and the woman bending over him was a golden-haired angel with lips the color of strawberries.

"I'm alive?" he asked, his voice hoarse and so scratchy as to sound less like a man's and more like that of one of hell's agents.

"You're alive."

"Where am I?"

"You're in heaven."

"Who are . . . ?"

"I'm called Isabella Angel."

"Angel? Of course," he whispered. "I knew you would be. . . ."

Chapter One

*Spanish territory
along the Mississippi River
July 1794*

Tomorrow was to be Catherine Caden's wedding day.

Tomorrow she was to marry the wrong man.

If the wedding had taken place immediately on Charles's arrival at Weatherby's Trading Post she might have gotten through it. But it hadn't, and now the night hours loomed ahead, filled with doubt and regret.

Bats darted across the midsummer night sky, swooping between the glow of the campfire burning beside the river and the trading post where Catherine stood at the window of her tiny loft room. She stared out at the Mississippi River where the Spanish boat her future husband had hired passage on was moored, and tried to remember why she'd ever thought she could marry Charles Forrest.

The dark, lazy water slapped at the riverboat, pushing it against the smaller pirogue as if trying to nudge it away from the bank. At feeding time she'd seen the horses back on Cadenhill, her family plantation in Georgia, do the same thing.

Catherine let out a deep sigh, wishing that she were back home. She wished that it were 1791 again and she were still sixteen, boldly falling in love with a laughing, golden-haired Irishman who refused her naughty advances and teased her about her taking liberties with his person.

That long-ago morning, on her way into Petersburg, she'd become caught up in a herd of pigs being driven to market. The pigs had spooked her horse and she'd been thrown. In the melee that followed, she'd expected to be killed by pigs' feet. Instead, she'd been caught in midair by a stranger with sun-streaked hair and teasing blue eyes, the most beautiful blue eyes she'd ever seen.

"Oh, I'm sorry," she'd finally managed to say. "I truly do thank you for saving me. You can put me down now."

"Begorra, lass! I don't think you want me to put you down right here," he'd answered. "No bigger than you are, little darling, the mud would likely cover you and not even the little people would find you in that muck."

"I'm Catherine Caden," she'd said with no attempt to keep the bemusement from her voice. "And I'm sixteen. What's your name, Irishman?"

"Patrick McLendon, darling. And I'm thirty. Do you always travel with such an unusual entourage?"

"Entourage? Oh, the pigs. Certainly not. I don't know where those dreadful things came from."

Later Patrick said he'd thought her small and pert, with impish eyes that were neither green nor brown, but somewhere between, and strawberry-colored hair that shone like a halo of silk in the sun.

She'd decided in that moment that he was the man she would marry, and she'd seen no reason to conceal that fact. In the middle of Petersburg she'd proposed, and quickly, before Patrick had known what she was doing, she'd closed her eyes and pursed her lips.

"I'd like you to kiss me, please, Patrick McLendon," she'd said and waited.

Caught up in the spirit of the moment, Patrick had joined in the game. "You wish to be kissed? Never let it be said that an Irishman refused to kiss a beautiful woman."

Afterward it had taken her weeks to convince him that she was serious, and in the end he hadn't been able to refuse. He'd spoken to her brother-in-law, Rushton Randolph, head of the family, and promised to come back for her.

Now, almost three years later, she was in the Louisiana Territory, about to marry a man she barely knew.

Around the trading post, stately cypress trees dressed in hanging wisps of gray Spanish moss stood like sentries keeping out the marshy swamp and wild animals that prowled its wilderness. There was something wonderful about this new land, something challenging and alive—like Patrick.

If only she were seeing it with Patrick.

If Catherine's life had gone according to plan she'd be Mrs. Patrick McLendon, experiencing the most exciting time of her life with a bold adventurer. But that was not to be; Patrick was gone, and Charles was here.

Charles. During the few short weeks that Charles had stayed at Cadenhill, Catherine had come to enjoy his company. She'd thought to continue those pleasant feelings, expecting them to grow. But yesterday, when he stepped off the flatboat and made his way up from the dock to meet her, she had realized that he was little more than a fancy-dressed stranger. She'd begun to have second thoughts.

"You needn't worry, Catherine," Mrs. Weatherby was saying now as she laid the wedding gown across the rope bed. "It's not unexpected. Every young bride has an attack of the vapors on the night before her wedding. You're only nineteen and away from your mother. It's normal."

"Where's Charles?" Catherine turned away from the window. She'd known that he was disappointed when, after supper, she'd refused his invitation to walk along the river. But she'd listened to him complain about the humidity, about the muddy water, about the danger of meeting the pirate, Stone, as he made his way upriver from New Orleans, until she couldn't listen anymore. She'd pleaded a headache and retired.

"He and the flatboat captain are having a drop of spirits with the minister and Mr. Weatherby," Mrs. Weatherby answered. "They're full of the tales about that river pirate. I told them they don't have to worry. He only robs the Spanish and their friends—after they've completed their business with the folks along the river. Stone is very careful that none of the little people suffer."

"He sounds like an odd pirate," Catherine commented, wishing that he'd come sailing up the river and steal her away. That would solve her problem and she wouldn't be responsible. A pirate's life sounded like a grand adventure.

"Your Mr. Forrest wants to wait until another boat comes down the river. Traveling in a group is safer."

"Yes." She sighed. "Charles is conscientious. He was personally selected by President Washington to come to New Orleans and deal with the problems over river trade. He has a bright future."

Catherine couldn't decide whether she was trying to convince Mrs. Weatherby, or herself. Conscientious was certainly not a word anybody would ever have used in describing Patrick, and Catherine would have gone with him anywhere.

"He said that you'd met the President. Imagine that," Mrs. Weatherby went on.

"Yes, I met him three years ago in Augusta when he was visiting each of the new states."

Three years ago, Catherine thought, when she and Patrick had danced at the festivities honoring the President, and when, in order to protect Cadenhill, her sister, Amanda, had surprised everyone by marrying a man she barely knew, a man she said she didn't love.

But Amanda had been wrong. She'd been in love with her new husband, Rush, even then; she just hadn't known it. As Catherine waited for Patrick to send word from New Orleans, she'd watched their love grow.

Patrick had promised to come back for her, but he hadn't. Then, the report had come that Patrick had been accused of murder by Spanish officials, who confiscated and sold his ship. Some time later she received the terrible news: Patrick was dead.

Catherine wondered if she would learn to love Charles. She knew little about love, only that she didn't feel about Charles the way she had about Patrick.

Of course, she'd been only sixteen then.

And Patrick had been a man who was bigger than life, spouting blarney and romantic nonsense. Everyone had told her to forget the Irishman. But she hadn't, even after the news of his death, and she'd refused to believe that Patrick was truly gone.

The unbearable months had passed and, little by little, she had lost her confidence. Until finally she'd retreated into a private world that held no joy and no future.

Everything had been different before the war, before Amanda married Rush, before Patrick came. She'd been a child, barely aware of the revolution. When Papa was home, her mother had laughed and life had been good. They'd visited neighbors, traveled down to Augusta. Then Papa had been wounded and Amanda had been the one to ride the fields and see to the planting.

Cadenhill had been Catherine's entire world then. But after Papa died, nothing was ever the same. There were no more parties, no money for new dresses and little social activity. Catherine had begun to grow up, to understand that there were dark spaces that nothing could fill.

No one had time to see Catherine's hurt, or understand the loneliness of a girl caught between childhood and an uncertain future.

Then one sunny day Patrick had come to Petersburg, and the world was bright again.

Catherine had fallen in love and Patrick had finally stopped resisting her and allowed himself to love her, too. But he'd sailed away, never to return.

She hadn't expected ever to marry. Then, en route to New Orleans to accept his new post, Charles Forrest had come to Petersburg to visit Amanda's husband, and delayed his departure to conduct a whirlwind courtship of Catherine.

Eventually, she'd agreed to consider his proposal. He hadn't seemed dismayed when she told him about her betrothal to Patrick. In fact he'd understood her commitment, even agreeing to confirm the details of Patrick's death before they were wed.

There seemed to be little reason not to agree to marry Charles. Because of him, she would learn the truth, and maybe then she could forget Patrick and get on with her life. At least she'd get away from Petersburg, where everyone looked at her with pity. Charles had spoken with Rush. He'd even talked with Judge Taliferro before he finally departed, leaving Catherine behind for a second time.

But Charles had hardly left when the doubts began. How could she have promised to wed anyone when she still felt connected to Patrick?

Then Catherine learned that the Weatherbys of South Carolina were journeying across country to open a trading post on the Mississippi just upriver from Natchez. She couldn't wait any longer for word about Patrick. She would accompany her mother's old friend, Mavis Weatherby. One way or another, she'd get on with her life. Reluctantly, but with her daughter's happiness in mind, Iris Caden had agreed to allow Catherine to make the trip.

To Catherine, the wagon trip had been glorious. Even the rough living at a trading post was exciting. The river was the connection between the Northern wilderness and the Spanish-held port on the Gulf.

Sailing ships, flatboats, Indians and traders on horse-back stopped at the post on their way down the mighty river—all people who might know something about Patrick.

But no one did. Finally, after six months of asking about Patrick McLendon, only to be told nobody had ever heard of him, Catherine had resigned herself to the truth. The Weatherbys, with Catherine's best interest at heart, sent word to Charles of her presence. Weeks later, Charles arrived, confirming that Patrick had been mortally wounded while defending his ship.

Catherine hadn't expected Charles to have news of Patrick, and his report had depressed her far more than she'd allowed him to know. It hadn't given her the peace of mind she'd expected. She didn't *feel* Patrick's death. Something deep inside still told her he couldn't be dead. The feeling wouldn't go away.

Now Catherine was letting Mrs. Weatherby attribute her unease to bridal jitters. The older woman, trying to reassure her, gave her arm a gentle squeeze of understanding. "You mustn't worry, Catherine. You'll do fine. Charles is a lucky man."

"Yes," Catherine agreed sharply, no longer sure that either of them was lucky. Mrs. Weatherby uttered a few more platitudes, to which Catherine couldn't respond. She didn't know when her hostess left.

Catherine paced the tiny room. She wished for her sister, Amanda. She even wished for her mother. She hadn't truly known what to expect when she agreed to accept Charles's proposition. Every woman was supposed to marry, and he'd seemed like a good choice. But faced with the ceremony, Cathering felt despair come crashing over her like the Broad River slamming against her papa's mill in a storm. Each new wave of fear further underscored her doubts.

Perhaps she'd tell Charles that she needed more time to renew their acquaintance. But they already knew each other better than many couples did on their wedding day.

The truth was, she couldn't find a reason good enough to justify a further delay, even to herself. And though the Weatherbys were kind, she'd worn out her welcome.

Catherine recalled how Mavis and the minister's wife had explained very carefully what would be expected of her on the wedding night. All she had to do was submit herself to her husband, be a dutiful wife, and love would come.

Catherine didn't tell them that there was a time when she'd tried desperately to force another man to make her his wife, a man whose kisses and firm body she'd welcomed, a man who'd refused to soil her when she'd been more than ready to learn all the mysteries of being a woman.

The slim brown-haired young man downstairs would make a proper husband. He came from a good family and had a promising future in the government. Even if Catherine felt nothing for Charles, she could learn to be a good wife. Passion wasn't required to make a marriage. Besides, living in New Orleans would surely offer enough excitement to fill her life.

The room grew more and more stuffy. Feeling the tension crawl up her backbone like a many-legged spider, she finally accepted that she was not going to be able to sleep. She needed air. A walk along the river, alone, would be calming. Sliding over the windowsill she crept down the slanted roof to the section over the woodshed and dropped quietly to the ground.

By following the tree line she avoided the open yard between the trading post and the river, where moonlight shone as bright as day. As she made her way to her favorite rock near the dock where the flatboat was moored, she could hear the crewman talking and she sat down to listen.

"*Oui,* and he is big, a very big man, with great hands and powerful arms...."

"He don't smile, Frenchy, and he don't speak much," Catherine heard the second man say in a low guttural voice.

"*Sí,*" a third man agreed. "This is why my cousin, the Spanish governor, Colonel Grancois Louis Hector, Baron de Carondelet, says he is called Stone."

"Hah! You just spread out the man's name to make it sound as if you are personally acquainted with the governor," Frenchy said.

"But I am. He is my honorable cousin."

"You may be Spanish, but he is no cousin of yours, you bragging fool. Too bad the boat, she isn't already loaded with the pelts. We could make much money."

"*Sí,* and you'd have the captain after you from behind, and Stone waiting in front. He never touches the boat until the Spanish have paid for the goods they carry."

"Ah, you're such a coward. You're just as afraid as Monsieur Forrest. He almost soiled his fancy trousers so worried is he about that golden-haired Irishman."

"So am I," the Spaniard replied. "It's said that he travels with leprechauns. He claims to have the magic to protect him."

Golden-haired Irishman who traveled with leprechauns? Catherine crept closer. Stone was an Irishman? Tales of the river pirate had spread up and down the river for nearly eight months. She'd known the outlaw had long hair and a beard, but until now, nobody had said that he was an Irishman. And the only Irishman she knew who claimed he traveled with leprechauns was Patrick.

"Well, one thing about the pirate, he's good for our purses," the gravelly voiced speaker said. "The captain, he don't get nobody to sign on now unless he pay good coin."

Catherine didn't wait to hear any more.

It was too much to hope that this pirate was Patrick, but the man they called Stone might know Patrick's fate. More certain than ever that her impending wedding would be a mistake, she desperately reconsidered her situation.

If Patrick were dead, she had to know, without doubt. If there was a chance Patrick was still alive, she would find him. If it took asking Stone for help, she'd do it.

Besides, marrying Charles wouldn't be fair to him.

But if she remained here, the Weatherbys would likely follow her mother's wishes and insist that she go through with the ceremony. The only way she could avoid that was if she weren't here in the morning. She had to leave, look for Stone herself. But first she'd go downriver to Natchez-under-the-Hill. That was where all the criminals gathered, there she'd pay for information. Somehow she'd get to Stone.

As she worked out the details in her mind, the three sailors settled down until eventually the night was quiet. She heard Charles leave the trading post and go next door with the minister with whom he was staying overnight. Mr. Weatherby and the captain left the post, too, and started down the path to check the security of the boat.

Catherine scrambled to her feet and dashed back inside to her room. By the light of a candle she penned two letters. The first was to her mother, begging her to understand why Catherine had to end her engagement to Charles. The second letter was harder. She composed and discarded several, before finally settling for a brief note apologizing to Charles for running away.

When the house was quiet once more, she crept back down the stairs and, with her money sewn into the hem of her skirt and a few necessities tied up in her shawl, slipped into the night. She'd take the one-man pirogue. Surely she could handle the small dugout.

But she couldn't take any chances on Charles coming after her. With a knife she'd borrowed from the store she sawed through the mooring rope, allowing Charles's flatboat to move lazily off downriver, trusting that the sailors would sleep through its departure. Once she found Patrick, he'd compensate the captain for his loss.

With the crew already licking their lips over the goods on board, and the captain having been invited to sleep in the store, luck might make her escape possible.

Catherine climbed into the shallow boat, picked up the pole and pushed off.

"Stone, you Irish rogue, why don't you go back and get her, whoever she is?" Isabella reached into the fireplace and withdrew a burning branch to light the pipe she held between her teeth.

"There is no one waiting for Stone," Patrick answered. *And to the world Patrick McLendon is dead.*

Stone watched Isabella, appreciating the voluptuous body that spilled from the satin wrapper that hung open as she leaned forward to throw the branch back into the fire. Isabella Angel was truly beautiful, and he knew the envy that he aroused in the other men who frequented her establishment in Natchez-under-the-Hill.

Patrick still didn't know why Isabella had taken him in when he escaped from prison, but she had, offering safe haven to Pharaoh as well. Later, she'd teasingly explained that she couldn't resist a man so given to pretty words he must have kissed the Blarney stone at least twice.

From that chance remark had come the name by which Patrick was now known, and Stone was forever welcome among the various gambling dens, saloons and trading offices that lined Water Street.

Isabella's building, like the others, extended over the river in the rear, with a secret escape hatch for quick exit by delinquent sailors. That was where the similarity ended. Heaven's exterior was as elegant as that of any London bank. Part brick and part wood, her house had an ornate balcony, trimmed with iron, wrapped around its front. Inside, fine rugs covered her floors and satin brocades hung at her windows and covered her beds. Slaves under the careful eye of Patrick's old cellmate, Pharaoh, kept the peace, ejected the riffraff and did Isabella's bidding.

After months of searching for the man who'd sent him to jail, Captain Hector Lopaz, Patrick was tired, so damn tired. The Spanish army captain had disappeared.

Now, underneath Patrick's constant feeling of weariness there was a strong sense of unease. He'd learned to live with looking over his shoulder a long time ago, but this curious prickling sensation was new and he could find no reason for it. His life on the river had always put him in danger, both from the elements and from those who hunted for the Irish pirate with a price on his head.

For weeks he'd had the feeling that he was being watched, that there was someone standing behind him. He'd turn and find nothing. Even Jillico, the Indian boy who'd been his constant companion since they broke out of prison eight months ago, had begun to avoid approaching him without warning.

"I said," Isabella tried again, "why don't you go back for her, Stone?"

"For whom?"

"The wench who fills your heart and keeps you from being wholly mine."

"You know me too well, Bella. But I can't go back. The man I once was is no more."

"Then what's wrong?" Isabella came to stand beside him, looking down at the man she'd taken into her bed and into her heart.

"I'm not sure. But something isn't right. I can't put my finger on it, but like the storm, it's coming."

"More superstitions?" She sat on the bed beside him, letting her fingertips play across his bare chest.

"Maybe." He might have told her that when he wasn't dreaming of Catherine he'd begun to dream of another woman—a shadow figure who never came clear. Where Catherine brought joy and light, the other woman brought a sense of foreboding.

"Who is she, Stone, this woman who haunts you when your mind runs free? Does she love you?"

"Once, she loved me—perhaps. But that was in the past. I gave her my word I'd return, and I didn't."

"But you were in prison. Now you're free."

"Yes, but I was accused of murder. I lost everything—my ship, my name. Now I'm a different kind of criminal, a thief. I couldn't ask her to marry a murderer then or a pirate with a price on his head now."

"So you come to me and wish for her."

"Of course not, Bella. No man could wish for a more beautiful, exciting lover than Isabella Angel."

"No other man, but you." She stood and walked back to the fire, drawing on her pipe and staring vacantly into the flames as if she, too, were remembering. "That's all right, Stone. Perhaps that's why we get on so well, we respect each other's secrets."

"That we do, darling. Now come and give us a kiss." And with those words, he forced away his melancholy. He'd never taken Catherine, never loved her completely, though she'd made his life hell because he'd constantly refused. But whenever he was with Isabella all he could see were hazel eyes that sparkled with mischief, and a small, pert face filled with sunshine. She'd been hardly more than a child, yet she'd stolen his heart and he couldn't sever the tie that existed between them.

"There's a storm brewing, Stone."

"I know. I'd better be away from here," he replied, pulling on his rough canvas trousers and heavy blue shirt, "Time to take care of business." Soft boots, his riverman's neckerchief and captain's cap, and he was ready to go.

"Sometimes I think you're only half here anyway, my pirate," Bella said with a low laugh. "You allow me to borrow you for a while, then that river claims you or you hear a report that your Lopaz has returned, and you're off again like some wild bird caught in the wind."

He gave a low, wicked laugh and kissed her, giving her bare bottom an intimate caress. "Keep a light in the window, darlin'," he quipped as he went through the door.

The men were already waiting on his boat. Quickly they shoved off, making their way to the other side and upriver to the narrowed section of the Mississippi known as Necktie Bend. From the cliffs beyond, they could pick out their victims, and from the shore they could board any unsuspecting boat caught by the current and stranded on one of the shifting sandbars.

The rain made their prey easier to stop, but it made identification of the Spanish vessels harder. Americans and Frenchmen from the Northwest were allowed to pass. The men had grumbled about that at first, until they learned that Stone only robbed pirates or Spanish traders and officials. Only one man made the mistake of questioning Stone's peculiar code of ethics, and he never did it a second time.

Spanish coins were widely available, and cargoes of slaves, brought upriver by the pirates and listed as cattle on the Spanish records, made easy prey, though Stone never sold a human being. His band of followers had become larger than he could care for until he bought an indigo plantation from a Spanish nobleman whose wife longed to return to Spain. Stone had given the men free rein of the place and set them to growing food, caring for the indigo and clearing new land for the planting of cotton. He was rapidly accomplishing his goal of obtaining land and a home without stealing from either the French or the American traders. But there was still a price on his head and the man who was responsible had disappeared.

Until he could clear his name, Patrick could never return for Catherine. Patrick McLendon was Stone, the river pirate, and Stone would continue to plunder the river and rob the corrupt officials who'd stolen his dream, all the while waiting for Lopaz to return.

Chapter Two

Catherine hadn't realized that the current was so strong. When she'd watched men poling their small craft past the trading post it hadn't looked that difficult. Now she strained her arms trying to lift the pole from one side of the dugout to the other, finding to her dismay that more often than not she had no control over which way the small boat moved.

Matters worsened when she heard the distant rumbling of thunder. Like faraway cannons firing, the muffled sound announced the coming storm over the sound of silent moving water. Black, billowing clouds slid quickly over the moon, closing out the thick green forest on the other side of the river. With the darkness came fresh gusts of strong air currents. Lightning brought scattered bursts of light in the distance.

The water began to swirl, as if some great hand were stirring it from the bottom, slinging out foam-edged ripples that slapped the boat back and forth. Catherine gave up any attempt to direct the craft and sat down, holding on to the sides as it whirled and twisted like a leaf in the current.

Not once, from the time she'd left Petersburg, had Catherine been afraid. But now she had a feeling that the grand adventure she'd been ready to embrace was likely to be her last. She was beginning to understand Charles's fear of this great river.

Catherine couldn't imagine what Charles would be feeling if he were in the pirogue with her. He'd been terrified enough over making the slow journey up-river, before the storm. According to the captain, Charles had spent most of his time on the pallet of skins in the center of the craft, worrying because he'd never learned to swim.

That image had added to her already grave doubts. Even now, to Catherine, there was something wonderfully alive about the spray on her face, the wind behind her that bounced the craft along like a leaf dipping on the currents of wind. Though she recognized the danger, she wasn't truly afraid.

Even through its most crucial moments, the journey was oddly exhilarating. There must be something wrong with a woman who might be facing death, yet felt so alive, Catherine thought. If she were going to die, she would do so sharing the kind of adventure she might have had with Patrick.

Patrick. For a moment, as clearly as if he were sitting in front of her, she felt his presence and the strong certainty that he was alive and waiting for her. She so wanted Patrick to still be alive, could she have failed to accept the reality that he was probably lost to her forever?

"Don't worry, Catherine," she said aloud to bolster her sagging courage. "You're going to find Patrick and get married. He'll build you a fine house in New Orleans just as you planned."

It would be a fine house, she decided, calming herself, as if she were in the eye of the storm and seeing the future clearly. And a new life—with Patrick.

The boat took another swing about, snapping forward again, then bouncing across the top of the waves as the heavens opened and the storm hit full force.

In minutes, Catherine was being thrown from one side of the boat to the other. It was all she could do to hold on to the sides. For one brief moment she decided that she was being punished for her wickedness. If she survived the journey, she'd apologize to Charles and—and . . . no, she wouldn't promise to go through with the wedding. Promising that would be a sin. It wouldn't be fair to Charles.

It was beginning to look less and less likely that she'd ever see either Charles or Patrick again. Then, just as Catherine was ready to say her final prayer, the pirogue slammed into a fallen tree that extended into the water. The roots were still embedded—albeit unfirmly—on the riverbank, but Catherine could see and hear the muddy earth being washed from around its base.

Her small craft caught the branches and remained tethered there. She heard shouts in the darkness. As the lightning flashed she caught a brief glimpse of a flatboat rushing by. The boat Charles had hired? No, she'd released it first; the vessel should have been in front of her.

Dared she call out? Little good that would do, the boat was already past and not even an experienced crew could stop their momentum and move the big trading boat back upriver to where Catherine had been ensnared.

Suddenly the tree gave way and her boat moved off downriver again—still connected to the tree. Catherine's clothing was plastered to her body. The brisk wind was cold, slamming the raindrops painfully against her face like sand in a storm. Her hands were growing numb. Soon she wouldn't be able to hold on and she'd be swept overboard. Knowing how to swim wouldn't save her now.

She'd been fooling herself all along. She was lost.

"Oh, Patrick," she cried, "why didn't you make love to me? I'm going to die without ever having known what it would be like."

From his place on the cliff Patrick watched his men moving toward the flatboat aground at the end of the spit of land now underwater. This was only the first of many in this storm that would be caught on shifting fingers of earth just beneath the surface of the river.

His men would pretend to help the victims by taking them to shore. Then, after the rescue, the boat and its goods would be theirs. The crew would be lucky. There were no floaters in the water when the pirate, Stone, boarded a ship. He only wanted goods and information. Goods meant money, the only power the Spanish understood. After he questioned them about Captain Lopaz, the crew would be set free.

Then, in a flash of lightning, the river lit up like daylight. That was when he saw it, the pirogue, caught in the branches of a tree like a snared bird. Straight ahead was Necktie Bend, the sandbar and the flatboat. There was a slight form in the boat—a child perhaps—hanging on for dear life.

Patrick descended the hill and mounted the horse corralled on the back side of the cliff in the area known by all the river pirates as the Devil's Punch Bowl. There was no time for a saddle. He was probably already too late. Nevertheless he urged the horse into a mad gallop along the bank. For once he was glad to have the lightning, for when he reached the sandbar where he'd expected to find the tree, it wasn't there. Somehow it had cleared the narrows.

Where was the tree? Where was the boat?

Another mile and the river would pass Natchez, where the water was deepest. Perhaps that depth would slow the current and save the occupant.

Patrick peered at the rushing water through the rain, his heart pounding in his throat. As a sea captain he knew what it meant to be caught in a storm, to be swept up by angry water that held you at its mercy. He knew what it meant to be a child alone and afraid. Then he saw the pirogue slam into a temporary barrier of debris near the shore and hang there, its occupant knocked into the bottom of the boat.

Reining his horse to a stop, Patrick slid to the ground and plunged into the icy current. For a moment it took his breath away. Because the tangle of limbs and trees extended to the shore, Patrick knew that he would be swept by the eddy into the crush of flotsam. Taking a deep breath and shielding his face he allowed the swirling current to bounce him against the shore and hurl him into the tree trunk.

Catching a limb, he held on, gradually moving himself toward the boat. The occupant had disappeared from sight, washed overboard, most likely. After what seemed like an eternity he reached the pirogue, caught the side and pulled himself over. The occupant was lying in the bottom of the boat, apparently lifeless.

The tree was groaning. There was a crack, and the mass dislodged itself and was swept away once more. Patrick lifted the victim's head from the water, then flung himself over the prostrate figure, becoming a human shield. Time passed. Patrick didn't know where they were. He only knew that the body against which he was pressed, though cold and still, was alive. He could hear a low moan now and then.

At last there was an abatement in the storm. The water still rushed downriver, but the rain had stopped and Patrick found that he could sit up. There was no pole for directing the boat and the shallow craft was half-full of water.

He had to get the child out of the water and warm her up, or she'd die. Lifting the lifeless form, Patrick pulled the slight figure against his chest and drew her close. With one hand Patrick tried to bail water from the boat but it was filling faster than he could bail. They were going to sink.

He reached down and pulled the waterlogged figure farther up against him. Then he realized his mistake: this was no child—this was a woman.

"Damn! A woman!" A woman, alone, was the last thing he'd expected.

The pirogue was still moving but it was sinking lower in the current. They'd reached deep water, and ahead he could hear the sound of music and laughter. Natchez-under-the-Hill. He had to get to shore. He'd take her to Bella. She always took in the abused and neglected. She would know what to do with an unconscious girl.

Patrick swore again. Getting himself to shore was one thing, but towing a body through the current was something else. Still, with the deep water up ahead, if he could float, and angle his body toward the shore, perhaps he could use himself as a rudder. It was the only chance the girl had.

Using his jacket, he tied her body to his, her back to his chest, like two joined spoons. He said a small prayer and fell backward into the cold water, gasping as the current momentarily covered his face. Small though she was, she seemed uncommonly heavy. It was her clothing, her skirt that threatened to drown them. With difficulty, he managed to drag it off and let it sink.

Now, flying headfirst down the river, Patrick tried several adjustments of his arms and legs until he found a position that seemed to angle him slightly toward the far shore.

The sounds of music were lost in the roar of the water. His ability to judge distance and position were swallowed up by errant waves that crashed over them and spun them around. Still, little by little, the darker shadows of the shoreline began to inch closer, until at last his head crashed against something solid.

Another blow to his head left him half-addled. Not now! Not when they were so close. He didn't want to think he'd found a log that would keep him from reaching shore. Frantically he reached behind. Wood, a wooden beam. No, he decided, piling. He was beneath a dock, or a building. They'd made it.

"Ahoy, the dock!" he yelled. "Help!"

The current still tugged at his body, trying to dislodge his tenuous hold. "Help! Somebody up there, there's a man and a girl down here!"

"Where are you, matey?"

Thank God, somebody had heard him.

Moments later a rope was thrown down and he managed to tie it around both him and the girl before he lost his grip on the piling. The current swept them beneath the pier to the other side. Slowly, their rescuer managed to pull them back through the posts and up to the wooden dock.

Patrick began to breathe a sigh of relief when the rope made a sudden downward bobble. Then, in an attempt to regain their lost ground, the rescuers gave a mighty jerk, pulling Patrick's head into the bottom of one of the dock supports with a crunch.

"Take us to Heaven," he managed to say, as they pulled him over the side and laid him out on the dock. Then he slid into darkness.

Catherine stretched, winced and allowed her fingertips to slide back and forth across the satiny sheet that covered her.

She could hear voices, hushed in conversation. Feminine voices.

"Is she going to be all right, Isabella?"

"I think so. It's Stone I'm worried about. He has a nasty knot on his head, a cut over his eye and he's still asleep."

The first voice was young and a bit crude. The second, more polished and older. Catherine wondered where she was. She decided that she'd probably like this Isabella, who was concerned about Stone.

"Stone!" Catherine opened her eyes. It all came crashing back to her, the boat slamming into the tree, throwing her down, hitting her head against the side. From then on, everything seemed hazy. She had an impression of a man, of being close to a man's body, of the strong sensation of familiarity and trust. Then came water and more water, and finally darkness.

"Stone?" Catherine repeated, her voice gravelly as her throat protested her trying to speak.

"Well, she's awake now," the younger woman said. "All it took was hearing Stone's name. It'll bring the dead to life again."

"Sally! Stop that. Our guest would probably like some hot soup. Please fetch it for her."

The woman, Isabella, came to stand beside Catherine's bed. She turned a warm smile to Catherine, a smile that didn't quite reach her eyes. "You're a friend of Stone's?"

"I've never met him."

"Well, for two strangers, you certainly were close when they pulled you out of the river last night."

Though her green eyes were narrowed in concern, Isabella was still very beautiful. She had an astonishing mass of flaxen-colored hair that was arranged in exquisite curls, cascading down the sides of her face and across the soft pink wrapper she was wearing.

"Last night?" Catherine frowned, forcing her unwilling mind to focus on the fleeting memory of her rescue. "I'm afraid I don't remember. Please..." She swallowed hard and licked her lips. "Please tell me what happened."

"Two sailors fished you out of the water, wearing only your petticoat. You were tied to a man who apparently was trying to get you to shore. Don't you remember?"

"Only my petticoat? My money—it was sewn in the hem of my skirt. He must have taken it."

Isabella swallowed a smile. "I don't think so. The man who rescued you wouldn't steal your money or your skirt."

Isabella held a glass of water to Catherine's lips and lifted her head so that she could swallow. The water was soothing, but movement only made her head swim. She sank back into the soft pillows with a moan.

"I don't remember anything after my boat hit the tree. What did the man say?"

"He hasn't."

A cold sense of dread fell over Catherine. "Is he dead?"

"No, he's just unconscious. He had a lick on the head. Don't worry. He's a very strong man. He'll be fine, I'll see to it."

Catherine felt herself slipping back into sleep, but she recognized the note of distress in Isabella's voice. It was the same kind of false confidence she'd felt when she'd tried to convince herself that Charles was a fine prospect as a husband.

The second time Catherine awoke she found the girl called Sally sitting by her bed.

"Are you ready for a little broth, darling?"

Darling? That was a familiar greeting from a stranger. Catherine tried to lift herself onto her elbows. "Please."

The girl put down the bowl she was holding and packed pillows behind Catherine's back so that she didn't have to support herself.

"How long have I been here?"

Sally spooned hot chicken broth into her mouth as she answered. "A day. You slept the clock around, then woke up this morning and went directly back to sleep again. Your body needed time to gain strength.''

This time Catherine glanced around. She'd never seen a bedroom quite like the one where she was resting. The walls were covered in lilac fabric. The bed was of polished wood that seemed to smile in the sunlight coming through large glass-encased windows that stood open to the hint of cool air.

Elegance beyond her imagination was displayed in the furnishings. But it was the girl who caught her attention. She was young and very blond and she was only half-dressed. The tops of her breasts spilled over her chemise, and her undergarments were openly displayed so as to look as if she'd just stepped from her bed. But her hair was artfully arranged and her face gently blushed with color. Stockings, slippers and a lilac wrapper completed her wardrobe. Catherine was confused.

"Where am I?" she asked.

"Heaven."

Catherine shook her head. "I can't be dead."

"You came pretty close."

"Well I'm not likely to make it to heaven, so where am I?"

"Well, darling, there are them who might argue with you about this being heaven. You're in Natchez-under-the-Hill."

"Then I made it."

"Depends on where you're going. Being as you were brought here instead of coming of your own free will, maybe you really don't understand."

"Who brought me?"

"The two sailors who pulled you out of the water. He said to bring you to Heaven. That's what they did."

"Who said?"

"Stone. He apparently floated downstream with you tied to his body. Course if it were me, I wouldn't have to be tied. Just let me plant my body next to his and I wouldn't even charge him for the privilege."

"Charge him?"

Sally filled Catherine's mouth with soup again.

"Say, you sure do ask a lot of questions, don't you?"

"I don't mean to pry," Catherine said in a low voice, "but what kind of place is Heaven?"

"It's a house of pleasure, darling, and the closest thing to real heaven our gentlemen callers will ever find."

"Gentlemen? I find it hard to believe that there are any gentlemen here."

"Well, there's them who pretend to be legitimate when they ain't, and them who don't make any bones about being what they are. We don't ask questions."

"You work here?"

"That I do. Working for Isabella is a good way to make money, darling, if that's what you're aiming for. Then when you're ready to take a husband, you can pick the one you want."

"Me? I didn't intend to work here."

"Oh? Isabella likes her girls to be well filled out and have golden hair. You have a ways to go on the womanly body parts, and your hair is more red than blond, but I suppose that's close enough."

"About Stone," Catherine said hesitantly. "You say he brought me here?"

"That he did."

"And where is he now?"

"He's in Isabella's room, at the end of the hall, where he always stays when he comes. But he ain't usually dazed when he gets here."

"I'd like to talk to him."

"Wouldn't we all. But he's off limits, even if he was in a mood to talk."

"What does that mean? I only want to ask him about—someone."

"He's still sleeping but even if he were awake, you'd not likely get past Isabella. Stone's hers and everybody knows to leave him be."

"But I only wanted to talk to him. I'm not interested in him. As a man, that is."

"What's your name, darling?"

"Cath—" She stopped herself. Suppose Charles were looking for her? She'd do better to use another name. "Cat," she corrected, "Catrina O'Conner, and I'm looking for my fiancé, Patrick McLendon. I'm hoping that Stone might know him?"

"Cat O'Conner, huh? Well I guess you do have cat's eyes. And your man has disappeared." Sally looked at Catherine for a long time, then gave her a sad smile. "Maybe, darling, but I've been down that road myself. If you're with child, this is as good a place as any for you to stop off. Isabella won't turn you away. And nobody will know you're here. Isabella has already seen to that."

"Thank you," Catherine hastened to say, "but—"

"Just you rest. It's time for me to get downstairs. Our guests will be arriving soon. The gents will be looking for me. Then at midnight, Isabella will entertain."

Sally took the tray with the empty soup bowl away. When she opened the door, Catherine heard the sound of a pianoforte and laughter.

Bruised and sore, she slid her feet from beneath the covers and sat up. Through sheer determination she managed to stay upright. But sit up was all she could do. After watching the corners of the room cave in she lay back down. Maybe she'd wait a bit longer before confronting the pirate. If Charles should come looking for her, Isabella would protect her. Sally had made that clear.

Tomorrow, she'd ask him about Patrick.

Tomorrow, she'd check out the place called Heaven.

Chapter Three

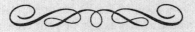

"Are you certain she wasn't on the barge?"

Charles Forrest was furious as he faced the rescued crewman from the missing flatboat they'd found on the riverbank just beyond Necktie Bend.

He'd found it hard enough to accept the finality of Catherine's disappearance, but that she had hidden herself on the flatboat to flee him and their impending marriage was simply too insulting for him to comprehend. Had it not been for her note, he would never have believed what she'd done.

"What happened, Frenchy?" the captain asked the burly first mate.

"Somebody cut the rope. We got washed away in the storm."

"*Sí!*" the Spaniard agreed. "And the boat got hung on the sandbar."

"An' before we could get free, that pirate, Stone, sent his men to board us. When they found out we were carrying little cargo they took our boat and left us on shore."

"What about Miss Caden?" Charles asked again. "Where is she?"

"Don't know, my frien'," the Frenchman answered. "It was all we could do to stay afloat. If she was on board our barge she was either stolen by that pirate, or washed overboard during the ride downriver."

"Maybe she took the small pirogue," the captain suggested. "It, too, was missing."

"Don't be a fool," Charles snapped. "A woman, alone? In a storm? It was one of your crew members who stole the barge and cut the pirogue loose so we couldn't follow. I want Miss Caden found and I want her found now!"

"Then, *señor,* you'd better find that pirate. Sure as my name is Carlos de Ortega, she's in his lair right now."

"And he has my barge, Mr. Forrest," said the dismayed captain who'd brought Charles to the trading post.

"I think your crew is right," agreed the Spanish captain of the ship who'd promised to transport them back downriver. "We'd best shove off. When we get back to New Orleans you can petition the governor to look for the woman."

Charles reluctantly agreed. If Catherine were with Stone, she was already lost to him. Unless—unless he could turn this to his advantage. If he found Catherine, he'd find Stone. Delivering the pirate to the authorities would gain him badly needed favor from the governor.

He'd simply offer a generous reward for the return of Catherine Caden.

The boat they'd hired passage on was stopping at Natchez-under-the-Hill, a good place to announce the reward. The Spanish captain they were traveling with seemed unconcerned about docking his goods-laden boat among such notorious criminals. That suggested to Charles that he might be well known there.

"Captain, might we not overtake the pirate at Natchez-under-the-Hill? I believe the village is known as a safe harbor for thieves. There is already a reward for Stone's capture, which I'll double if you find my betrothed."

"Well, I am a personal friend of the captain of the Spanish garrison nearby. Perhaps I could send for him and report your missing bride-to-be."

The men on board the flatboat concurred with the captain's decision to put in for the night. They doubted that Stone would be waiting for them; he was much too wily for that. A night in the taverns was an unexpected treat. Charles was satisfied that the story of the reward would travel fast enough once the crew reached Natchez-under-the-Hill.

Either way, Catherine would lead the governor to Stone. Stone would be destroyed and the governor would be in Charles's debt. And Catherine—well, Charles would deal with her when the time came.

Catherine was awakened by music.

She listened to the strains of what sounded like a harpsichord for a moment, then a sudden silence followed and she wondered if she'd been dreaming. No, she'd been rescued and brought to this place, as had been the man who was her rescuer. It was all coming back to her. She'd been found by the very man she'd been seeking: Stone, the river pirate.

Carefully she slipped her feet from beneath the satin sheet to the thick rug covering the polished floor beside the bed. There was a creak as she slowly stood, balancing herself against the high bed as she tested her feet. Her body was sore, bruised, but it still seemed to function.

At the door she paused, pressed her ear against the wood and listened. Nothing. She tested the knob. Unlocked. It opened easily. The girl called Sally had said that Stone was in Isabella's room, at the end of the hall. The music had begun again, loudest at the far end of the corridor; Catherine slipped out into the candle-lit hallway and hurried in the other direction.

A series of open doors revealed small, unoccupied rooms like the one in which Catherine had been sleeping—tastefully decorated rooms that might have been found in any luxury home in Augusta or Petersburg. There was nothing crude about Isabella's house.

A male laugh, followed by a softer female one, pealed from behind one closed door and Catherine scooted past. Somewhere behind her, footsteps sounded. She glanced frantically around. She was about to be caught, or worse perhaps, be mistaken for one of Isabella's girls. She took a deep breath and opened the door at the end of the corridor, praying that she wouldn't find her hostess inside.

At first glance the room seemed to be empty. While the furnishings of her bedroom had been lush, this room bespoke elegance such as Catherine had never before seen. Panels of white, painted with tiny pink roses and lavender forget-me-nots, hung from the walls, caught in the center by satin ties that made the walls look as if they were windows, draped with gauzy curtains. The bed was enormous, hung with matching tiers of fabric that swayed back and forth, caught by the night breeze flowing through an open window. This had to be Isabella's room.

From the bed came the distinctive sound of a man snoring. A man wouldn't likely be snoring if he were with a woman, at least Catherine didn't think so. She had to be in the right place, Isabella's room. The occupant of her bed had to be Stone.

Catherine glanced down at the sheer nightrail she was wearing and wished she'd stopped to find a wrapper with which to cover herself.

Feeling like an intruder, she tiptoed toward the bed, timidly reaching for the netting and drawing it aside. Fervently she prayed that the occupant of the bed *was* Stone, the river pirate, not some customer. Stone was her last hope to find Patrick.

A single lamp threw a watery light across the lower half of his body. The sleeping man was big. His huge arm was laid across his face, revealing only the bottom of a light-colored beard. His hair was thick and curly. The sheet, lying loosely across his lower body, revealed a large chest scarred with red streaks that weren't recently made.

A soft gasp escaped her lips as she realized that the man had been badly beaten in the past.

The man groaned and moved his arm, revealing his forehead, discolored just above his right eye where he'd suffered some heavy blow. There was a jagged wound at the hairline. His skin gleamed with a sheen of sweat. As she watched, she felt her knees go weak. A strange shiver raced up the back of her neck.

He licked his lips and whispered a name.

Catherine took a step closer. Still half-shadowed, and covered by his long hair, his face wasn't revealed. She wasn't yet ready to believe what every part of her was screaming. "Are you Stone?"

"Angel? Of course I am." He let out a deep breath and tried to moisten his lips again. "Water."

Catherine reached for the pitcher, poured a small amount of liquid into the goblet beside the bed and stepped up onto the bed stool to reach the man. She lifted his head, pushing back the mass of unruly hair

Her heart stopped and every part of her body stilled with dizzying sensations as she pressed the goblet against his lips, allowing the water to trickle inside. As if she were in a dream, she replaced the glass on the table and reached out her hand to catch a drop of water that trickled down the injured man's face.

She still didn't believe it, even as she felt the soft hair curl around her fingers. She closed her eyes and opened them again, deciding that her mind was playing tricks on her, that she wanted something so badly she was willing it to be true. Then he moved and for a brief connecting second his eyes flew open and there was no more doubt. She'd found Patrick. Patrick was the pirate, Stone!

"Patrick!"

"Ah, Catherine. Sweet Jesus. I know you're in my dream. Don't tempt me any longer, darlin', come close," he whispered and pulled back the sheet in invitation. "I'm so cold, warm me."

He was nude, his glorious body exposed in a way that Catherine had wished for, but never expected to find. Like the marble statue in Papa's study, her Patrick was magnificent, even in his injured condition, a condition that in no way stilled his great physical response to a woman.

Her hand played across his face, touching, reassuring her that he was real, that she wasn't conjuring up the man she'd wanted to find. He'd said he was cold, but he wasn't. He was warm, too warm.

"Please, Catherine. I need you."

She didn't hesitate. This was Patrick, not some pirate called Stone. Catherine had come across a wilderness to reach him. He'd saved her life. She didn't care where they were, or what might happen. Patrick needed her; nothing else mattered. She blew out the lamp, slid into bed and pulled the sheet over them both.

Moments later his arm was around her, pulling her face to his chest, pressing her against his body as if he wanted them joined. She felt the force of his touching her, not the polite teasing that they'd shared in Georgia, but the unleashed power of his need. Catherine had never been so close to a man, not even back in Georgia, on the bank of the Broad River, or in the barn when they'd kissed.

And it was no longer just Patrick who was on fire.

"What's this?" he muttered in a voice that was more a growl than a question. He caught her nightdress and pushed it up around her neck. Their skins touched, melded. Fire met ice and engulfed Catherine with such heat that she knew she would surely burn up.

"It's all right," she whispered, in a voice so shaky that she didn't recognize herself. "I'm here now, Patrick. I've found you."

"Ah, Catherine, I've waited so long." His kiss was rough, urgent. Then he groaned and fell back. "No, I must be gentle. I promise."

Given the chance, Catherine would have told him she didn't care. But he covered her mouth again, even in his feverish condition, governing his actions by settling her in the curl of his arm so that his other hand could steal across her body, touching her face, her neck, her breasts.

"Open your eyes, Patrick," she finally pleaded. See me, she said silently.

But Patrick didn't comply. He knew that he was turning Isabella into Catherine as he'd done so many times and that opening his eyes would dispel his fantasy.

And then Catherine saw the moisture begin to bead his forehead. His fever was breaking. She tried to use the corner of the bed cover to wipe the perspiration from his skin, but the silk fabric slid away and her fingers were caressing his chest, following the line of the scars, finding his lower body and the enlarged part of him that had once pressed against her so urgently. Her skin was absorbing his heat and simmering with the fire of his touch.

Catherine's eyes stung with a mist of tears that rolled down her cheeks. There was such intense joy in being with Patrick again. Joy and gratitude. Never had she given up that he was alive, even when everyone told her he was dead. Even when a stranger had sailed his *Savannah Lady* into port. She'd still refused to believe that he was gone.

Privateer, adventurer, pirate, whatever he was, she was here, with him, in his arms, and nothing else mattered—not where he'd been, or why he hadn't come back for her. He was Patrick, her laughing, blue-eyed Irishman, and she trusted him with her life, and her body.

She was aware of every part of him, lying beside her, her breasts being seared by rough skin, fingertips skimming the rounded curves, seeking and teasing her now taut nipples. When his hands left her breasts and moved lower, she wondered at her body's reaction, the involuntary arching of her back, as if she were reaching out for something that she'd craved but never experienced.

Catherine's breath came faster. Somewhere in her mind she knew that what was happening was probably not the best thing for a man who'd been injured. But he was strong and there was a need in him that went beyond his condition, a determination that seemed to match her own and she knew that there was no stopping him. Even if she'd wanted to, and she couldn't.

He was sliding his hands along her hips, down her legs and across her knees until he reached the inside of her thighs, which parted involuntarily. She panicked for a moment, reaching for his arm and holding on as if she couldn't decide whether to stop him or urge him on.

Slowly, either from his weakened condition or from some inner control, his fingers played along the inside of her thighs, skimming across the moist, tingling area between, touching her lightly until she thought she would die.

Patrick wasn't cold anymore. His body was fiery hot, and she couldn't tell whether it was from the fever or the heat raging between them. Then she felt him touch her most private place.

Without thought, Catherine pressed against his hand, urging him on, lifting herself to meet the intrusion that had coaxed the flame higher. Of its own volition her hand left Patrick's arm and sought that part of him pressing itself against her thigh as he turned his body toward hers. His leg slipped across her, dislodging her hand just as it gripped his maleness.

With a groan, half of pain and half of passion, Patrick lifted himself totally and pressed against the most heated part of her body, found and entered her with a sudden fullness that seemed more than she could take.

As if he'd suddenly wakened, Patrick stopped and held himself above her, barred by the barrier he'd encountered. Then that fleeting realization passed and in one sudden push he was inside.

He knew as he plunged inside her that he was caught up in a fevered dream. He knew because night after night, imprisoned in that dark, airless cell, he'd had that same dream, of holding Catherine in his arms, of loving her, of losing himself in that warm, wonderful body that he'd walked away from. But now, as before in his imagination, she was here and he was loving her, and he could hear her soft mewing cries.

"Patrick... Patrick, Oh, Patrick—"

And then he felt it, the powerful, dizzying whirlpool of sensation that caught his body and spun it into a place of quaking heat that he'd always believed existed, but never truly found. Faster and faster, hotter and hotter, and finally a thrust of tightness that ripped his control and spilled over into some great plunging release.

Then there was stillness, contentment, connection, even as he fell back into sleep, the first real, relaxed sleep he'd had in so very long. He'd apologize to Bella for calling her Catherine. She'd forgive him, she always did. Until the next time Stone made love to her, when he'd close his eyes and pretend that it was Catherine in his arms.

But tonight, caught up in a dream, tonight he'd have sworn that it really was his Catherine who'd come to him. But Catherine was back in Petersburg, Georgia, waiting for Patrick, who could never return.

Catherine lay for a long time, nestled in the crook of Patrick's arm, listening to him breathe. He seemed calmer now, cooler. As if their mating had removed the evils festering inside his body and made him well. Catherine liked that thought. She sighed in pleasure and closed her eyes. Tomorrow they'd talk. Tomorrow would be soon enough. Tonight she'd found him and that was enough.

Chapter Four

"Where is the girl, Sally?"

"I don't know. She was in her room just before I came down tonight. Then, after you sang I brought a gent up for a short time. Afterward I checked on her and she was gone."

Isabella glared at the open door and back at Sally. "Well, that's a fine thank-you. We take her in and she runs off in the middle of the night. I'd better check on Stone."

But her progress was halted by the voice of Pharaoh, coming from downstairs. "Where you going, Captain Lopaz, suh? Miss Isabella don't allow no soldiers in her private quarters."

Captain Lopaz? The intruder was the newly assigned assistant to the commandant at the nearby fort, the man who'd beaten Stone and arrested Pharaoh. And he was here.

That was to be expected. Everyone in any position of authority came to Heaven, sooner or later. Isabella groaned and chastised herself for not finding out the man's name yesterday so she could have warned Stone that his enemy had returned.

And there was Pharaoh.

In the weeks since Pharaoh had arrived, he'd gained back his strength and his pride, improving to the point that she'd made him her house manager. With Pharaoh at the door and Stone, injured, in Isabella's bed, Captain Lopaz's arrival could be a disaster. She held her breath, searching her mind for answers.

"How may we be of service, Captain, sir?" Pharaoh was asking politely. There was no immediate response from the captain, so perhaps he didn't recognize Pharaoh as the slave he'd sent to prison.

"There is a woman missing, upriver. Her future husband believes she may have been taken by the pirate, Stone. He has offered a large reward for her return. I've been told that a man and a woman were found in the river and brought here," the captain said. "I've come to question the pair."

Isabella thought about the woman Stone had brought here. Stone had never done anything like that before. She could be the missing woman, but Lopaz was too late. She'd already gone.

Still, if the soldiers were allowed to search, Stone would be discovered and she couldn't let that happen.

"Sally, tell the captain that I'll be down shortly, and send Pharaoh to the kitchen until he leaves."

As Sally left to comply, Isabella dashed down the corridor and into her room. "Stone! You must get away!"

But it wasn't Stone who sat up sleepily. It was the girl. She was in Isabella's bed, where Isabella expected to find Stone. For a moment Isabella was stunned into silence.

"Where is he, you foolish girl?" she said at last.

Catherine looked around in sleepy confusion. Patrick was gone. "I don't know. He was here earlier."

There was a commotion behind Isabella in the hall. "You can't go in there!" Sally was saying.

"Get out of my way, woman! No more lies. He got fished out of the river last night and was brought here. Everybody knows that head of yellow hair. Give me that lamp and step aside."

"Why, Captain," Isabella said smoothly. "I hadn't expected you to call so late."

"Move aside, woman. I want to see who you have in your bed. If it's Stone, I'll take him into custody and see that he's hanged. Then I'll get back to New Orleans and collect the reward."

Catherine leaned back, hiding herself among the pillows. The Spanish captain was looking for Stone—no, she corrected herself, not Stone—Patrick. She understood the truth now; Stone and Patrick McLendon were indeed one and the same. And she'd caused Patrick's injury when he brought her here. It was because he'd rescued her that he was about to be caught.

Isabella looked as if she were going to argue, then smiled and stepped back. "By all means, Captain, see who is occupying my bed."

The overlarge man shoved Isabella away and jerked the hangings from the bed, exposing the frightened and confused Catherine. She stared at the soldier, turned her head into the pillow and covered herself with the sheet.

"A woman?"

"My niece," she said in resignation, trying not to let him see her casual perusal of the room. As the captain waved the lamp about, she noticed that the rug beside the bed had been moved, exposing the corner of the trapdoor.

"Where is Stone?" he was demanding, "and don't tell me that he hasn't been here. I know that he has."

"Why, Captain, I don't know what you're talking about. As you can see, there is no man here. Now, suppose we go back downstairs and leave this poor frightened child alone," Isabella said, stepping between the girl and the captain in an attempt to hide the escape tunnel from discovery.

"Your niece is quite attractive." The captain gave Catherine a piercing glance that said he was not completely convinced that he wasn't being fooled.

Lopaz would accept Isabella's story for the moment. If this girl was the one the American claimed had been kidnapped by Stone, she wasn't going anywhere—and neither was Stone. Come morning, Señor Forrest would be on the flatboat heading downriver. He didn't have to know about this girl just yet. Lopaz gave an imperceptible nod and allowed Isabella to draw him into the hallway. He could wait. Two rewards were better than one.

Once the soldier was gone and the door was closed, Sally rushed toward the bed. "Where is Stone? Isabella is going to have your hide for this, you foolish girl."

"I don't know. And his name isn't—" Catherine broke off. She didn't understand what had happened. She'd gone to sleep in Patrick's arms, only to be awakened by the clamor in the hallway. She'd only just discovered that Patrick was gone when the door burst open.

' I think you'd better return to your room before Isabella gets back." She pulled Catherine's arm, forcing her to stand, then let out a gasp.

"What's wrong, Sally?"

"Blood. On the sheet. What did you do to Stone? Is he injured?" She took a step closer, studying the sheet, then lifting her eyes in question. "You—you made love with Stone?"

"No!" Catherine felt a flush of heat color her cheeks. "Yes. How did you know?"

"The sheet. You were a virgin. Why? He's never touched another woman since he's been coming here. Why you? Isabella isn't going to like this."

Catherine was embarrassed. She stood watching while Sally quickly stripped the bed and remade it before leading Catherine back down the corridor to her room. This time when the door was closed she heard the lock click.

Where was Patrick? What had happened and why had he left her here? Had she found Patrick only to lose him again?

Below the floor, in the escape tunnel, Patrick crouched, his head aching as he forced himself to make sense of what little he'd heard. When the sound of voices announced the arrival of the soldiers, he'd awakened. The intruders had gathered noisily beneath Isabella's open window while the captain issued instructions to his men and discussed their plans with a stranger who seemed to be responsible for the search.

"Señor Charles, you wait here."

The voice he'd heard seemed familiar.

"We have no way of knowing whether Stone is alone, or with his gang of cutthroats. If your woman is with Stone, we'll find her."

Woman?

In the darkness, Patrick had sat upright. He recognized that voice. Lopaz! It was he, the man Patrick had been searching for, waiting for. Lopaz, the man who'd nearly beaten him to death. At last they were to meet again—at a time Patrick was not at his best.

Patrick would have to be ready. For now, he didn't want Lopaz to know he had survived. Patrick hadn't killed anybody then and Stone hadn't stolen anybody's woman now. But that wouldn't stop the captain from punishing him and anybody protecting him.

That included Isabella.

Patrick had realized that he wasn't alone in the bed, but if he roused Isabella she'd try to protect him. Better he disappear, he thought, quickly and quietly.

Painfully, unsteadily, he'd dressed. Making as little noise as possible he'd found the well-oiled trapdoor beneath Isabella's fancy Persian rug, and dropped into the secret space. From there he'd made his way to the hatch that led to the water's edge.

Isabella had shown him the exit long ago, but this was the first time he'd ever made use of it. He'd laughed at her when she threatened him with being sold into slavery if he tried to leave her, but now he was grateful for the means of escape. In Natchez-under-the-Hill, a man was protected from the law, whichever country the law represented. Protecting oneself from others was the real danger.

Patrick wished his head didn't ache so. There was a nasty cut at the hairline, and a puffy area surrounding it. Even a casual touch set off waves of pain that clouded his memory and probably his judgment as well.

Everything that had happened since he dived into the river was such a blur. There'd been someone trapped in a pirogue—a girl. He'd brought her to Heaven where he'd thought she'd be safe. Or had it been part of the vivid dream he'd had? In his feverish state he'd imagined that the woman was Catherine, that she'd come to his bed.

Catherine Caden, his Catherine, the woman he'd planned to marry. He'd been so certain that it was Catherine he was kissing, making love to, holding in his arms. But that couldn't be. He'd left Catherine back in Petersburg. It was just another dream, triggered by his rescue of the girl in the river. He wasn't strong enough to meet the captain tonight.

He'd have to hope that the girl wouldn't be found and that Isabella wouldn't be implicated. His relationship with the owner of Heaven was more than simple friendship, it was a matter of honor. She'd taken him in and given him safe haven. Now that had ended. With Captain Lopaz's arrival he couldn't even trust Heaven anymore.

Patrick McLendon dropped the final distance below to the riverbank. Once he got back to his plantation, Rainbow's End, he'd decide what to do. Perhaps it was time to consider making a secret trip downriver to New Orleans. It was time he called on the American representative from President Washington. If anyone could help him clear himself of the charge of murder, President Washington could. Using the last of his energy, he stumbled down the bank.

"Stone?"

"Jillico?"

"Yes. You are hurt?"

"I seem to have had a lick in the head. I'm still seeing stars. How did you know?"

"I know."

"Yes, you're like one of the little people. I keep expecting you to start wearing green and grow a long red beard."

"My people do not allow their facial hair to grow."

"I know and I guess you don't have a pot of gold, or an extra wish or two to be granted, do you? Never mind. Let's get out of Heaven, my friend. I seem to be hallucinating about a hazel-eyed angel, and I know she isn't real."

Chapter Five

Low spirals of fog wafted across the stage like smoke, circling the ankles of the performers like disembodied fingers holding them to the floor.

The humming of the drums was joined by a low wordless chant that ebbed and flowed like the beat of a heart. At first, the dancers seemed to cower from some unseen attacker, then as if seeking a way out, they peered into the darkness outside the light. The drumbeat grew louder, the pace faster, the movements of the dancers more frantic.

Beyond the candles, the audience, made up of the more affluent and curious of New Orleans's fledgling young society, eyed each other in alarm. What was happening here was no stage show, no bawdy entertainment. This was more like an eerie reenactment of some secret ritual.

This was all dance, chants without spoken words. There was a sense of unrest in the music, reminding the audience that many of their slaves brought that same kind of dancing with them from their homelands. Whispers began to be heard as the drumbeat peaked.

Nine months ago the dance director, a handsome, well-educated man had mysteriously appeared in New Orleans. His claim to be a stage actor and performer had quickly caught the fancy of one of the local businessmen, who turned a store on St. Peter's Street into the city's first theater.

The stranger brought in refugees from islands in the Southern oceans to make up his cast of blacks, and weekly performances were immediately sold out. Soon, the theater was joined by the first newspaper, *Le Moniteur de la Louisiane,* which printed the playbill and brought in such a response that the theater was enlarged.

What had started out as New Orleans's newest claim to civilized society had, this night, become something fearful.

Suddenly a puff of colored smoke ignited in the center of the stage, and under its cover appeared the man called the Dancemaster. There was much speculation about his nationality. He was tall, Indian perhaps, or some half-breed mixture, and a spectacular specimen of maleness. Wearing only a scrap of cloth covering his male parts, the dancer crouched and waited, motionless until the whispers subsided.

Then like a snake he writhed and twisted, uncurling himself, without moving from the spot where he'd appeared. The chains of hammered copper and strands of pearls around his neck caught the glow of the candles like the eyes of some jungle predator in the night.

From somewhere outside the shadows a ghostlike figure moved slowly and majestically onto the stage. This figure, a woman wearing little more than a length of gauzy fabric wrapped around her body, seemed to move in a trance. Her face was concealed by her painted mask, to which a fall of long white animal hair had been attached.

She began quick little movements around the circle, as if she, too, were searching for someone, then, disappointed she would turn away, always keeping her back to the man in the center. After several passes she cried out and collapsed to the floor in what appeared to be a faint.

The Dancemaster let out a scream, leaping into the air and coming down on his knees at a spot near the woman's body. He brandished a spear over her, lifting both arms as if in a signal to the dancers that the time had come to attack. Then, as if awakening from sleep, the white-faced woman rose. The man held out his hand. She clasped it and walked toward the front of the stage where she pulled the mask from her face, faced the patrons, then held the mask up in clear view. There was a shriek from the audience.

The theater owner started down the aisle, got a close-up look of the mask and came to an abrupt stop.

The woman's real face was painted as white as the mask. But every eye in the house was riveted on her disguise. For it wasn't a mask at all, but a human head.

The drums suddenly stopped. The dancers fell to their knees with their arms extended before them on the floor as they blew out the lights.

Chapter Six

"So your name is Cat O'Conner, and you knew Stone before you came here?"

"Yes," Catherine said bravely, "he and I were . . . acquaintances."

Isabella was standing by the door, more angry than she'd ever been in her life. She just couldn't figure out this girl Stone had rescued and put in her care.

Sally's bizarre explanation of why the girl wound up in her bed—that Stone had reopened his wound and called out, drawing the girl to him—made no sense. This time Isabella intended to get to the truth.

"Strange, Stone never mentioned you. How well did you know him?"

Catherine debated her answer. She sensed that Isabella cared for Patrick. If Catherine told the truth, she might cause Patrick further harm and hurt the woman who'd befriended her. Still, if she lied, she might anger Isabella and find herself ejected from the one place where Stone was likely to return. Catherine didn't hesitate. Better placate Isabella than be sent away before she found Patrick again.

"I didn't know Stone as well as I would have liked," she admitted, mixing truth with fiction as she went. "I was running away from a man I chose not to marry, when I was caught by the storm. Stone saved my life. Nothing more.''

''But you were in my bed.''

''I went to your room to thank you for my life. Stone was already gone. Before I could get back here, I heard the captain come. I thought Stone might be hiding from the captain so I—I blew out the candle and took Stone's place. I'm very sorry if I caused you any grief.''

The girl's explanation still had holes in it that Isabella could climb through, but for now, she decided it was better to accept it than assume that Stone had brought her there because she meant something to him.

''And what did you plan to do when you ran away from this man you were to marry?''

''I—I was coming here. I thought perhaps you might—might—give me a job. I believe I could be an asset to your...establishment.''

Isabella bit back a laugh. The girl had a way about her, as if she were ready to take on the world. She was interesting, with her lively face and proud manner, but she was obviously wellborn. Isabella didn't want to agree to her employment until she'd spoken with Stone.

Catherine saw Isabella's disbelieving expression and hastened to add, ''Oh, I didn't mean with the men. I'd thought to play the harpsichord, or perhaps cook or clean. I'm very experienced.''

Isabella took one look at Cat's hands and confirmed her suspicions that Miss Cat O'Conner was making up her story as she went. She might play the harpsichord, but hard labor was not a thing of which she could claim experience.

"Do you sing?"

"Some," Cat agreed, hoping privately that God wouldn't strike her speechless for her lie. She could at least play the harpsichord, thanks to her mother's insistence that at least one of her daughters learn the kind of social graces expected of a lady. More than that, she'd have to improvise.

"And you're Irish. Well, we might work something out there, at least temporarily. Cat O'Conner, the Irish colleen. My clients might appreciate something a bit different. What about dancing an Irish jig?"

"No, I don't dance." Enough was enough. Cat didn't expect to stay around long enough for Isabella to find out how badly she sang. If dancing was required she was sunk.

"You've already told them she's your niece—why not let her stay?" Sally asked. "Having somebody new to entertain them might just divert the sailors from turning her in for the reward."

Isabella frowned, then nodded. She still didn't believe the tale she'd just heard, but short of waiting for Stone's return, she had no way of learning the truth. Until then, she'd just keep Cat O'Conner close by.

There was more to Stone's actions than he was telling. But then there always was. Meanwhile she had the very real problem of keeping the Spanish captain from discovering the truth—no easy task since he was the second-highest-ranking officer at the fort. But she'd always managed to outwit any man—except Stone.

Isabella thought of Stone and allowed a sigh of regret to escape her lips. Stone, the one man in all her life that she truly loved, would never belong to her.

But for now, she was certain that he didn't belong to anyone else, either. And it just might be that, one way or another, she had something he wanted.

Even if it was a saucy hazel-eyed minx who called herself Cat.

"Why did you collapse tonight, Moria? That was not a part of the reenactment."

"I don't know. I felt very strange. I told you that I was not an actor. While you and your members of our family were learning how to perform on the stage, I was learning to open my mind to the spirit world."

"Ah, Moria, there are more spirits in the world that we are aware of. On the island where I come from, there are people who are believed to be the living dead."

Moria shivered. Ever since he'd come back, since she'd seen him so clearly in a vision, she'd both feared and waited for him to send for her. She'd thought she was prepared, until they met on the green mound of earth in their old village. From that moment she'd become caught up in his spell so completely that he never disappeared from her mind again.

But recreating the coming of the Sun King was a thing she didn't understand. She pulled on her loose-fitting Indian tunic and turned to go.

"Wait, why do you flee?"

"I must. I am needed."

"How do you know?"

"The Great Spirit has called. There is a man who is hurt, and I must heal him."

"What about me?"

"I don't know the answer to that yet, Simicco."

She felt her bones quiver as he placed both hands on her shoulder blades and held her motionless.

"Come to me, Moria. Come lie with me."

"We cannot mate," she protested. "It is forbidden. We both belong to the royal family."

"Yes, I know. And I ask you to come to me, not as my wife, but as my honored concubine."

"No," she snapped. "I will be your equal or I will be nothing."

"So be it," he answered and watched her go.

The pirogue slid through the dark water of the bayou like a shadow. Night animals sang their song of life undisturbed by the intruders. Jillico poled the craft without a ripple of water to announce their presence. Patrick lay against the bow of the boat and wished that he'd stayed behind.

Once he'd recovered from the wound he received escaping from prison, he'd started a search for Captain Hector Lopaz, the man who'd nearly ended his life. Lopaz's superior, the official who'd ordered Patrick's arrest and confiscated the *Savannah Lady,* had never expected his actions to be questioned. But according to sources, they had been. Afterward, the official had sold his military commission and returned to Spain. Lopaz had been demoted and reassigned, and told to consider himself lucky that he wasn't thrown in his own jail.

Now he was back, and he was charged with arresting the pirate, Stone.

Patrick sighed. The means had finally come for him to even the score. But he didn't delude himself. He was in a country under foreign rule and he had little clout.

Refusing to face Lopaz went against everything Patrick knew. The man had been within his reach, and Patrick had turned away, to protect those he cared about.

Somehow it wasn't the turning away that was keeping his pulse racing, it was the caring and the responsibility it brought. Responsibiity for his ship and his crew was the kind of duty he understood. Men had shared a common bond that made them stand together. But women? His point of reference here was nonexistant.

Except for that one brief moment when he'd believed Catherine was in his arms and he'd felt his heart surge with strength.

Catherine, so alive, so positive. She'd never cared where he came from, or why. It didn't matter that his background was as poor as the most worthless of those people sent from English jails to settle the colony called Georgia. She made him feel good. She'd trusted him to return, and trust was a thing he'd known little of in his life.

Dear God, he hadn't trusted that kind of devotion, hadn't allowed it of himself. He'd thought that Catherine's obsession was temporary, that of a child for a new toy. A girl like Catherine wouldn't want him, not when she got over her infatuation and realized what he was.

Yet in the privacy of the night, in his most secret dreams, he'd allowed himself to get caught up in a dream. Because he'd wanted her—so much.

Like tonight, when he'd felt that Catherine was in his arms, he'd allowed himself to believe. But, even in his dream, she couldn't remain there. Day would break and she'd be gone. But for now he held her, closing his eyes so that he could recapture that energy, that strong belief she'd had that they were meant to be together. The night sky disappeared into darkness and finally he slept.

Once Jillico reached the safety of one of his frequently traveled waterways, away from the big river, he made the sound of a bird and listened to hear it repeated along the route.

By sunrise he and Patrick were so deep in the swamp nobody could have found them. And yet their route had simply paralleled the river, never carrying them more than shouting distance from the great body of water called the Mississippi. Reaching solid land now, Jillico beached the boat carved from the trunk of a great cypress tree and signaled their arrival again.

Silently men appeared from the shadows and lifted the protesting Stone, carrying him to the crude shack being used for shelter while the plantation house was being built.

"Is he hurt bad?" one of the slaves asked.

"No, I'm all right," Stone kept protesting, "it's just this ache in my head."

Jillico ignored him, giving the men instructions to be careful of Stone's head wound. "I don't think so. He managed to slip out of Isabella's place and make it to the river. His head is too hard to break. He just cracked it a little the night of the storm."

The slave examined Stone's head, then lifted his face in question. "Jillico?"

"The medicine woman, Moria, comes," Jillico answered and turned to greet the Indian woman already entering the hut. "Greetings, Moria."

"Why have you sent for me?"

Stone tried to study her. There was something familiar about her dark, expressionless face. She waited in the shadows, showing neither concern nor curiosity. Yet Stone couldn't escape the strange conviction that she'd been expecting them, nor could he get past the feeling that he'd seen her before, and not long ago.

Finally she stepped forward and touched his head. Then he knew. She was the shadow woman in his dreams, the strange new presence who seemed to stand in Catherine's shadow.

"What do you want?" he tried to ask. But if he did, she didn't answer. Her examination of his wound was followed by a discussion between her and Jillico. It was obvious that Moria's way prevailed.

Patrick was taken to bed, stripped of his clothing except for his pants and bathed in a cool, odd-smelling water. A cup of even stronger liquid was foisted upon him, after which he slept briefly.

Throughout the morning, between times of sleep, he studied Moria. He couldn't fix her age. She might have been a mature girl, or a very young woman. He only knew that, although she sighed frequently, she seemed intent on accomplishing her purpose. But he'd bet she regretted her mission.

At all times he could feel her eyes on him, her will imposing itself on his. And he fought her control.

By noontime Patrick was sitting up, drinking more of Moria's bitter-tasting concoctions and swearing oaths that would have embarrassed the most seasoned sailor.

When Jillico next joined his friend, he did so with timidity. "Are you better?"

"Better than what? Of course I'm better. If you'll just get this witch out of here with her poisons and bring me a pint of ale."

"Then the bad dreams are gone?"

Patrick caught back the orders he'd been about to deliver and studied his young Natchez friend. "What bad dreams?"

"About the woman in the river, the woman called Catherine? You talked about her in the boat, calling her name repeatedly. I feared she'd stolen your mind."

Until then Stone hadn't been certain. He remembered the storm, remembered diving into the water and reaching the runaway pirogue. He had vague recollections of the girl's continued presence.

"And her name was Catherine?" Jillico prompted.

"No. Catherine is someone I once knew. I don't know who the wench I rescued was. Just someone who was about to die."

"Do you know that you took a chance with your life, going to Isabella? It is no longer safe for you there. Captain Hector Lopaz has been transferred to the fort—to find you."

At last the man he'd been waiting for had returned. "Does he know about me?"

"No," Jillico said softly, wondering if he was doing the right thing, "I do not think he knows about Patrick McLendon. But he brags that he will find Stone and that the governor will reward him by restoring him to his place of authority and allowing him to return to the city."

"Where has he been?"

"He was sent to the outpost at Pensacola."

"And now, Lopaz is here, at my mercy. First he imprisoned Patrick. Now he wants Stone. And, my friend, were it not for you, he might have captured him."

"Were it not for you, I would be dead."

Patrick considered their situation. Jillico and Pharoah had become the family he'd never had. They'd looked after one another. But this association with Stone could bring ruin to his friends. "You must go, Jillico, else you place your people in danger."

Jillico made a crude sound and slapped his thigh.

"For nearly a hundred years the Natchez have fought to occupy the land at the head of the deep water. First came the fort, then settlers and finally a town. Governments and people like Lopaz change, but our people go on losing the most in this battle we fight for wealth and possession."

"I am sorry, my friend. I wish I could change what has happened."

"It cannot be changed. After the last great war between the Natchez and the French, we fled into the swamps like dogs."

Like me, Patrick thought. But the time had come for him to fight back. "Tell me, Jillico, why didn't your people retake Natchez after the French left?"

Jillico looked startled at his friend's question. "My father asked the same question. He was told that the remaining wise men of our tribe met and decided that the strangers brought nothing but greed, illness and death. When our Sun King was taken prisoner, it was agreed that the Natchez would forever remove themselves from danger. Some joined other tribes. Some of us learned their languages and how to live among the intruders. We survive and we wait."

"Your Sun King?"

"It is not your concern," Moria said. "You cared for Jillico and now we give you our protection."

"But I bring new danger to you. Captain Lopaz will try to hunt me down from his base at Natchez-under-the-Hill."

"Perhaps," Jillico said, "but he must survive the swamp."

Patrick thought about the snakes, the alligators, the moving earth that was firm one moment and a quagmire the next, and nodded.

"There's another man with Lopaz, an American who claims his woman ran away with you, Stone. He's offered a large reward. I think that it isn't safe for us to ride the river for a while."

"Reward?" Patrick was puzzled. "The girl in the boat, the one I saved? She must be the one the American is seeking, and, bloody hell, I took her right to him."

"No. Isabella has her. She'll be safe. At least for now."

Stone looked out the window at the fields knee high with indigo. The plants were heavy with leaves from which the blue dye would be made and bean pods containing the seed for next year's crop. With little effort, Patrick McLendon had become not only a river pirate, but a planter as well.

Now he'd come full circle. Traveling the river was never his choice; it had only been the means to reclaim that which was stolen from him while he awaited the chance to find Captain Lopaz and force him to admit the truth. But Lopaz had disappeared, until now, and Patrick had needed a home base. It had seemed a fair exchange to use Spanish coins to buy land the Spanish had stolen from the Indians.

The planter who'd sold him the plantation had already sown the indigo seeds. Indigo was one of the few products for which there was a market in the Old World. But for Patrick, the crop of his dreams was cotton, and one day, when his name was clear, he'd set about growing it.

Across the clearing that joined the road to the river, Patrick's house was slowly taking shape. He wasn't certain why he'd even begun to build a manor house, unless it was a part of the illusion he still maintained in his secret heart—the dream of Catherine.

The plan to return for her had died, but not the memories of the time they'd spent together. Those remembrances had haunted his mind unmercifully, but never so vividly as during his night of pain in Isabella's bed. He'd imagined that Catherine had come to him, lain in his arms, joined her body to his. Even now, it seemed as real as if it had actually happened.

Patrick was tired, so damned tired. Nothing in his life was turning out the way he'd planned. He'd had dreams, but never in his grandest hope had he expected to meet a woman like Catherine who'd want to marry him.

The adventure of the sea had always lured him because it represented movement and change. Perhaps becoming a planter was a false dream that he was never supposed to realize.

But, damn it, why did Catherine still fill his mind and his heart? Catherine was the sunshine and Captain Lopaz was the nightmare, a fog of darkness that seemed to follow him and cloud his dreams with pain.

Now, just as Patrick was in a position to seek revenge, Jillico was suggesting that they give up their foraging for a time. "Perhaps you're right, Jillico.

Now that Lopaz has returned I have to make plans. I do not want to fail. For now, we'll become planters, and let him look for Stone. We'll let him live with failure for a time."

Jillico looked at the man he'd come to know as Stone, curiously. It wasn't like him to back away from a fight. Perhaps his head had been hurt more seriously than it appeared. That, or Stone was up to something. Either way, Jillico had followed the golden-haired man faithfully, ever since Jillico had been beaten and thrust into the cell with Stone, who'd protected and cared for him.

Jillico would have brought him to the swamp when they'd first escaped, but Moria had forbidden it. Instead, he'd taken both men to his friend Isabella in Natchez-under-the-Hill, where he knew nobody would ask questions.

On recovery Stone had made up his mind to recoup his losses by robbing from the Spanish who'd stolen his ship. Jillico, tired of the life his people were forced to live, joined in the cause. But Stone wasn't a true thief. Many times he gave back the goods and sent the traders on their way. Even then Jillico had known that their continued forays along the river were a mask for some purpose that he had not yet learned.

"Planters?" Jillico questioned suspiciously.

"We must do something to feed our friends. Every day more of them come, hiding from the pirates who've stolen them and the owners who've bought them. Like us, they deserve their freedom."

Stone's assessment of the situation was accurate. The Spanish turned a blind eye to the pirates who plied the Caribbean, stealing men and women, and labeling them as cattle on the cargo bills. For a fee, the

Spanish allowed them to be taken upriver to be sold as
slaves to the growing number of local plantation
owners.

The idea of owning men was abhorrent to Stone.
He'd seen his father live and die as little more than a
slave on a rich man's estate in Ireland. Stone offered
the men asylum and a share in what he had. In return
they began clearing the land and building a barrier
along the river to protect the land from flooding.
What they were building was nothing like Cadenhill,
the Georgia plantation where Catherine had been
reared. But it would be—someday.

Patrick didn't know why he measured everything in
terms of Catherine. She'd never see the primitive
plantation he'd laughingly dubbed Rainbow's End.

What he really needed was some of the luck of the
Irish, maybe a few of the little people to guide him.
What he settled for was a pint of strong, home-brewed
ale.

The drink didn't help his head. It didn't even help
him resolve a plan to deal with Captain Lopaz. What
it did, after several pints, was send him back to a state
of sleep that brought no dreams and offered no
promise of Catherine.

Catherine watched Sally wrestle with the curly mass
of hair that was neither red nor blond. It had never
been easily styled. She'd thought to pin it up and cover
her scraggly attempt with lace, but Isabella had de-
creed otherwise.

"She can't be angelic, Sally. And she doesn't have
the kind of body to vamp. So you must make her into
an innocent coquette, pouting and childlike. Other-

wise the gents will think I've put the cleaning lady on
stage as a joke.''

Catherine winced. Cleaning lady? No matter that
she'd asked for just such a job, being so described only
eroded the meager confidence she'd been trying to
build. Singing to her little sisters was different from
entertaining a boisterous gang of rowdy thieves. Back
home in Petersburg she'd never felt dowdy. She'd been
a Caden and that made people see her differently.

"Hold still, Cat. You're going to be surprised at
what I can do with these rags and a little hot mud.''

"Hot mud? You're going to put hot mud in my
hair? She said make me look like a flirt, Sally, not a
pig.''

"I've heated the mud until it's pliable, like dough.
Now I'm rolling it in squares of calico. I'll tie it in your
hair and let it dry completely. When I take it down,
you'll be beautiful.''

"I'll be ready for an apple in my mouth and a ser-
ving platter,'' Cat said crossly. She had made up her
mind not to complain. She'd allowed herself to be
laced into soft white leather boots without comment.
The high tops and lace stockings were elegant indeed.
When Sally had trussed her in a garment that drew in
her waist and pressed the air out of her lungs, she'd
kept quiet. The lacy corset had pushed her breasts up
so that they peeked out from the top of her low-cut
dress, making Cat swallow hard and remember how
Patrick had touched her there so intimately. But tying
mud-filled rags in her hair and forcing her to wait patiently while the mud dried had to be the final insult.

The dress that Isabella had provided was a deep
emerald-green, a color the like of which Catherine had
never seen. It picked up the green in her eyes and

hugged her body, nipping in at the waist and draping itself along her bosom.

"Close your eyes," Sally instructed as she helped Cat sit back down before the mirror. "Don't look until I tell you."

Catherine complied. Anything to get this evening behind her. She'd agreed to sing and entertain so that she could stay until Patrick returned. But now that she was going to have to actually perform she had butterflies the size of buzzards flitting around her stomach.

"Why are you helping me, Sally?"

"Oh, I don't know. Maybe because not much happens in my life and I admire anyone who goes after what they want. I've been here three years, Cat, and I've seen all the other girls marry and move on. I keep waiting and hoping—"

"For what?"

"I don't know. But I think you're my good luck charm. There's something about you that makes me smile. You're like sunshine."

Sunshine. That was what Patrick had called her. Catherine's mind rushed back to Patrick and their time together. Why had he left her without speaking? Had he been horrified to find her in his bed? Why hadn't he returned? Why was he pretending to be a pirate? Nothing made sense. But nothing had made sense about her feelings for Patrick from the start. She'd loved him from the first moment she'd seen him. She trusted him.

Patiently Cat waited while Sally ministered to her hair, untying the rags, pulling a large-toothed comb through her tresses and poking and pinning until at last she stepped back and said, "All right, have a look."

Catherine gasped. The woman staring back at her from the wavery mirror was a stranger, a beautiful, provocative stranger. "I swear my hair has grown. I must be wearing a wig."

"Nope, it's just the curls. I sprinkled them with starch water before I rolled them in the hot mud. Now they stand alone. Inside and out, you're truly beautiful, Cat. I can see why Stone cares for you."

"You can? I—I barely know Stone."

"You can tell Isabella that, but I saw the evidence of how well you know him. And I know Stone. He would never have bedded you, even if he was sick, if he didn't care about you."

But he thought I was Isabella, Catherine wanted to say. Still, she believed that in the deepest part of his heart he'd known that it was she, not Isabella, he'd been with. And he'd come back for her, she was certain.

On that high note, Catherine allowed herself to be escorted down the back stairs and around to the door at the back of the large area that Isabella called her drawing room. She waited in the shadows for Isabella to introduce her.

"Tonight, my friends, straight from the halls of the most famous pubs in Dublin, the Irish colleen, Cat O'Conner."

"Sure, and I'm the king of England!" a patron called out.

Catherine took a deep breath and wished she'd never volunteered the fact that she could play. Washing the dishes seemed infinitely more appealing.

The slave called Pharaoh stood in the hall behind her. "You just let 'um look at you, Miss Cat. Dey'll love your playing."

He was right, she was Cat O'Conner and she would make them all sit up and take notice. That ought to get Patrick's attention. Cat squared her shoulders, gave a tug to the top of her dress and stepped into the light. She took her time arranging herself on the bench before the harpsichord, took a deep breath and began to sing.

Chapter Seven

Cat O'Conner's first song was "Barbara Allen," a folk song about a girl who didn't appreciate the man who loved her until it was too late. Her voice was as weak and thready as worn-out sackcloth. She knew that she was much too tense and if the expression on her face was a reflection of her desperation she must look more like the grim reaper than a dance hall entertainer.

The sound of Pharaoh's words snaked from behind the piano like a whistling wind. "Your name is Cat. Play with them, girl, like a ball of yarn!"

Cat straightened her shoulders, tilted her head and pretended the man sitting nearest her was Patrick. She gave him a flirty wink and launched into a boisterous rendition of a song she'd heard Roman, the grist mill operator back home, sing about a drunken sailor. The mood of her audience changed from indifferent to jovial. By the end of her half hour of entertainment, the bright-eyed girl with the sunshine smile had her audience in the palm of her hand.

Catherine Caden let her fingers trill across the keys for the last time and stood. She bowed her head, stunned by the exuberant appreciation of the men, and backed into the hallway behind her.

"I did it, Pharaoh. I really did it, didn't I?"

"Dat you did, ma'am. And a right lively performance it were."

"I never knew that I could sing."

"A fine voice ain't always the measure of entertainment, ma'am, it's de spirit of the heart that counts most."

Catherine hurried past the drawing room and up the stairs to the bedroom, considering Pharaoh's words. When she'd sung "The Girl I Left Behind" there hadn't been a sound in the place. She knew without being told that every man there was picturing someone, somewhere, he'd left behind—mother, wife, sweetheart. From a distance, she heard Isabella's deep voice singing a song in French and heard the men clapping enthusiastically.

Heaven was a special place and she was learning it meant different things to different people. For her it was a waiting place, a safe haven where she'd stay until Patrick returned.

Later, when she heard the heavy thud of feet come up the stairs, she tried to close her ears to the sounds of the man in the room next to hers. Now she understood what was happening. She'd learned in Patrick's arms. But the guttural moans and the haste of the act seemed at odds with what she'd felt with Patrick.

As the room beyond went silent, Catherine felt the flutter of her heartbeat. Her arms were crossed across her breast, her hands holding her forearms as if it were she experiencing the passion that had exploded beyond the flimsy wall of her bedchamber.

"Oh, Patrick, where are you? Are you all right? Did you leave me voluntarily or were you taken away from me?" She'd asked Sally about Patrick, but Sally replied that nobody had heard of him. Stone came and went as he wished.

Her questions went unanswered, filling her with anguish, yet all the while she was forced to remind herself that it was likely that Patrick did not know the true identity of the woman he'd bedded. He'd been caught up in some fever-induced dream. She had no excuse for her actions. Even now she could scarcely separate reality from the mind-numbing passion of what she'd felt. Was it always thus?

Did her sister, Amanda, share the wonder of her body's response with her husband, Rush? If so, why had she fought the idea of marriage so vehemently, giving in only when it became necessary to save the plantation? But Catherine had no one to ask. The miracle that she'd experienced with Patrick remained with her constantly and her body yearned to experience the sensation once more.

There was a knock followed by Sally's quick entrance into the softly lit room. A frown on her face spoke more of reluctance than delight. "Men! I'll be so glad when I can leave this place behind and submit myself to just one man. At least I can choose."

"You find it so very awful?"

"Yes, mostly. Though sometimes—"

"I found it very pleasant."

Sally looked at her curiously. "It can be, with the right man. And heaven knows—" she stopped and laughed lightly at her own choice of words before she corrected them "—at least some people in Heaven claim that Stone is considered a gentle man, for a pirate."

"Tell me about him, Sally...please. Has he always been a pirate?"

"Nobody knows for sure. He escaped from the New Orleans prison and came here. He was hurt. Isabella took him in. It was after he recovered that he began to rob the Spanish and their friends."

Catherine felt her heart lurch. "He was in jail?" He was in jail. That was why he hadn't come back for her. He couldn't. "For how long?"

"How long was he in jail? I don't know. I only know that the Indian, Jillico, brought him, and Pharaoh here, and he's been coming here ever since."

Patrick had been in jail. The ship captain who'd sailed Patrick's ship had said Patrick had killed someone. Catherine hadn't believed it then and she didn't believe it now. Patrick might have killed someone in self-defense, but he was no murderer.

"He's innocent, of course," Cat said with utter conviction. "I mean, he may be a pirate, but I'm certain he has good cause."

"Maybe, but the men he robs don't take kindly to losing their cargoes, to say nothing of their purses."

Catherine was assimilating the information she'd gathered. Patrick had been falsely accused of murder, put in prison and had his ship stolen, forcing him into a life of crime. She had to do something to help. Charles! If Patrick could take his case to Charles, she was certain that President Washington would intercede to clear Patrick's name.

Sally stood by the door, watching the myriad expressions ripple across her new friend's face. Sally was well liked by the other women in the house, but the secret she shared with Catherine made their relationship more like that of sisters. Still, she recognized the innocence of the girl and the stubborn determination that she'd already shown by making her way to Patrick's bed.

"I don't know what you're thinking, Cat, but these men are the most vicious, untrustworthy villains on the river. You may have known Stone before, but he is still an outlaw. Why don't you go back to that nice man who was looking for you and forget about Stone?"

"Charles? I can't marry Charles. I'm certain he is a very fine man, but...he doesn't like this country and—he can't even swim."

"Well, I suppose that could be important. But I wouldn't turn down a respectable man like that for an outlaw."

"Yes, you would, Sally. When you love someone, nothing else matters."

There was another knock on the door.

"Come in," Cat called out.

Isabella stepped into the room. "Never invite anyone in. You never know when one of the guests will slip up here, and unless you wish to perform a different duty, you must always make certain who is knocking."

"I didn't think."

"Working here is pleasant and rewarding, my little one, but there are certain things you will learn. Please leave us, Sally."

Sally scurried out the door, giving Cat a reassuring smile as it closed behind her.

"You did very well tonight, Cat O'Conner."

"I was so scared I could barely sing."

"Perhaps, but it fostered your innocent image. You make the men think of home, and their sadness translates to more visits to the bar and with my girls. I think we'll play on this by presenting you as a virgin and allowing you to suggest a certain promise of naughtiness with your songs."

"Then I can stay?"

"Yes, though why you'd want to remains a mystery. Which brings me to my question, why are you really here, Catherine?"

Because I'm waiting for Patrick. "Cat," she corrected. "I'm looking for someone."

"Not the man who was here with Lopaz?"

"No—someone else," she said, sensing that Isabella might not support her efforts if she thought that the end result might cost her the Irish river pirate she claimed for her own.

"You are not betrothed to this Charles?"

"No," she answered firmly. "I'm promised to someone else."

Moria slipped through the open window and came to stand beside Jillico, who was staring out into the blackness of the bayou.

"Why do you continue to follow the American? These are grave times for our people."

Night birds called, and the swamp creatures made little whispered sounds as they slid through the water. Hordes of mosquitoes swarmed around the two people, but the the juice of a certain bog plant that they had applied to their skin kept the creatures from biting.

"He isn't an American," Jillico corrected, "he's from Ireland, a country across the sea. And he cared for me when the foreigners beat and imprisoned me. He is my friend."

"The Natchez have no friends. We have learned to live among the intruders because we have to, but they are all our enemies. Yet you bring him into our midst and ask me to heal him."

Jillico let out a deep sigh. "The Natchez are nearly extinct. I believe that we must forge a different place for ourselves in this new world."

"No, you are wrong, Jillico. Our corn is ready for harvest and you are here, growing weeds that color the white man's clothes. What need have you for their coins?"

"Not I—Stone. He must feed the growing numbers of those who escape from the men who wish to make them slaves."

The woman moved in front of Jillico and looked at him sadly. "I have tried not to see what the visions foretell, but that cannot be. What will come will come, and I cannot stop it. You have brought this golden-haired man here, and because of him, the vision is destined to come true."

"What are you saying, Moria?"

"I came today because you sent for me to heal this man, but I warn you that his indigo will never leave the river. Bad spirits come here, and to our people. We must make sacrifices to the Great Sun."

"Moria, why do you say such evil things? Stone saved my life."

"Yes, and for that, I thank him. But I give my help only because he brings the White Woman back to us."

Jillico stiffened. Not since his father was a young man, when the French governor ordered the Natchez tribe to vacate their village so that he could build a plantation, had the White Woman appeared. She'd led the Natchez to retaliate, but eventually the French armies had overcome the tribe, capturing their ruler, the Sun King, and sending him, along with most of his young warriors, into slavery on the plantations of Santo Domingo in the Caribbean.

"Moria, the White Woman is only a legend handed down by the elders of our tribe. Who knows the truth?"

"The truth is as it always was. Long ago the Great Sun was absolute ruler of our people. He was aided by the White Woman, and along with his brothers and sisters, called Suns and Women Suns, they ruled our tribe."

"Yes," Jillico agreed, mentally recounting the tale. "I know. Even the great French king learned of the Sun King's power and proclaimed himself Sun King of his people across the great water."

"And now the Sun King has come back to us. He waits only for the return of the White Woman and our people will rise up and take back what is ours."

"The Sun King has come back? From where? How?" Jillico was startled. Since his escape from the Spanish prison, he'd left his people to become Stone's assistant, joining in the raids willingly, living on the piece of land Stone had bought and named Rainbow's End. "Why have I not learned what is taking place?"

"Because you have turned your back on your people. You wish no longer to belong to the Natchez nation. Only because the man you follow is in favor with the Sun King has he been allowed to live."

"Stone? How is this possible?"

"Because the Sun King was returned to us on the Irishman's ship when it came from the island in the South, where the cane is grown."

Jillico wanted to protest. But he knew that most of the men brought in from the islands on Stone's ship were slaves—forced to accompany their masters, either willingly or unwillingly. Was it possible? Could this slave revolt in the Caribbean have returned their leader?

Had the Sun King reappeared as he had long ago when his people were in chaos? No, the Sun King would be an old man now, too old to lead. Still Moria knew many things. Her words were foreboding. Jillico felt a chill fall over him.

"How will he know the White Woman?"

"She comes in fire, as a cat, or perhaps she walks on cat feet. This image is less clear. All I know is that she will follow Stone."

"Cat?" Jillico didn't tell Moria of Stone's mutterings about someone he called Catherine. He thought her to be Stone's woman, and he didn't like the feelings he was picking up from Moria about this Cat.

"The White Woman is coming—soon. And I cannot stop her."

Jillico looked at Moria and frowned. She'd always seen what others could not, but he'd never taken her visions seriously. The Natchez had seen the French come, then the Spanish and now the Americans. His people were too few now. They'd lost their power and their will to fight.

"Why are you sad, Moria?"

"Because, unless I can stop her, she will take what should be mine."

"I don't understand."

"Neither do I, Jillico. I only know that I cannot become the Sun King's mate while the White Woman lives."

Inside the crude hut, Patrick listened intently. He didn't understand all the mumbo jumbo about the White Woman coming on cat's feet. Moria's healing power was apparently only a part of her powers as a medicine woman. Patrick knew the Indians believed in visions and dreams, but the return of the Sun King seemed more than just a vision.

He'd heard the rumors about a man who roamed the city streets by night and lived in the swamps by day, a man hiding from both the Spanish and the Americans, and he'd been puzzled by the strange stories. Now he was beginning to understand the large numbers of slaves fleeing upriver. Slaves from the Caribbean islands. Slaves who spoke a language that even the Spanish didn't understand.

Could there be a connection between the man in the bayous, the Indians and the slaves? So far the mysterious man had remained unidentified. And he'd remained hidden. Obviously he wasn't a planter or he'd have made his intentions known.

Patrick tried to recall the men who'd boarded and taken possession of his ship. But when he'd resisted having his goods replaced with those of the fleeing plantation owners, he'd quickly been imprisoned below deck, so that he knew little of what happened until they'd reached the port at the base of the river. He'd been turned over to the Spanish authority who'd charged him with murdering one of the more outspoken planters and released him to Captain Lopaz to be killed.

At the time Patrick had thought it odd how little concern the other planters exhibited. They'd said practically nothing, almost as if they were afraid.

Patrick moved and winced. The pain in his head was easing, though the powerful dream he'd had remained. Another dream about Catherine. But Catherine couldn't have been there, in Isabella's bed. Catherine couldn't be in Heaven. Still his body responded to the thought with such need that he forced himself to stop and consider other things. Now he had Lopaz to deal with.

He was bothered by Moria's prediction that his indigo would never leave the river. Sale of the anticipated crop would cover the next payment on the land. He had counted on that when he agreed to the exiting planter's terms. Disaster would be imminent if the leaves didn't make it to market.

For now he'd force himself to go slowly, to force Lopaz to admit the truth and clear his name. He'd have to proceed carefully in order not to find himself back in jail. Besides, he wanted Lopaz to suffer first, really suffer. Until his crop was in he'd avoid the river and the lure of robbing the Spanish. Until the indigo was harvested he'd wait, and plan.

Two weeks later the caterpillars invaded Patrick's indigo fields, systematically devouring every plant in their path. While Patrick made plans to burn his affected fields in an effort to stamp out the invasion of insects, Captain Lopaz was deciding to claim the now famous Cat O'Conner for his bed.

Sadly, Catherine was learning that being headstrong and opinionated counted for little when she didn't have the Caden name and authority to back her up. Every question she asked about Stone was met with blank stares. And he hadn't returned.

Every night for two weeks Captain Lopaz had come to hear Cat O'Conner sing. Every night he'd invited her to supper and every night she'd declined.

"I absolutely refuse to have anything to do with that horrible man," Cat said firmly. "I am an entertainer, not here for—for a man's pleasure."

"Cat, you don't understand," Sally said fearfully. "He can close Isabella's business. He can arrest her and send all of us packing."

"He's just a man. We have Pharaoh to protect us."

"Yes, and Lopaz has the entire Spanish army at his disposal. He may be out of favor with the governor, but he is still an officer and there's little love lost between the citizens and the outcasts who live in Natchez-under-the-Hill."

"You don't understand, Sally. I don't—I wouldn't know how to—"

"You don't have to bed him. At least not yet. He only wants you to have supper with him."

"Just supper, nothing more?"

"That's what Isabella insisted on and he assured her that he'd respect your innocence."

"But what if he finds out that I'm not a virgin?"

"How can he?"

Catherine couldn't answer that question. Her mother would have said that there would be some mark on her forehead that proclaimed her shame. Except it hadn't felt like shame. And all she could see when she looked in the mirror was the woman Sally had created, a woman who presented herself on stage as a creature made of saucy sunshine, all the while suggesting naughty night dreams.

Catherine studied the men in the audience each night, hoping beyond hope that one of them would be Patrick. But he was never there, at least not yet. And if she didn't have a meal with this odious man, Heaven might be closed. Her mother had always warned her that if she didn't mend her outspokenness she'd lose her place in heaven, but she'd never taken the threat seriously.

Until now. But if Heaven was closed, she might not be there when Patrick returned. And he would come. In her secret heart, Catherine knew that they'd be together again.

They had to be.

"All right, I'll do it."

Singing to Isabella's clients was one thing; it was impersonal and Catherine could allow her mind to pretend whatever she liked. But being shown to a seat directly across the table from the dark-skinned Spaniard was a different matter.

She'd thought of him as a loud bully. But in fact there were those who considered him to be quite handsome, in a cruel, cold way. She suspected that many of the women who went to his bed went willingly, the first time. But, according to Sally, if they had a choice, there was no second time.

"Good evening, *señorita*. Please sit down."

Catherine allowed the man to draw up her chair. She felt the unwelcome caress of his fingertips as he slid them across her shoulders before he backed away.

"I look forward to hearing you sing this evening. Your songs bring great enjoyment to this dreary assignment I've been posted to."

"Oh, haven't you always been here?"

"No, I preceded your arrival by only a few days. It seems fate has placed us together."

Pharaoh poured wine into the glasses, delaying his duty as long as he could before withdrawing.

"And where were you before, Captain?"

"Originally? Madrid. Most recently, the settlement at Pensacola in the southern Spanish territory."

Cat took a sip of her wine and put her glass down once more. Her inaudible sigh told the captain that he was going to have to move slowly if he intended to gain the information he was certain she had.

"Tell me about New Orleans," she was saying. "Have you been there?"

"Yes. New Orleans is a wicked, wicked place, *señorita*. One of the more interesting places to visit is the Slave Theater."

"Slave Theater? You don't mean something like a slave market, do you?"

"No, this is an actual theater. The wealthy planters of Santo Domingo had little to entertain themselves and they trained some of their slaves for the stage. During the revolt they came to New Orleans with the man who owned the theater. Unfortunately, he was killed by the American on whose ship they traveled."

Patrick. The man was talking about Patrick.

"You're certain," she said tentatively, "that he's dead?"

"I was there. Just as I'll be there when the pirate Stone is captured. Once I've put him in prison, I'll take you to New Orleans. With him on the loose, even reaching the city is a risk."

"Is he that wicked?"

"He is a very cruel man. I'm told he is a frequent guest, here, *señorita*. I guess you must have seen him when he was here."

"Me? Oh, no, Captain. I'd be scared to death of the man. Besides, I've heard he's left the river." She put on a frightened face. "Have you seen him?"

"I don't think you'll have to worry, Miss O'Conner. I've been sent here to capture him. It's only a matter of time before one of my people will locate him."

"Really? I thought all these people looked out after each other."

"When the purse is big enough, all loyalty is forgotten, my dear."

In spite of her plan to remain impassive, Lopaz's certainty alarmed her and a frown creased her brow. There was a cruelty about her supper companion that simmered just below the surface.

Across the table, the captain studied Miss Cat O'Conner curiously. He didn't believe for one minute that she was Isabella Angel's niece. Isabella's manner and bearing were impeccable, but they had been learned. This girl's refined upbringing was genuine, yet she, too, was fascinated by Stone.

All women seemed to be fascinated by the criminal element. In Lopaz's country the wellborn females wore veils and attended hangings where they pelted the criminals with rotten fruit. But Lopaz would have wagered that this girl was more sheltered. She could barely disguise her distaste for him, but her interest in Stone was obvious.

"Stone is an evil man, my dear. You mustn't allow yourself to be deceived by his appeal. If he wants a woman, he takes her. It matters not that she is promised to another man.''

"Really? I hadn't heard that.''

"I recall one incident,'' Lopaz fabricated, trying to strike fear in the girl, ''when Stone coveted the wife of a wealthy planter. He eventually stole the man's wife and his land. In disgrace the Spanish nobleman was forced to take his wife and return to Spain.''

"But you're here now, Captain,'' Cat said, trying not to let his words upset her, ''and you will protect us, won't you?''

Something about the man's boastful manner told her that his story about Patrick was meant to intimidate her. In spite of his present activities, Patrick was an honorable man. She could attest to that. He would never have allowed himself to dally with another man's wife.

Catherine would have pursued the matter, but Pharaoh brought their food, after which the captain turned the conversation away from Stone to tales of New Orleans, and his hope to return to his former position of authority once he'd completed his assignment to take the pirate into custody.

But Captain Lopaz was growing weary of the charade. He intended to do more than protect the runaway bride. If he couldn't charm the information he needed out of her, he'd get it another way, after he'd enjoyed her virginal young body.

When thick sweet coffee was finally served, Cat tried to excuse herself by saying that it was nearing time for her performance. Just as she was poised to make her escape they were interrupted by a messenger who appeared at the table.

"Captain, come quick. There is a man at the dock who has news of the pirate. He reports that the Natchez have taken Stone into the swamp."

Captain Lopaz stood eagerly. "Can he guide us?"

"So he says."

"Ready the men while I say good night to this lovely lady."

Catherine felt her heart twist. Someone was going to lead the Spaniard to Patrick. No! Not if Catherine could stop them. Not if Catherine could get to him first.

"Surely you won't depart at night, Captain. How will you ever find a man in that swamp in the darkness? It isn't safe."

"I appreciate your concern," the Spaniard said, stretching himself with pride. "I will be quite safe."

"Yes," the messenger agreed. "We go into the swamp with one of the Indians, a Natchez. He escorts us to a place where the slaves are hiding. There we will find the pirate."

"But," Catherine continued, taking the captain by the arm, "why not wait until morning?"

For a moment the captain was torn, reluctantly planting a moist kiss on Catherine's hand before turning away. "Good night, *señorita*. I will return triumphant and we will resume our evening."

The captain was not out of the house before Cat was seeking Pharaoh in the kitchen. "Please, Pharaoh, you must help me, quickly."

"Of course, Miss Cat What do you need?"

"A guide. There must be someone in Natchez-under-the-Hill who knows where Stone and the slaves are hidden."

"Why would you wish to know?"

"Because, because—" She searched her mind for a reasonable answer, then settled for the truth. "I know you won't believe this, but I came here to find Stone. His real name is—oh, it doesn't matter. But Captain Lopaz has found an Indian who has agreed to lead him into the bayou to find Stone. I have to get there first, to warn him."

Pharaoh studied the girl, convinced that if he refused to help her she'd likely dash onto River Street and be kidnapped by the first sailor she asked to take her into the swamp. Yes, he knew where the slaves were hidden, he'd given many of them directions to Stone's burgeoning plantation. But to tell this girl? He couldn't take a chance.

"Just let me tell Miss Isabella, den I'll get word to him myself. You go on with your singing."

Catherine breathed a sigh of relief. Pharaoh knew where Stone's stronghold was. He knew how to reach Patrick. "No. I must come with you. I must! Get me some men's trousers, a hat and a frock coat. I won't slow you down, I promise. Trust me, Pharaoh."

Though Isabella voiced strong opposition to Pharaoh's plan, the black man reluctantly agreed to let Catherine come along. Before the Spanish garrison had readied itself for travel, Cat and Pharaoh were poling a pirogue down the Mississippi and into one of the bayous that was almost hidden from view by brush along the water's edge.

Instantly they were in another world, a quiet, foreign world of silent movement, swishing water and biting insects. At one point Pharaoh pulled to the bank and instructed Catherine to cover her face with mud as protection from the swarms of vicious winged creatures.

It seemed as if they'd followed the twisting waterway for hours when a flight of birds overhead interrupted the silence. The ground rumbled with the
footsteps of frantic animals in flight, as they suddenly parted the brush, jumping the waterway at its
narrowest and plunging in where they were forced to
swim.

"What's happening, Pharaoh?"

"Don't know. 'Pears the animals dey spooked over
something." He sniffed. For some time he'd thought
he smelled the remains of a campfire. Now he was beginning to understand that the strong odor of fire was
intensifying.

"Are you certain you know where you're going?"
The unrest of the animals was beginning to affect
Catherine's already tenuous control over her fears.

"Yes, miss. You just set there still and quiet. Likely
dey already knows we's coming."

"You mean Stone is close by?"

"Stone, or one of his kind. I been hearing they signals. Pray it's Stone."

But it wasn't Stone who surrounded them the moment the dugout beached itself on land, but a circle of
Indians, as wary and uncertain as their captives.

Neither Pharaoh nor Catherine could decipher their
excited chatter. A certain amount of awe, mixed with
apprehension, seemed to dictate their movements as
they argued over what they ought to do. Catherine finally determined that it was her they were concerned
with. She heard the phrase White Woman repeated
over and over. At last they could see the light of a fire
in the clearing ahead.

"I'm here to see Stone," Catherine repeated as firmly as she dared as they reached a clearing in the forest.

"And who are you?"

The woman who stepped into the light was like a shadow, dark and beautiful. She gave the illusion of movement yet she remained absolutely still. She was like the earth, giving the appearance of solidity when it shimmered beneath the weight of Catherine's light step.

"I am Cat O'Conner."

"Cat—she comes on cat feet, in fire. Yes. I am Moria. We have expected you. Please come."

Behind the woman great smoke was belching into the sky, chased greedily by orange flames. The world seemed to be swirling as the fire raced across a low-growing field, reaching the black water, then being lifted by invisible air currents that bent the scraggly plants with its force.

"What do you mean, expecting me?"

"You're the White Woman. We knew you'd come. You are welcome."

"I'm white, yes, but I don't understand. Where is Patrick?"

"Patrick? Who is Patrick?"

"Patrick—Stone. The pirate called Stone. I've come to warn him."

"You've come to warn me of what?"

The deep weary voice that asked the question wasn't laughing. It wasn't even laced with the amusement she'd remembered from all those months ago. But it was Patrick, her Patrick, his face smudged with soot, his golden hair hanging in damp curls against his furrowed brow. "Tell me, boy, warn me of what?"

"This is the second time you've called me a boy, Patrick McLendon. Are you blind?" Catherine pulled the felt hat she was wearing from her head and turned her face toward the light, toward the man she'd come so far to find.

He stood, looking at her, allowing his eyes to record and understand what he was seeing. This muddy-faced person was a woman—no, not a woman, but *the* woman he'd dreamed about, the woman he'd carried inside his head for months.

Patrick told himself he was tired. For most of the day he'd been overseeing the burning of his diseased fields, separating them from those not yet infested by the caterpillars.

It was at dusk that the flames had gotten away from his men and raced toward the river. He was tired, hallucinating again. He was seeing what he wanted to see, not what was there. For a moment he allowed the hunger in his eyes the freedom to see and believe, then forced that weakness away.

"No," he protested sharply. "You can't do this to me again. You're not Catherine. You can't be. She's in Petersburg. This is a trick."

The brush parted at that moment as a wild hog charged into the clearing, screaming her rage at having her habitat upset. Catherine's nerves, already on edge, shattered completely and she began to laugh. For a moment Patrick stared at her in disbelief. It *was* Catherine, his Catherine. He'd recognize that laughter anywhere. While the screeching pig disappeared into the night, he opened his arms in welcome.

As she flew into them he swung her around, shouting joyfully. "Ah, Catherine, darlin'. The first time I saw you, you were surrounded by pigs. Do you always travel in such strange company?"

"No stranger than a man who's friends with the little people."

And then he kissed her, muddy face and all.

Once he'd tasted, satisfied himself that she was real, that this was no dream, he slipped his arm around her shoulder and turned to Pharaoh. "How did you get here?"

"Not now, Patrick," Catherine interrupted. "Now you must listen to what we've come to tell you."

"Yes, Señor Stone," Pharaoh said tightly. "We come to warn you."

"Warn me of what, old friend?"

"The Spanish captain, Lopaz. He is behind me. Someone has betrayed you, Stone. You must flee."

Patrick looked around at his burned fields and half-finished house. Catherine was here and Lopaz was behind her. She'd come to warn him. Because of him, Catherine was in danger. If Lopaz found them together, Catherine would disappear as completely as Patrick McLendon had vanished.

Patrick's grievances with the man were quickly forgotten. He had to save Catherine. Patrick nodded his head in agreement. "Yes, Catherine must go, quickly."

Catherine looked around at the destruction. "But what about the fire?"

"Everything here is lost, anyway," Patrick said. "I am not cut out to be a planter. I was only fooling myself."

"Except for the cane," one of the slaves said. "We gonna save the sugarcane."

Jillico appeared beside the native woman. "Hurry, Stone, the time has come."

"Yes," Moria agreed sadly. "The time has come."

There was more here than Patrick could fathom. "The time for what, Jillico?"

But it wasn't Jillico, but the woman who spoke. "It is time for the White Woman to return."

Chapter Eight

"Pharaoh, you will take Catherine back with you. Take her to Isabella."

"No, Patrick. I won't go."

"You will go, Catherine. Lopaz is a dangerous man. You don't know what he will try to do."

"Oh, but I do know. He'll try to get me into his bed."

That stopped Patrick. Reluctantly he decided that Catherine was right. For now, the only way he could protect Catherine was to keep her with him.

"All right, you will stay for now," he agreed, turning to Pharaoh. "Thank you again, old friend. Make certain you're not seen. Are you sure you won't be in trouble over this?"

"Only Miss Isabella knows and she say, 'be careful.' She know about de slaves and me helping them get to you for safety."

"The slaves! How can we protect them?"

"Do not worry. Dey'll be hidden until de danger is past. Go now, Stone, and take care of dis woman who loves you."

Patrick insisted that Catherine be placed in his pirogue. She was right about the danger to her. Patrick knew Lopaz, probably better than anyone. Patrick had had firsthand experience with his cruelty. Protecting Catherine was more than simply a matter of his desire for her. It was his responsibility and he had no intention of delegating the task to someone else.

They got into one of the larger flatboats, with Jillico at the bow and a man Patrick didn't know at the stern. The other Indians and the medicine woman, Moria, followed.

Catherine settled herself in Patrick's arms and released a sigh of contentment. Patrick tried to question Jillico about their destination but was quickly signaled to silence. Like ghosts, the Indians disappeared into the night, carrying Patrick and Catherine to safety.

The wind dropped. Behind them the fire would reach the second bayou and burn itself out, revealing the location of Patrick's burned-out plantation to anyone traveling on the water. For now, what was left of his cotton field was safe, for it was behind a section of trees. He couldn't be certain about the fate of his house. It mattered little now, for he was heading away from it as quickly as the small boats would take them, with no promise that he'd return any time soon.

Had it not been for Catherine he'd have stayed and faced Captain Lopaz. Without him, Patrick had little chance of clearing his name of the charge of murder. But Catherine's safety was more important than his honor.

Flight was alien to Patrick. He'd never left anything unsettled unless he was going forward to meet new challenges. From his first desertion at fourteen, when he'd signed on a trading ship, abandoning his native land, he'd set his sights on making his fortune.

The trading ship was captured by pirates who allowed a brash young Patrick to join their crew. Years passed and Patrick's fortune and reputation grew. And then one day he'd bought his own ship and become respectable. He'd never returned to Ireland, falling in love with the brave new country that had thrown off its oppressor and claimed independence.

Then, he'd fallen in love with Catherine. She'd never understood why he'd left her behind. But it had to do with his promise to her family to do the honorable thing. Honor was important to Patrick. That same honor made him refuse her love until he could offer her the kind of life she deserved. And he'd come so close to doing that. But fate played funny tricks. Instead, he'd lost his ship and his good name. Then as if all the luck of the Irish had deserted him, an insect with an insatiable appetite had turned his dream into ashes.

Suddenly, like the sun peeking out in the midst of a thunderstorm, Catherine appeared. Unafraid, she'd turned her back on her own world and followed him.

"I knew they were wrong when they said you were dead," she whispered.

"Who said?"

"The man who bought the *Savannah Lady* and sailed her to Charleston. Officials there sent the report to Rush."

"Then why in God's name did you leave Cadenhill and come to Louisiana?"

"Why did I come? I was sure that you weren't dead. I had to find out why you hadn't come back. Now I know. You were in jail."

"You know that?"

"Yes, I just don't know why."

"Captain Lopaz charged me with a murder I believe he committed. He wanted to cover his tracks and steal my ship while he was at it. He tried to kill me."

"Now he's come back to finish the job." Catherine shivered and snuggled closer.

"No, it's greed that brings him here, and the desire to regain favor with the governor. I don't believe that the captain knows who Stone is. He thinks Patrick McLendon is dead, as perhaps he must remain."

"Fine. I didn't come all the way across the country to be a widow. I'll be Catherine Stone. One name suits me as well as another."

"Shhhh!" Moria's voice carried across the silence.

Patrick held Catherine tighter. Brave, determined, always ready to go after what she wanted, Catherine had forced Pharaoh to bring her to warn him. And now Patrick was taking her God knew where, and to God knew what. It made his heart sing to know that she trusted him enough to go without question.

In the darkness he couldn't see her. But he could feel the ever present energy that surrounded her, just as it always had. She nestled into the curve of his arm, pressing her cheek against the rough sailor's shirt he was wearing. Her arm rested against his and she lay silently content to be in his care.

As always, he felt an overpowering need to protect and cherish her. There'd been a time when he'd built invisible walls to separate them, walls she seemed neither to see nor to acknowledge, a time before he allowed himself to imagine a future such as had existed on her family plantation, Cadenhill.

When he'd bought his plantation and called it Rainbow's End he'd been fooling himself into believing that such a life was possible. And that foolishness had nearly taken away the instinct that had accounted for his survival. Now he was being hunted by the same man who'd nearly killed him. There was no more time for dreaming of a future. Dreams only softened him and made the danger greater for the woman he dreamed of.

The woman he dreamed of?

Catherine sighed and with her fingertips traced the edge of his cheek along his beard. Her breathing slowed as she fell asleep with her hand resting on his face, content now that she was where she'd set out to be, in Patrick's arms again.

Patrick pulled her close, his large, rough hand burrowing beneath her coat and holding her tight against him. Her skin was like warm satin beneath his touch and he reveled in the feel of it, just as he had in his dreams. She would always be sunshine and satin.

Dreams? Like that night at Isabella's. As he breathed in the soft, feminine smell of her, and felt his body adjust to her closeness the dream started to clear, like an early morning fog lifting in the sunlight. Suddenly he was no longer certain of what he remembered.

Had he been dreaming, or had Catherine actually been there, in his bed, in his arms? Had their lovemaking been real? Had he done the thing he'd sworn not to do? He was stunned.

He didn't understand how it could have happened. But nothing about his relationship with Catherine had ever made sense to him—how she could have crossed a wild unsettled land to reach the Mississippi, how she could have found her way to Heaven, and to him.

As the first rays of light peeked over the trees Patrick heard the onset of a breeze. Like a sigh of contentment the air ruffled the branches of the great live oaks, tangling in the wisps of gray moss as if it had found its place of refuge.

A spindly-legged blue heron watched curiously from his place among the cattails. He seemed part of the illusion that there was land beneath the lush green grass. He didn't move as they passed and Patrick had the feeling that they were sliding through a liquid, lonely dream.

"Will Lopaz be able to find us, Jillico?" Patrick's whisper carried across the black water.

"No."

"Where are we going?"

"To a spiritual place, known only to the Natchez."

"What about the guide who's bringing Lopaz? Will he know?"

"No, only the old ones know of the Sun King's temple."

Catherine was still sprawled against Patrick, her eyes still closed in sleep. Even with the muddy face and men's clothing she was beautiful. He'd never felt such completeness as he did holding her in his arms, feeling her head pressed against his chest. But that couldn't be.

He lay, convincing himself that his need for her had triggered his dreams. They couldn't have made love. Even half out of his mind with fever he couldn't have disgraced her that way. Still, the nagging doubt plagued him, forcing him to swear that even if what he'd remembered was real, it couldn't be allowed to happen again. He couldn't turn her into the kind of savage he'd become.

But he knew, even as he made his vow, that if it were up to Catherine, they'd be together again. She'd never once hidden behind subterfuge, or womanly wiles. If she wanted a thing, she went after it. Just as she'd come after him.

At the time she'd burst into the clearing and ripped off her hat he'd been so startled to see Catherine with Pharaoh that he hadn't thought anything through.

They were fleeing civilization, hunted like criminals both by the Spanish and by an American who believed that his betrothed had been kidnapped by the pirate named Stone. The American's reward, added to the one offered by the governor, had been impossible for the guide to resist.

As harsh reality set in, Patrick realized that his situation was even more precarious than before. Catherine might have found him, but she couldn't stay with him. As soon as he could make proper arrangements he'd have to send her back to her family. Stone's purse wouldn't make the payment on his land, but it would see Catherine back to Petersburg.

He could accept the loss of Rainbow's End, but not what would happen to Catherine if she remained with an outlaw. Starting over again wasn't new for Patrick McLendon. He'd done it before.

Then Catherine opened her eyes. A slow, smile spread across her mouth, and the day seemed infinitely brighter than before.

Catherine wished she were alone in the dugout with Patrick. But perhaps that would have been a mistake. She wouldn't have been able to keep her hands from touching his firm body, running her fingertips along the scars she'd examined so intimately that night they'd spent together. They'd capsize and drown. She blushed and lowered her lashes, fearful that he could read her thoughts.

Though she knew full well that he didn't remember what had happened between them in Isabella's bed, every nerve ending in her body was responding to his presence. He'd thought the woman in his arms was Isabella. She wished he'd known that it was Catherine. She tried to hold back the twinge of jealousy she felt. Isabella had offered Patrick a safe haven when he most needed it. Catherine couldn't resent her for that. Once they got to wherever it was they were going, she'd tell him the truth about that night.

She allowed herself to watch him without reacting, allowed her gaze to drift to the sky overhead and the thick growth along the bank. Soon enough they'd come to a stopping place and for now she could fill her eyes and her thoughts with his presence.

When the sun was straight overhead, the natives beached the pirogues and Jillico gave Patrick and Catherine permission to stretch their weary legs while food was prepared.

"Be careful," he instructed Catherine, who was looking for privacy in order to deal with certain natural functions. "There are snakes."

"I'll accompany you." Moria seemed to materialize beside them.

Catherine looked up, caught between the warning and the urgency of her need. Patrick, unsettled by the strong sense of danger raised by Moria's offer, walked to Catherine's side. "No, I'll go."

Catherine hesitated. She knew it was foolish to feel uncomfortable with the native woman, but she did. She gave Patrick a hesitant nod. Even having such a discussion wouldn't be considered proper in Petersburg, but she was not in Petersburg now, and this was Patrick. "Thank you."

"I won't intrude. Come."

Moments later they were in a private area, where moss hugged the riverbanks and silence stretched tightly across the clearing.

"I'll be beyond the tree limbs, Catherine, out of sight, and sound. Don't be afraid."

And she wasn't. Feeling embarrassment with Patrick was foolish. They'd shared life's closest moment and soon they'd share more. Silly qualms were out of place here in this wild country.

Catherine took care of her needs quickly and hurried back to Patrick. At last they would have a moment of privacy, a moment to hold each other and exchange a kiss. She felt her heart quicken as she saw him waiting, so serious, so stiff.

"Patrick," she began, then stayed her step as his stern expression found hers. "Aren't you pleased to see me?"

"I'd be lying if I said no, but you shouldn't have come here. It was dangerous for you to make such a journey unescorted."

"But I had proper chaperons. I came with the Weatherbys who run the trading post up the river."

"I can't believe your mother approved of your actions. What about my old friend Rush? As your sister's husband he should have stopped you."

"Nobody could have stopped me, Patrick McLendon. I had to find you."

"You should have remained on Cadenhill until..."

"You returned?" He was right. She'd promised. Telling him that she'd given up and agreed to marry Charles seemed wrong now. She'd gone back on her word, but the question about his fulfilling a promise hung between them.

"And I didn't," he finished, feeling the weight of his guilt. After his escape he could have sent word, but what would he have said? He'd been branded a murderer and until he could prove otherwise, he had had no right to claim Catherine. He'd thought then that it was better if she believed him dead. He couldn't expect her to forgive him for bringing her pain, yet she had. But more than that, he had no right to censure her for her actions.

Catherine wanted him to open his arms, to hold her and say that what was past was past, that they'd only go forward. But suddenly another lie was between them now, one of her making—her engagement to Charles. And she couldn't bring herself to admit that she'd lost faith in Patrick's promise to return, not if she expected him to believe in her promise to wait. She'd hold her confession until they'd resolved this strange new barrier between them. When the time came, he'd understand, the same way she understood about Isabella.

She parried with a question of her own. "Why did you let me think you were dead?"

"It was better that you should have. There are things you don't understand."

But she understood more than he knew. The thing that came most clear was that Patrick had changed. His blue eyes weren't laughing anymore. He was serious and staid. She desperately longed to find the man she'd fallen in love with and searched for a way to bring back only a glimmer of that glorious adventurer. Tension sliced the air and fed the anxiety that surrounded them.

"I understand," she improvised, "that Stone has been accused of stealing some plantation owner's wife."

"Plantation owner's wife? Who told you that?"

Shaking her finger at his surprised expression, Catherine warmed to her ploy and went on, "And I want you to know that I expect that sort of thing to stop as soon as we're married. I won't have my husband accused of frivolous dalliances!"

Frivolous dalliances? That was too much. Patrick tried to remain serious, he did. The situation was serious. but this was Catherine and suddenly he was back on the banks of the Broad River with the woman who disregarded every convention and stole kisses like a child stealing strawberries from a berry patch. He couldn't contain his amusement.

At the sound of his laughter Catherine's heart melted. Nothing had changed. He was still her love. Her lips trembled as she tried to maintain her serious position in the face of the absurdity of their exchange.

"And another thing, Patrick McLendon, you're to stay away from Heaven. You will have no need for such a place in the future."

Were it not for her dirty face and the devilish sparkle in her eyes, Patrick might have let her go on, giving orders, feeding her own position of authority like a banty rooster in a henhouse.

But they weren't on the banks of the Broad River, and the time for playing was gone. It was the hardest thing Patrick had ever had to do, but Catherine must go back and it had to be willingly. He had no trust that she wouldn't jump in the river again if he returned her against her will.

"Catherine, my love, I wish things were that simple. But everything has changed. My life is no longer my own and it may never be."

Catherine stilled. She didn't like the expression on Patrick's face and she knew he wasn't going to be dissuaded.

"You're right, Patrick. Your life is my life and there's nothing you can do about that."

"I can see that you get back to Petersburg where you belong."

"I belong here!"

"No, this is a lovely dream, Catherine, but it isn't real and you can't stay. I may never clear my name and you can't marry a murderer."

"And you can't send me back if I choose to stay."

"How will you live?"

"I have a job. I work for Isabella Angel, in Heaven."

"You work for Isabella? I don't believe it."

"Why not? You're a pirate. Why can't I work in a saloon?"

"Because you don't belong here. I don't want you here."

"You don't want me here?"

"I don't want you here."

And this time she believed him. The truth was that however much he might want her, he was rejecting her. Patrick knew how to walk away, he'd spent his life doing that, never allowing himself to believe that someone could want him unequivocally.

She'd disguised herself as a man, rubbed that awful mud on her face and arms to keep from being eaten alive by mosquitoes as big as bats and come through a swamp to get to him, only to be rejected. She'd been wrong in pursuing him. Now, all she could do was find a way to save face.

"All right, Patrick. I understand. You don't want me. I'll go, but not back to Petersburg. I like this land and its people and if I can't stay with you, I'll find another way to live. Because I'm a survivor, just like you."

With every moment she stood there, her soul reflected in her eyes, Patrick was finding it harder to hold back. But he couldn't let himself give in to a promise he couldn't keep yet. Lopaz was too close. One more touch, however, and he'd not be able to send her away.

"No, Catherine. As soon as I can make arrangements I'm sending you back to Petersburg and safety."

Back? He would send her back? She refused to believe that until she saw the determination in his eyes. But he was wrong about that. She hadn't come this far to go back. Catherine Caden lived in Petersburg. Here, she was Cat, and Cat wouldn't be dictated to.

"Try it," she warned, the pain of his wanting to get rid of her forcing her to hurl words before she stopped to consider. "I'm staying. One thing you don't know, Irishman, is that I am betrothed. You didn't want me. I found someone who did. My future husband might have something to say about where I reside."

"Your future husband?"

Catherine had reached out, finding the first thing she could think of to hurt him as his words had hurt her. But she'd found the one thing that might stop Patrick. She could tell that from the sudden tensing of his body. So be it. If Patrick wouldn't keep her, Charles would. At least that would stop her being sent back to Petersburg until she could sort out the mess she'd made.

"Yes, his name is Charles Forrest and he's in New Orleans, waiting for me to arrive. He's asked me to marry him."

"Then it's true? You're the woman being sought by the American? But you were running away from him the night of the storm."

"I wasn't running away," she snapped. "We had a misunderstanding and the boat was swept away. Then you tied me up and took me to Isabella. I found that I liked working there more than I did being promised to either one of you."

Catherine blinked back the tears and whirled around.

"Catherine, wait. You can't be serious."

"Who's giving the orders now, Stone, or Patrick?"

She swung around and sprinted into the forest, heading back toward their temporary camp, losing her battle with the tears as she fought her way through the thick growth of honeysuckle vines. Finally, winded, she stopped and leaned against a tree, gasping for breath.

She'd thought she was alone, until there was movement in the brush, and the dark-haired woman called Moria stepped out from behind the tree. "Forget Stone! You have a higher mission."

"I had a mission, and I've fulfilled it. Stone has been saved. Now I'll return to Natchez-under-the-Hill."

"No. That cannot be. I do not understand why you are the chosen one, but the legends foretell your coming and I know you to be the woman for whom we've waited."

"What kind of nonsense are you spouting? All I want to do is get out of this swamp and wash myself with sweet-smelling soap."

Moria glanced around, took note of the curses coming from the brush where Patrick was searching for the woman he'd said he would protect. Moria was torn between her desire to take the woman away and her fear of what would happen if she interfered in what had been prophesied. But she was the only one who knew the full prophecy. The Natchez were her people. Only she could help them, not this outsider. She'd followed the Sun King's wishes. But now, Moria would make her own decisions.

"Quickly," she whispered. "Follow me. I'll get you away."

If Catherine hadn't been hurting so badly she would never have followed the strange woman, never have gotten into her boat. But her heart was shattered. All she wanted to do was wound Patrick, as he'd wounded her. He didn't want her. He was sending her back. If Patrick truly loved her, he would never send her back to Charles. Perhaps that was her mistake.

Men were different from women. Men didn't love so deeply or so completely.

"How long will it take us to get back to Natchez?" Catherine asked.

But Moria didn't answer. Instead she seemed to be listening, concentrating intently on some sound that Catherine couldn't hear. Perhaps she did have some magical powers, for the bushes seemed to part, allowing them to travel down tributaries that were not there before the dugout nudged a path.

Catherine had never seen any human being remain so still. At first Catherine had thought she was old, but now she realized that she'd been wrong. An old woman couldn't move the boat as Moria was, effortlessly, skillfully. Her thick dark hair fell down her back like the black water beneath their boat, reflecting the threads of light that sifted through the trees. In the shade she appeared dark and elusive. In the light she radiated strength like the blade of a knife. And always she was silent. Like a chameleon, she adapted herself to her surroundings as needed.

By late afternoon Catherine began to realize that something was very wrong. "Moria," she began, trying not to give in to the fear that was mounting, "please, talk to me. You're making me worry."

"There is no need for you to worry, White Woman. You will soon understand everything."

"Why do you keep calling me White Woman? I have a name—Catherine."

"You had a name. Now, White Woman, you must wait. The Sun King will answer all your questions."

Chapter Nine

"Where is she, Jillico?"

Patrick charged back to the riverbank, his expression murderous.

The Indian looked up in surprise. He'd been gnawing on a piece of dried meat and washing it down with water. "Who?"

"Catherine. She ran away from me. I thought she'd be here."

Jillico frowned and looked around. "Moria went to find berries. Perhaps they are together." He quickly gave instructions to the natives to begin a search. Soon they learned that Moria, Catherine and one of the pirogues were missing.

"Moria's taken her," Jillico finally admitted in exasperation. "Why would she do so without me?"

"Why?" Patrick demanded, cursing himself for driving Catherine away. In his effort to keep from giving in to his desire for the woman who'd risked her life to save him, he'd put her in danger. He should have known that she'd never take orders, not even when they were for her own good.

"She thinks she is fulfilling a prophecy."

"Where is she taking Catherine?"

"To the sacred realm of the Sun King. Moria believes that your Catherine is destined to be the new White Woman who comes to take her place beside the Sun King and rule our tribe."

Patrick had faced starvation as a child. He'd battled the king's men in war, fought with the most feared pirate crew to sail the seas. He'd been through hurricanes and revolutions and he'd survived. But now he'd lost Catherine and he was helpless to stop whatever was happening.

"Sun King? White Woman? Jillico, I don't understand any of this. Catherine is the woman I love and I won't lose her, if I have to follow her through every bayou and swamp in this country. Either take me to her, or I'll go alone."

Jillico stared at his friend helplessly. Stone had befriended him and saved his life. Since then Jillico had been treated with respect and rewarded with his share of the purses they'd taken. He was becoming a wealthy man. But now he was being asked to go against his own people, to dishonor a legend and interfere with a request from their highest god.

"It will not change what is to happen," Jillico explained sadly. "You have lost her. But you should know that she will be honored above all women."

But Patrick was having no part of legends and prophecies. Angrily, he shook his head and began to move toward the water. "I don't accept any of this, Jillico. How could Catherine be in anyone's vision? Nobody knew she'd be here. She was to be my wife and even I didn't expect her."

"The vision goes back further than our memory, back to the time we existed in the thick air, the fog that concealed our path. Our people lived in chaos. And then the Sun King came, bringing the wind to blow away the mists and show us the way. With the Sun King came the mother of us all, the White Woman. And the Natchez prospered.''

"So what happened to her?"

Jillico's face fell. "It is said that when the outsiders came they took our lands and our people began to change. In the beginning, my clan lived on the great river at the place of deep water. In my grandfather's time the French came and claimed our land. We fought, but they were stronger. They killed the White Woman and took our Sun God away. The old ones survived by retreating to the villages where our ancestors built mounds of earth away from the intruders' eyes.''

"And you think Catherine is that White Woman? That's absurd." No more absurd than the knowledge that the shadow woman in his dreams had been Moria. But she was. He didn't know how he knew, but he did. And with that thought, he tightened the muscles in his jaw.

"The vision has been passed down that one day a white woman would return to our sacred place.''

"But she didn't come of her own accord, she's being taken there.''

"No. The sacred place to which she was destined to come was the site of your plantation. In that same clearing we once held the ceremony that signaled the beginning of our new year.''

Patrick was becoming very concerned. This had to have been a terrible coincidence. That he would buy a plantation that had once been the site of ancient Indian rituals could be a reasonable happening. The Indians had been here long before the white man came.

But the rest of the legend was too absurd to be believed. The coming of a white woman? "What about the plantation owner's wife who was there before? Couldn't she have been the woman in your vision?"

"No. The vision could not be realized until the Sun King returned. Once he came back we knew she would follow. It was foretold that, on cat's feet, she would come in fire to save the sun and we would know her because of her fearless manner and her hair, the color of the flames."

The burning of the indigo fields. Fearlessly, Catherine had come, to warn him about the Spanish captain, Catherine with her strawberry-colored hair—not red, perhaps, but given the other conditions, close enough. And her name was Cat.

"And what will happen to this White Woman?"

"She will bring wisdom and power to the Sun King."

Wisdom? Patrick wasn't sure about that, but power he understood. Whoever this Sun King was, he'd enhance his position of authority by having a white woman at his side, any white woman with red hair. And Catherine would fit that description very well. For a moment he allowed himself a smile. The man didn't know what he was asking for. Unless he broke her spirit, controlling Catherine was going to be a full-time job. A sense of dread fell over Patrick.

"Where are you, little people? Forget the rainbow and the pot of gold, just send me a little magic."

"Little people? Are they here?"

"Never mind, Jillico. I understand if you can't help me, but I ask you not to stand in my way. Just give me a boat and let me go."

"No, I cannot do that. I am bound by my honor to protect you. Perhaps this is also meant to be. I will take you to our ruler. It will be he who decides your fate, not Moria. Come."

Moments later the two men were poling themselves down the waterway, leaving the other members of their party behind as a buffer between them and the Spanish. Later Patrick would wonder how any man could know where he was going, or how to get back when he wished to return. But for now, he put himself in Jillico's hands, trusting him without question as he had refused to trust Catherine.

In the swamp behind, Captain Lopaz slapped at a mosquito and swore. "I don't believe you know where that renegade is. We've been mucking about in this swamp for two days."

"*Señor,* we would have been there by now if your men hadn't insisted on stopping so often."

Captain Lopaz knew the Indian was right but he refused to agree with his logic, reasoning that agreement elevated their guide to a position of authority to which no self-respecting Spaniard would agree. His men had never become accustomed to the rigors of this liquid wilderness. Now they were showing signs of unusual fatigue. This morning two men had become so ill that they'd been sent back. The captain was beginning to regret his hasty departure from the fort.

He'd brought thirty men, but carrying proper equipment would have required more boats than they'd been able to find. Believing their mission would be brief, they'd made poor choices in supplying themselves for the pursuit. They had already used up the fresh water, and the brackish swamp water was as unpleasant as the hordes of insects that fed constantly on their bodies.

As if the Indian sensed the captain's waning interest in the search, he stepped to Lopaz's side and spoke in a low voice, imparting the last bit of information he had, like a carrot before the Spanish donkey.

"The Green Mounds of Earth are near," the Indian said, "the place where the new leader of the Natchez reigns and where you will find Stone."

Find Stone. Lopaz liked that. Finding Stone and the girl would be enough to regain favor with the governor. But a new Indian leader? That was an added attraction. It was unlikely that the Natchez would mount a threat to the fort, they were too scattered, and too few.

Lopaz searched his memory for what he knew about the Natchez. He'd been told that long before the Spanish had come the Natchez Indians had suffered great losses trying to reclaim their land from the French. Afterward, they'd retired into the swamp and all but disappeared. There couldn't be enough of them left to worry about. Still, it might enhance his position with the governor to report that he'd quelled this potential source of trouble.

"A new leader? Who?"

"He is called the Sun King."

"And he's just come?"

"Yes."

"And where did he come from, this new leader?"

"On the Irishman's ship, from the island in the sun."

The Irishman's ship? The sea captain he'd killed? There was something disturbing about this connection between the Irishman and the pirate, Stone. Lopaz had wished a hundred times that he'd never laid eyes on Patrick McLendon. The inquiry from the American president about McLendon's death and the sale of his ship had been the start of Lopaz's trouble.

Lopaz knew the passengers on board the *Savannah Lady* believed that he'd been responsible for the death of the plantation owner on board. Only he knew that, for once, he'd been innocent. Blaming the Irishman solved two problems, by assigning guilt and removing any proof that the ship had been stolen. Lopaz and his superior had split the profit and shortly thereafter, the other man had returned to Spain, leaving Lopaz to answer the inquiry. In the end Lopaz had escaped blame for any wrongdoing, but doubt had been raised and as a result he'd been reassigned to Florida.

But the Sun King on that ship? He couldn't recall anyone that fit such a description. Of course he'd paid little attention to the slaves and it was possible that there'd been a stowaway that he might not have known about. Many stowaways who came in on foreign ships slipped away in the night and were never seen again.

"And Stone is in league with your new chief. Where is this Sun King?"

"In the village of the sun."

"God's blood, you heathen. You talk in riddles, and I suspect that you've been deliberately leading us in circles. If you don't get us to that village by noon, I'll feed you to the alligators! Now get moving."

The guide nodded and quickly resettled the soldiers in the low flat pirogues. He poled the craft carrying the captain, hiding the smile on his face. He'd take them to the village and collect his fee. He'd disappear before anyone knew he was there. Then later, he'd return. Although he was a commoner, he was now a wealthy man. Moria would look with favor on his courtship.

Catherine was already regretting her act of rebellion in running away from Patrick. The heat had become unbearable. There was hardly a breath of air and what she breathed in was so thick that she felt smothered. Perspiration was running down her face, streaking the mud. She knew she must look as though she were wearing war paint.

Wishing for a simple garment like the one her silent companion was wearing, she unbuttoned her coat and fanned her damp skin with her felt hat. Immediately a swarm of insects descended, forcing her to refasten the buttons.

Leaning over the side of the shallow dugout she scooped up the warm water, splashing it on her face to wash the dried mud away. Let the insects devour her. Nothing could compare with the pain of Patrick's rejection.

"No, do not put your hand in the water!"

At first Catherine was startled. Then, feeling her hackles rise at the dictatorial tone the woman was using, defiantly stuck her hand back in the water, caught sight of the snake swimming lazily across their path and jerked it back.

"Poison!" Moria said.

Catherine's second act of defiance had nearly been one of self-destruction. She settled back in the boat and let out a deep sigh of frustration. She'd never been one to feel sorry for herself. And she had no plans to begin now.

She could continue to sing at Isbella's, or she could travel to New Orleans. But Charles was in New Orleans and she wasn't ready to face him yet.

Glancing overhead she studied the sky for a long puzzled moment before she realized what was wrong. The sun was on the wrong side. If they were heading toward the Mississippi it should be behind her. It wasn't. The rays of light penetrating the forest were angling in from the front. They were traveling west, away from Natchez-under-the-Hill. The full understanding of her error was becoming clear. Instead of heading back to Heaven, she was being kidnapped.

"Stop this boat this minute!"

Moria neither relaxed her stance nor moved her gaze from where they were going.

"I demand to know where you're taking me."

The pirogue continued to snake its way through the narrowing tributary of water.

Catherine sat up and began to swing her feet over the sides, causing the flatboat to dip into the water.

"The gator would like that," was Moria's only comment.

Gator? Catherine pulled her feet back inside and took a quick angry breath. She hadn't come hundreds of miles, braved a wilderness, a storm and a house of pleasure to be eaten by an alligator.

This time she'd really done it.

"Oh, Patrick, where are you?"

But there was no answer. Only the throaty croak of a frog and a splash as he leaped into the water just ahead of the boat.

All right, Cat O'Conner, if you can't swim to safety, at least you can find out something about who this Sun King is and what he wants with a white woman.

She didn't want to think that he'd sent for her because he'd learned she worked at Heaven. But he wasn't likely to have a harpsichord out here. If he expected anything else, she might as well take her chances with the gators.

"Tell me about this Sun King."

"Wait. You will learn soon. Answers come to those who've learned to be silent and listen."

"You know that I belong to the pirate, Stone. He'll come after me."

"It matters not. What will be, will be."

Moria suddenly turned the boat into a thicket whose branches reached out and caught in Catherine's hair before parting to reveal a vee-shaped indentation along the shore.

Catherine pushed the escaping strands of hair beneath her hat and watched as Moria leaped to the bank and tilted her head, directing Catherine's attention to a well-worn path.

"You first," Catherine said.

"No, I will follow."

Any thought Catherine might have had about fleeing was quickly dispelled by the sight of a very large field of ripe corn. A plantation. She could get help. Catherine made haste toward the fields with Moria behind her. After a heated walk they circled the corn, its stalks heavy with ears tasseled brown and ready for harvest.

Catherine could see that she'd made another error in judgment, for beyond the field, rising above the clearing in the distance, were four green mounds of earth. Atop the largest mound was a huge building with a thatched roof. On what might have been called a porch on a normal house, stood a man magnificently bedecked in a cape of brown turkey feathers and an elaborate headdress.

"Go forward," Moria urged. "The Sun King awaits."

"I don't think so." From behind, the familiar voice spoke. "Not without me."

Catherine turned in a show of relief. "Oh, Patrick. I'm so sorry. I should never have run away. How did you find me?"

Moria turned toward the two men and gave Jillico an angry look. "How?" was her first question, followed by a sadder, "why?"

"Because I believe this to be wrong," Jillico answered. "It was not difficult to catch you. Two strong men can move faster than two women."

"You are a fool!" she snapped. "You cannot stop what is to come. I have seen the vision."

"You have seen what you choose to see, in order to gain power."

"Silence!" The voice of the man standing on the green mound carried across the open space and boded no pleasure. "Captain McLendon, I believe. I will speak first with you. Moria, prepare the White Woman."

Several braves materialized beside Patrick, escorting him past the silent watchers who'd gathered in the clearing. "Do what they say, Catherine. I'll find a way to get us out of here."

Only Catherine heard the words of the medicine woman, uttered under her breath, her lips curled into a deadly smile. "I don't think so, Mr. McLendon."

* * *

Patrick climbed the steps, narrowing his eyes as his gaze met that of the imposing figure looking down on him. Patrick didn't recognize him. "Do I know you?"

"No, Captain McLendon. I am Simicco, the Sun King. I owe you a great debt. Had you not come to my island, I would not yet be here. Normally I would kill you, but a Natchez always repays his debts."

Patrick reached the top step and studied his captor. The man was tall, very tall, with handsome features and dark, almost mahogany skin. His startlingly white teeth and short cropped hair gave him an intense look that must have struck terror in the hearts of his followers, and his enemies.

"You were on my ship? You're not one of the planters."

"No, I was one of their trusted slaves."

"You were a slave on a sugarcane plantation?"

"No, I was a slave, but I was taught to entertain. To the planters I was the Dancemaster."

"But you're an Indian."

"Yes, as was my father, before he was captured and sold into slavery by the French."

"An Indian slave?"

"Yes, Captain. You were already imprisoned and did not see me come on board your ship. I was owned by the man you killed."

"But I killed no man."

"Of course not. I killed him."

"Why?"

"It was necessary. I had prepared all my life to return. Then you came and you were my answer."

"And now you plan to kill us?"

"Us? Oh, no. I learned much from the white man. Do not kill that for which you may have use."

That macabre statement gave Patrick no reassurance. Have use? Was he referring to Catherine, or himself? What use could the Indian have for either?

Patrick rubbed his eyes. He'd gone without sleep for nearly two days. From time to time his head still ached as it had the night of the storm. Storm? It seemed only days ago that he'd rescued a girl from a runaway pirogue caught up in a sudden summer rainstorm. Now he felt as if he were caught in the middle of a different kind of storm.

This man was no ordinary slave. Patrick didn't have to be told that he was different from the slaves who'd sought refuge at Rainbow's End.

"Am I to learn what plans you have for Miss Caden and myself?"

"But of course, when the time is right. For now, you will accompany our young friend, Jillico. I think I will let him share your quarters while he contemplates the error of his impulsiveness."

"I won't allow you to harm Catherine."

"I don't intend to."

"Then what?"

"Soon, very soon you will understand."

What Patrick came to understand was that both he and Jillico would be prisoners, hands and feet bound, and guarded by two silent tribesman who had obviously been given orders not to allow them to converse.

Listening at the base of the mound, out of sight of the men above, Moria frowned. When she turned to Catherine she allowed her expression to reflect her disgust. Speaking in her native tongue Moria gave instructions to the women who'd come curiously forward.

Catherine found herself being led away from the settlement to a thatched hut, where she was held prisoner for the next two days. She was bathed and fed. Her pitiful men's clothing was exchanged for a loose cotton garment that was more comfortable. The absence of undergarments was a shock, but by the third day she was beginning to appreciate the simplicity of her clothing.

Other than two women who snickered as they administered to her needs, she saw no one. Any attempt at communication was met with blank stares and she finally gave up. On the third day the cooking fire outside her hut was extinguished and no food was prepared. The ground was swept clean. Fresh sleeping mats replaced old ones, and the two women began to whisper.

Clearly, something was about to happen.

Finally the two women led her out of the hut for the first time, directing her down a slope to a stream that collected in a pool deep enough to stand in.

They motioned that she should remove her clothing and get into the water. Torn between the need for a good bath and resentment over not understanding what was happening, she resisted.

"Remove your garment, White Woman."

It was Moria, standing beneath a tree on a rise just above the stream.

"Why, what are you doing? Where is Patrick?"

"You are about to be reunited," she answered with a mystic smile, "as soon as you are purified."

Moments later Catherine was totally nude, submerged in the water and subjected to vigorous scrubbing with fine sand. Her hair was rubbed with the sap from a pulpy plant, then rinsed. Next she was dressed in the same kind of garment the other women were wearing, except hers was made of fine white linen and beaded with shells and bits of colored stones. On her feet were moccasins detailed in the same design.

"Where are we going?" she asked, trying to elicit some response from her stony-faced captor.

"To a most sacred ceremony. Our people have been preparing for days, forgiving old debts, fasting, drinking of the black root plant. The time has come to end the old and begin the new."

"I hope you're providing a meal. I'm very hungry."

The other women looked at each other, but they didn't answer.

By the time they'd arranged her hair, tying it with feathers and colored stones, and drawn her back into the circle, the sky was darkening and a new fire was laid. Up close she could see the steps leading up the side of the largest mound, at least twenty, if she could judge.

The people hung back, watching silently as Catherine was led to the steps and prodded to mount them. The grassy mound showed signs of recent work. Fresh dirt filled holes left by uprooted trees and vines. The house at the top was not old, its thatch roof still unbleached by the sun. Though the village showed signs of age, much of it was new. In the distance were suggestions of other mounds still covered with vines and brush.

On the top step, Catherine paused. From the time she'd started her climb she'd refused to look up, using the time to gather her composure and her strength. She had no idea what awaited her, but she wouldn't let them know that she was afraid. A sudden breeze caught the red feather that had been woven into her hair and whipped it across her face.

Catherine suddenly remembered the horse her sister, Amanda, had entered in the New Year's Day race. The family desperately needed to win the purse being offered to pay off their plantation debts. Catherine had impulsively tied a red scarf to the horse's bridle, declaring it would bring good luck. As the animal approached the finish line, the scarf had come loose, spooking him, and he'd lost the race. Catherine couldn't help but wonder if the red feather was an omen of ill fortune to come.

"Give me your hand, White Woman."

Catherine raised her gaze to meet the eyes of a man who looked as if he'd just stepped out of the picture of hell she'd seen on the minister's wall back at the trading post. Where Patrick was laughter and merriment, a golden man who caught every joy and magnified its power, this man was dark and foreboding.

"My name is Catherine," she snapped, and stepped onto the top of the mound unassisted. "And stop calling me White Woman."

"As you wish, my lady of sun and fire. Welcome."

Catherine swallowed hard and turned to look around. She might be a prisoner of this man, but she had no intention of allowing him to control her.

She could see three other mounds, forming four sides to the clearing. A second building was being constructed atop the mound opposite.

"What are you building?"

"A temple."

"And this building?"

"The house of the Sun King and the White Woman."

"What have you done with Patrick?"

"Here, Catherine."

From the shadows beside the dwelling Patrick rose and stepped forward. He looked tired, gaunt, a strained look narrowing his eyes. Moria had said the men had fasted to prepare themselves for the ceremony. It was obvious that Patrick had been required to join them. She wondered what that meant.

Like Catherine, he'd been dressed as an Indian. He was wearing only a loincloth, his massive chest catching the glow of the flames like a glowing shield, reflecting the strange streaks of color that covered the scars on his body. His feet were bare and his hair had been pulled back and was held in place with a band around his forehead.

His eyes weren't laughing now; their deep blue color seemed to burn with intensity. And once their gazes met she felt that intensity rekindle the connection between them that had been there from the first moment they'd looked at each other. He might have thought to send her away, but nothing could separate them—ever.

She took a step toward Patrick. "If these people are looking for a king," she said, "I think they picked the wrong man."

Chapter Ten

In a melody of chimes that came from the shells now fastened around her legs and the hammered copper chains looped around her neck, Moria rose from one of the two thronelike chairs that had been placed on the platform. She was dressed in a white garment made of animal skin, also trimmed with a beaded design of colored stones and shells. In her hand she was holding a staff. "Silence!"

Catherine felt Patrick's hand tight on her arm, cautioning her to comply. Without words, he drew her away from the spot where she was standing at the top of the steps, and to his side.

Catherine could tell from the set of his chin and the tension of his stance that he was merely waiting. There was a power about him that defied control, the steel will that had made him survive the long months in prison, the calm fury that radiated from somewhere deep within. Fury, not carefree laughter now filled his eyes. This was a different Patrick and she understood that there was much about this man she loved that she did not know. And yet she trusted him with her life.

After surveying the spectators below, Moria took two steps forward to stand beside the imposing figure in the plumed headdress and cape made from turkey feathers. At the moment she reached the space beside the Sun King, she lifted her staff and watched it burst into a crown of fire.

From below a hushed ahhhh swept the watchers who fell silent in response.

"Quite a show," Patrick said in a low voice.

"I expected lightning to strike," Catherine agreed in a whisper.

After an appropriate length of silence, Moria began to speak. "For years our people have wandered in chaos and darkness, as did our forefathers. Many seasons ago, in the midst of evil, the sun came down to drive away the night and bring our people to plentiful life."

Catherine felt the power of Moria's words, spoken in the broken English and French her people had adopted in their years of dealing with the traders and intruders on their land. There was a slight lilt to her speech that suggested she might even have attended some kind of school sometime in her life.

But it was the power of the woman herself that most disturbed Catherine. She was more than a medicine woman, she was some kind of sorcerer, or witch. Her tone was somber, her speech a rolling rhythm that caught her listeners in its spell and overwhelmed them with the painful memories of life.

The people listened. Not a breeze ruffled a leaf. Not a child moved, nor did an animal cry out. A muffled drumbeat began. Catherine felt a sense of terror begin to slide down her back. What was happening?

"The Sun King has heard our cries and returned to our side. Now the White Woman has joined him. They will make us strong again. Our crops already grow.

Our children will no longer die from the white man's sickness. The Natchez will once more be warriors and we will reclaim our rightful place in our land.''

She dipped her staff and nodded her head. The drumbeat began to build, increasing in speed and intensity until it reached a fevered crescendo, then stopped.

The Sun King began to speak. ''For three days we have prepared. Our hearths are cold. Our council house is made new. We've laid fresh mats on the clean swept floor. Our bodies have been purified by fasting and the drinking of the black root. We've bathed in the great river. Now, the White Woman, she for whom we have waited, has come. Let the final celebration begin.''

Moria took up the telling of the events. ''In the clearing below, a new sacred fire has been laid. Four poles have been planted, symbolizing the four corners of the upper world where our ancestors await our coming. The oldest and wisest of our people will lead the ritual. It is time.''

She started down the steps, pausing dramatically, effectively, until every eye was riveted on the woman holding the still burning staff.

''A modern-day Moses,'' Catherine thought, not realizing that she'd spoken aloud until the feathered native turned his frown of disapproval on her.

At the bottom of the mound Moria raised her staff and began an incantation in the language of the Natchez people. She began walking toward the fire as she spoke, seeming not to see the people prostrate themselves as she passed. Inside the four poles she stopped, bowed her head, then touched the staff to the ceremonial fire, which blazed up with the force of a small explosion.

"Now," the Sun King said forcefully, "we sit and watch." He held out his hand to Catherine, who leaned back and pressed herself against Patrick's chest.

"Where?" Patrick asked.

"She sits here—" he indicated the chair Moria had vacated "—beside me."

Patrick glanced down into the clearing. Once the flames started licking the sky Moria turned and started back to the mound.

"I don't think that's too wise, King. Your medicine woman seems to think it belongs to her. Since Catherine is mine, I think we'll just watch the show from here on the ground."

"No!" The king turned a thundering frown on Patrick, making it clear that the occasion did not lend itself to levity and that his commands would be followed.

"Thank you," Catherine said brightly, shaking her head at Patrick in warning. "I am very curious about the ceremony. Who are those people?"

"They represent our past, our memories, our dreams and our wisdom. They dance to pay tribute to the Great Spirits that have brought our people from the far corners of the earth to this place of new beginnings."

Four old men wearing animal-skin loincloths and headbands made of white skin trimmed with feathers, and four old women wearing only white skins draped around their waists, had moved inside the circle, two standing beside each pole. Around their necks the men wore medallions of hammered copper, the women necklaces of shells.

More shells, strung on leather thongs and tied around the women's lower legs, clanked musically as they walked. On their heads they wore a special ornament made of corn husks that had been split into strands and allowed to hang down like a green waterfall. Both the men and the women carried green stalks of corn.

When Moria reached the top of the mound once more she raised her staff and faced the clearing. When the staff was dropped the drums started up and the Natchez began to dance.

Moria allowed a smile of triumph to lift the corners of her mouth as she turned—and caught sight of Catherine sitting in the chair she had vacated. Covering her displeasure with an almost imperceptible lowering of her eyes, she moved to the other side of the ruler and dropped gracefully to the ground.

"The ceremony begins, my king. The lookouts are in place and the sacred house is prepared."

"You have done well, Moria."

Patrick didn't miss the exchange. Though she'd spoken in their Indian tongue, Patrick had learned enough of the language from Jillico to know what she'd said. He hadn't revealed his knowledge and though he didn't understand why, neither had Jillico.

Jillico? Where was he? Earlier they'd been taken to the river and washed, dressed and returned to wait, this time in separate huts. He hadn't seen his young friend since. They hadn't been left alone at the river and each time Patrick had tried to talk, one of their guards had rudely instructed them to be silent.

Now he studied the village. The mounds weren't new. They'd been there, unoccupied, if he were any judge, for years, probably centuries. Only the fields had been tended. He could see the corn, hanging heavy with ripe ears. The stalks supported vines of beans. The Indians along the Mississippi were farmers.

But there'd been a time, according to Jillico, when his tribe had been fierce warriors, who sacrificed their enemies to the Sun King, often cutting off their heads and preserving the faces to be used as a kind of mask. There were no heads impaled on the poles surrounding the ceremonial fire, but there might have been.

There might still be. Patrick had a bad feeling about this. He couldn't allow the ex-slave king to make Catherine his coruler, and that was what was about to happen. It wasn't hard for Patrick to see the intense jealousy of Moria, and he wondered why she was making it so easy for Catherine to take her place of power.

Moria had actually brought Catherine here. Why hadn't she arranged an accident in the bayou and disposed of her competition?

Where was Lopaz?

And where were the rest of the members of the tribe? Even Patrick could see how few men, women and children there were below. Certainly, according to Jillico, time and unsuccessful warring had decimated the tribe. Even the white authorities had ceased to worry about the Natchez, concentrating all their concerns on the Muscogee and the Choctaw. He could only surmise that the remaining Natchez people had joined the other tribes and were no longer the warlike people they'd once been.

But now they had a new leader, who wanted to make them strong again, a leader Patrick had brought to Louisiana on his own ship to rekindle the legend of the Sun King. And part of that legend was coruled by the White Woman.

Catherine. Catherine who'd come to the Mississippi in search of him had been drawn into a world that could destroy her. All because of him.

She was watching the proceedings intently, trusting that all would be well. Where he saw disaster, Catherine saw adventure. She turned and smiled at him, her eyes beaming with excitement. There was no fear in her. Where another woman might have averted her gaze from the half-nude bodies, and censured their beliefs, Catherine exhibited only interest.

From the first moment he touched her he'd recognized that special quality about her. His awareness had only grown with their being together. When she'd lain back against him in the pirogue, the electricity had blazed more potent than ever. It had taken every ounce of his control to keep his feelings secret. He wished now that he hadn't held back. If he'd voiced his concerns instead of deciding that he hadn't the right to be with her, none of this would have happened.

But he was too accustomed to acting alone, making his own selfish choices, for that had been his way. Until now. All the selfish things he'd done had only increased his wealth and added to his success until he'd decided to do right by Catherine—give her up.

The one truly noble act of his life, had brought them to this disaster. God help them, for he could see no way that he could save Catherine from a fate he didn't want to think about. The Sun King needed a White

Woman, an outsider. And Catherine was the perfect choice.

But the nagging question kept coming back. Why was the White Woman the title given to the coruler of the Natchez?

The Sun King began to speak, explaining the dance to Catherine. "They praise Mother Earth for taking the seed into her belly and giving forth the corn. The others are allowed to join in the dance."

Now they will come, Patrick thought. But even when the rest of the tribe joined in, they were still few in number.

"Tell me, Your Majesty," Catherine was asking, "why do you elevate a white woman to such a place of honor? I wouldn't think that your people would welcome an outsider."

"There are those who would have us believe that the White Woman was an honored medicine woman who painted herself white," he answered. "That is false. The White Woman was a commoner."

"You do not know this to be true," Moria said in a tight voice.

"No!" The Sun King snapped. "My father told of the coming of the first Sun King and the White Woman who was his mate. They gave us rules and order. From her we learned that the wives of the nobles must come from the ranks of the most common of our tribes. Is this not so?"

Moria nodded her reluctant agreement.

"But," Catherine persisted, "if the White Woman were really white, who was the Sun King and where did he come from?"

"From the west—from the land of the sun."

"Then the Sun King was not a member of the Natchez?"

Patrick thought the Sun King might have admitted that the original White Woman was not an Indian, but the suggestion that his ancestor was not of pure blood brought a rise of indignation to their host and an indiscernible warning to Catherine.

Patrick had his doubts about the legend. If the original Sun King had come when the Natchez were in chaos, Patrick would have bet the chaos referred to a time of war when they were being defeated. The Sun King who suddenly appeared, bringing a white woman who instilled order in the tribe, could have been anybody, including the early explorers who had looted the Aztec and traveled east in search of more treasure.

Though a glance around this ancient village didn't suggest the presence of riches.

But where were the braves?

Where was Jillico?

And where was Lopaz?

The next several hours were the most difficult that Patrick had ever experienced, worse even than the time of his beating and the long months of imprisonment.

Members of the tribe brought shells filled with drink to Catherine and Patrick. Too long without food, they swallowed the fruited beverage hungrily, at first allowing their shells to be refilled with little thought to what they were consuming. Too long without sleep, Patrick feared, however, losing the keen eye he would need to get Catherine away. No one saw him begin to spill much of the liquid into the grassy surface of the mound.

The dancers changed periodically, disappearing into the shadows, then returning to dance more wildly, until finally they seemed to wind down into a kind of slow-motion shuffle around the fire.

The Sun King stood and held out his hand to Catherine, urging her to accompany him. She gave a concerned glance to Patrick, then seeming without will of her own, followed the Indian's wishes. She'd spent the past three hours trying to make sense out of what was happening. She wasn't so naive that she didn't understand what was in store for her.

The king referred to the White Woman as being the Sun King's mate, and the expression in this man's eyes said that time was drawing near. She was beginning to understand that the new ruler was following an age-old plan with which Moria didn't agree. And Catherine could see no way to halt the procession of events.

They descended the steps, and entered the circle of dancers. The Sun King directed the others out of the circle and began to dance. His motions were nothing like those of the others. Even the drumbeat changed.

Suddenly he gave a savage cry, startling Catherine as he threw off his plumed headdress and cloak, exposing the body of a man who was as lean and powerful as the wild creature whose posture he assumed.

Assuming the demeanor of a stalking animal, the Sun King crouched, feigned attack and backed away again, working his way around Catherine. He preened, stretched out his body, then drew it close again, always enticing, drawing Catherine into his spell. Then the dance changed, and he indicated that Catherine should join him in a slow shuffle step around the fire.

She shook her head in rejection.

But he continued to move back and forth, enticing, charming her with his eyes until she knew that she could no longer refuse.

At the same time her limbs felt heavy, as if they'd lost the power to resist. The tension was alive, everywhere. It swirled around them, making her skin tingle and burn, as if she were too close to the fire. It was the drink, she decided. It had taken away her will to resist. She fell into an unwilling step beside the dark, volatile man.

On the mound, Patrick watched, as if he were seeing the players on a stage. He knew their lines, and though he would have changed the scenes, he could not. The drinks. There'd been something in the drinks that had taken their will. He'd been such a fool. If he hadn't been so concerned about being responsible for bringing Catherine here, he would have realized that what was happening was more than simply an attempt to intoxicate.

Now the Sun King was standing opposite Catherine, moving his body like some kind of snake, seductively, menacingly, moving ever closer. But she wasn't responding to the man, only the rhythm of the drums. Her head was flung back, her eyes clouded as if she were in a trance.

"Damn!" Patrick stood, or tried to. Assuming the same stance as Catherine, he wobbled unsteadily, as if he were unable to move. Then he caught sight of Moria and the look of evil in her eyes. She wasn't worried. She wasn't even concerned. Something was going to happen to Catherine.

"Moria, all that nonsense about the White Woman was a lie. She's not going to become the coruler of the king. She's going to be a sacrifice, isn't she?"

"Of course. I couldn't allow it to be any other way. A virginal sacrifice to the Sun King."

"And you approve? Of Catherine and what is his name, anyway?"

"He was given the name, Simicco, which means savior. As for your woman? What care I? Come morning we will all bathe in the river again, according to custom. Then comes more feasting. Then he will lie with her. Her child, not Catherine, is destined to become the next White Woman. Then the people will believe and return to the village. And I will take my place beside the Sun."

"Maybe, but what about the prophecy?" Patrick said, trying desperately to find a way out. He pretended to struggle forward, holding to the corner of the throne until he could stand steady.

"I will see a new vision. Who is to know?"

"But what about me?"

"You too, will die when the right time comes. Royalty always commands sacrifice. Until then, I will enjoy your services. You see, Simicco was correct about the line of succession. The nobility may not marry their own kind. They must take a commoner as mate to father their children."

Patrick's mind reeled under the sheer bravado of the medicine woman. He'd always trusted his life to fate and the little people, but this time he was going to need a real helping hand, and he was too far from Ireland to trust to the luck of the Irish.

"And Jillico? What have you done with him?"

"He's been imprisoned. Poor Jillico has become too much a white man. He's served his purpose. It is regrettable, but he will join you in the ceremonial pit."

"No! This can't be happening."

But one look at the couple swaying around the fire to the drumbeat told him that Moria had been in command all along. She was willing to allow Catherine to be with Simicco in order to fulfill the prophecy that would restore power. But somehow she had to deviate from the plan in order to rid herself of Catherine.

Moria had planned well and she was willing to wait.

Patrick wasn't. He'd find a way to stop what was happening. But first he had to get to Catherine. He had to break the spell that Simicco was weaving around her. His captors expected him to be incapable of intruding. That was what he intended. With unsteady steps he started toward her. As he reached the side of the mound a searing sensation sliced into his lower leg. He felt his leg jerk to the side as he stumbled and fell.

God's blood! he'd been shot. The cry he let out was as savage as that of Simicco and startling enough to the half-conscious natives that they fell back in terror, ignoring the command given by Moria to stop him.

When Patrick plunged down the steps, Catherine pulled herself back from the edge of the hypnotic trance in which she'd been drawn. With the last bit of reason she could latch on to, she knew she had to get to him.

Giving a sudden push against the pole holding up the thatched roof of cornstalks, she felt it give way. The cornstalks fell into the fire and burst into flames.

There was a hush as the corn burned.

The drums stopped.

The watching natives disappeared into the forest, trembling in fear. The corn was sacred. Only the Sun

King or the medicine woman could offer the corn as a sacrifice to Mother Earth. As if the spirit gods were registering their disapproval, the sound of more explosions filled the air. Smoke from the fire swirled upward, joining new puffs of smoke, and falling debris.

Voices screamed and burning gunpowder exploded.

The world was suddenly on fire.

Chapter Eleven

Half-running, half-stumbling, Catherine forced herself toward Patrick, reaching him at the base of the steps where he'd fallen. She wished she hadn't tasted the fruit punch, for now her head was swimming as she tried to help Patrick.

"Patrick, please! We must get away! Now!"

Overhead bursts of gray smoke exploded. The sounds and the smoke were not part of the ceremony, but of gunfire. The Indians were screaming in confusion as people were falling to the ground, shot by men approaching from the river.

From the top of the mound Moria watched. She'd expected chaos, but not so soon, and not that which would kill her people. Still, her vision had not been clear. She recognized the arrival of the Spanish soldier who wished to capture Stone. She quickly rethought her plan, seeing a new way to reach her goal.

During the confusion, she would arrange the death of the White Woman and let the Spanish take the blame. Then all that stood between her and the Sun King would be gone. The old ways would be gone. She, along with Simicco, would set new laws— together.

From the moment she brought the woman into camp, nothing had proceeded as she'd planned. Simicco had delayed the Green Corn Ceremony, following precisely the plans of old ways, disregarding her counsel as if she were not a person of importance.

He couldn't know how long she'd waited for her vision to come true, how long she'd dreamed of him, seen his face. Then one day Simicco had come to the village, tall, strong, defying argument as he told the Natchez people of his journey across the water to fulfill his destiny as the Sun King.

On that day Moria had known *her* destiny. That first night she'd come to him, he hadn't turned her away. Instead, he'd listened to her plans for their future. And he'd agreed, willingly, or so she'd thought. And he'd lain with her, not as a king, but a man.

Simicco was hers. She'd believed that the old way, that of nobility taking a commoner for a wife, was no more. But then Simicco had refused to put those ideas aside. His father, the enslaved Sun King, had carefully prepared his son, and Moria couldn't change his mind-set.

When she'd been summoned by Jillico to treat the white man she'd found a way to control what was to come. She'd bring back the White Woman, but she'd let her die. That would be enough to make Simicco see the error of his way. Moria had sworn that the return of the White Woman would never stop her from ascending to her rightful place as wife of the Sun King.

But Simicco had looked on this woman called Cat, and delayed, following each step of the old ceremonies. And in that delay, he'd become completely smitten with the girl. But Moria took heart. The great spirit had sent the captain. Instead of bringing a powerful army, he'd come with only a few poorly equipped men, arriving in the midst of the ceremony, frightening the people. Now—

With pride she watched as Simicco suddenly became the fierce warrior king, inciting the tribe to retaliate, drawing them back into battle with the intruders. Now was her chance. If the Spanish captain didn't kill Stone and the woman, she would.

Moria pulled a knife from beneath her tunic and started down the steps.

At Catherine's urging, Patrick forced himself to stand, swallowing back a reaction to the waves of pain that radiated from his lower leg and ankle. Blood from his wound was trickling down the leg that had been injured by his fall.

Catherine, unaware of the extent of his injury, tried to support him, but her head was still swimming from the effect of the drink. Behind them the captain was shouting orders. He and his soldiers had burst into the circle and were fighting hand to hand with the Natchez, who'd finally come to their senses and begun to resist.

"Where is Stone?" the captain was demanding of a man only a few feet away.

As the man motioned toward Patrick, Patrick pushed Catherine behind him and forced himself to stand on the ankle that screamed with pain. There was to be no more running. The time to face the Spaniard was now.

"Stone is here, Lopaz."

The captain followed the sound of Patrick's voice, waiting for the smoke to clear. "So, I've found you,

Stone. And your woman, the missing bride. Nobody escapes from me with their life."

"You're wrong, Captain Lopaz."

Lopaz took a step nearer, narrowing his eyes in shocked disbelief as the truth began to dawn on him. "Irishman? But you're—"

"Dead? No. Though I should have been, because of you."

"How?"

"Are you surprised, Lopaz? Taking Stone, the pirate, to the governor would be a feather in your cap, but bringing in the Irishman might cause questions. I can't refute your accusation of murder, for I have no witnesses. But your superiors might listen to what I have to say about bribes, and about you stealing my ship and selling it."

Patrick glanced casually about. Lopaz was beginning to see that he'd made a mistake. But he had no graceful way to back down.

Moria had started down the steps above them, knife drawn. But she'd stopped halfway. The only player not accounted for was the Sun King. As far as Patrick could tell, death from one direction was as likely as the other for him and Catherine. Captain Lopaz wasn't going to let him live and Moria would destroy Catherine. He wouldn't have made a bet on their chances.

At that moment an explosion occurred behind the captain, engulfing him in smoke. From out of the darkness a figure materialized, darted forward to reach Patrick, sliding his arm behind Patrick's back in support. "Come, hurry!"

"Jillico, old friend," Patrick said with a grin, and leaned against the boy. "Do you turn away from your people?"

"You are my brother, Stone. I do not turn away from you."

"Aye. I believe we both must be doomed. We are like dolphins who don't know not to swim with sharks."

"Stop!" Moria's voice cut through the darkness, halting their progress. "Do not do this, Jillico! The girl must die."

"I will not let you harm them, Moria."

"I must." She stood tall, her face stamped with the truth of her convictions, caught full force by the flames. "The girl must not be allowed to deliver a child. It will mean the end of our people."

"No, my sister, you are seeing the end and you are the one who has caused it. The last of the Natchez are being killed because of you."

"Jillico, can you not see? Our people were scattered like ashes on the wind. Because of me, they will come together once more and we will be strong."

"No, Moria. The other tribes prosper, but for the Natchez, this is the end."

The smoke cleared then to reveal Captain Lopaz, his pistol still drawn. But behind him stood the Sun King. "You have defiled a sacred ceremony, Spanish dog," he said, "and for that you must be punished." He drew back his hand, letting his knife fly, catching Lopaz in the side just as the captain attempted to fire his pistol at Stone.

The ball from the Spanish gun hit Moria in the chest, just above her breast. She had a startled look, as if she couldn't believe it had happened.

"A new world is being forged and I cannot change what is to come, Simicco," she said and walked slowly down the stairs. As she reached the grassy ceremonial

ground she closed her eyes. "And neither can you."
She slumped into the Sun King's arms.

"Get Patrick to the river," Jillico said to Catherine, sliding Patrick's arm around Catherine's shoulders. "I must see to my sister. Go, I'll catch up."

"Your sister? But—" Catherine began to object, but heard the shouts of the Spanish soldiers and knew they had no time. With Patrick sparing the weight of his hurt leg by leaning on her they stumbled into the forest, skirting the cornfield until they had left the fighting behind.

The flatboats, still loaded with munitions, were beached by the bayou. Patrick settled himself into a pirogue with Catherine crouching before him. He poled the boat into the water and away from the fighting.

"What about Jillico?" she asked.

"He'll come. He knows this swamp better than any of us. Right now we have to put as much distance between us and the Natchez as we can. I didn't see Simicco behind us, but I don't trust him."

"Let me look at your ankle, Patrick. How badly are you hurt?"

"Not now, Catherine, darlin'. It's just a sprain. Sit there and let me take you away from here."

"Darling? I like that. I like the thought of going home, too." And she lay back in the dugout, resting her head against a barrel that was covered by a damp, musty blanket.

Her mind still swam from the effects of the drink.

She hadn't understood all of what had happened back there, but apparently Patrick had. Had it been up to her, she might have tried to help Moria, but Patrick was more important. Patrick had always been the star on which she'd focused her journey. Nothing had changed.

She could still hear the pounding of the drumbeat in her head. Now the rhythm blended with Patrick's slapping the pole into the water and lifting it out again. There was something soothing about the sound and motion.

There was no moon, or if there was, its light couldn't penetrate the thick arbor of tree limbs overhead. The darkness was complete. Yet, as they moved through the silence, she began to pick out shapes. She could even see Patrick, the outline of his beautiful golden head and his bare chest, still streaked with paint.

He was taking care of her, just as he'd said. And she'd taken care of him. She wanted to stop him, lean her body against his and feel the strength of his arms around her. But there was a tenseness about him that warned her not to get too close.

She smiled. Like the porcupine they'd passed along the shore when they fled into the swamp, Patrick was always warning her off, showing her that she didn't belong with him. He'd bristle and hold her at arm's length. But that would change now. She'd known they were meant to be together from the start, and nothing had happened since that first day to change her mind. He was, quite simply, her heart, her life.

Catherine's eyelids began to droop and she knew that she was about to fall asleep. That wouldn't do. Patrick was in pain. They were still too close to the Spanish and they didn't know where Simicco was. She had to remain alert, even if it meant talking to keep herself awake. She couldn't think that it mattered. Either they'd been seen and would be followed, or they hadn't been. And there was only one direction that led back to Rainbow's End. She started to talk.

"Where are we going, Patrick?"

"Away from danger."

"I think we should go to New Orleans, to see Charles. As the American representative, he is bound to help us."

Charles? Catherine's betrothed was President Washington's agent?

Patrick was concentrating with every part of his mind and body on moving the boat down the waterway. He knew that he might pass out at any minute. There were likely to be snakes in the trees overhead, fleeing natives in the swamp beyond. But Catherine's suggestion that they go to see the man who expected to marry her came at him with such a jolt that the boat shimmied from his reaction.

"Go to New Orleans? To see the man you were to wed?"

"I could never have married Charles. I know that. I must have known it at the time. But you were supposed to be dead, and when I didn't hear from you I had to find a way to come here myself. I used Charles and for that I'm sorry."

Patrick grimaced. Already exhausted, he'd fallen into a pattern of movement that was automatic. He pushed the pain back into that hidden place inside him where all his hurts had been banished. But Catherine's suggestion had stunned him and he could find no rational explanation for the anger he felt at her mentioning Charles.

"And now you're suggesting that we go to the one place where I'll be arrested? Why?"

"To ask Charles for his help. Don't you see, Patrick, he's our only hope."

Maybe, Patrick wanted to say. But if he were in Charles's place he'd have a hard time helping the man who had taken Catherine from him. In fact, he doubted that Charles would even stop to listen to Catherine's plea.

"What makes you think that Charles would intervene? I wouldn't take any man representing President Washington as a fool."

"My father was a brilliant man, Patrick. He represented President Washington. But there were those who thought him a fool."

"Not from what I heard. I was told that he was a very wise man."

"Wise, yes. Impractical and foolish? Yes, that, too. You know he was shot, not in one of the battles for independence, but returning from a meeting called to work out a peaceful settlement. And he did. He put his duty over his personal needs. I believe Charles is that kind of man. He just doesn't know how to swim."

Patrick was past making sense out of Catherine's chatter. He realized that she was trying to keep herself awake and trying to take his mind off his leg. She was accomplishing neither.

"I don't know, Catherine. Right now, all I want to do is get us back to Rainbow's End. Pharaoh and the others will be able to protect us from what's left of Lopaz's men."

"The others? The members of your pirate crew?"

"Yes, and the slaves who've joined us."

"Caring for the slaves I can understand, but why did you become a pirate, Patrick?"

He poled the craft in silence for a moment before he finally answered. She deserved to learn the truth. "After I got out of prison I was determined to find Lopaz and force him to clear my name. And I had people depending on me."

"But before? I'm thinking that you're no stranger to a life of danger."

"How did you know?" He seemed startled.

"Oh, I don't know. There's a hurt driving you. You try to cover it up with foolishness and a devil-may-care attitude. But it's there. You said once that you only had a drunken father and two older brothers. You didn't care much about them, or was it that they didn't care about you?"

"Care about me? No, after my ma died, I was just in the way, another mouth to be fed. One day I just left. I doubt they even looked for me."

"Tell me about her, your mother."

And as they made their way through the black night, Patrick poled the boat and forced himself to tell her about the mother who died and left him. About the woman who'd been abused and misused by a man who didn't care about her. About another man who'd seen her washing clothes in the brook and used her, leaving her with his child.

"You? You were that child. Was that why your father hated you?"

"That's what he said. But he was an evil, cruel man. He hated my brothers as well, and they were his own sons."

Catherine couldn't imagine a father not caring about his children. She couldn't imagine any child growing up without someone to love him.

To Catherine love was the most basic good motive for all mankind. It was goodness and nurturing. It was respect and caring. Love was that inner sense of strength that came to life like the seed in the ground. It flourished. Love was goodness and nurturing. Love was Patrick and the way they made each other feel. And, she admitted with childish delight, it was excitement and adventure and the promise of the joy of a new day—together. That was love.

Beyond that, she had no need to define love. Except to know that, even in the midst of danger and the horror they'd left behind them, this moment was right.

How else could she feel such confidence when they were sliding through the night, hurt, hungry, probably lost, with her at one end of the boat and Patrick, suffering in silence, at the other? It was because they were together, and they had the luck of the Irish on their side.

She let out a deep satisfied sigh.

Patrick heard her sigh and echoed it with a mental sigh of his own. In his mind he was still seeing Catherine and Simicco dancing, sizzling with the jealousy it caused. Patrick knew Catherine well. He knew her passion and her honesty. What Simicco had put into their drinks, he didn't know, but he knew it had clouded her judgment and made her behave in a way that she would never have done of her own free will. For no matter what happened, Patrick knew that Catherine was his.

What would have happened had Lopaz not shown up? Would Catherine be sharing Simicco's bed now? Would he be with Moria? He felt himself shudder and bit back an outcry from the pain of his injuries, refocusing his attention on Catherine. She'd grown quiet now, and in spite of her attempts to stay awake he was sure she'd fallen asleep.

Catherine was his, had been since their first kiss and those that had followed each time she found a way to seclude them in the darkness of a veranda, in the barn, by the river. She'd been in love, and for Catherine there'd been no holding back.

He'd been the one to hold back. Honor, restraint and fear had kept him from loving Catherine, until one afternoon by the lake when he'd nearly lost control. He hadn't entered her body, nor planted his seed within her, but he'd touched and caressed and led her into such a state of desire that he'd finally given in and promised to come back for her.

Then she'd come after him, coming to his bed after he'd rescued her from the river. His head had been hurt, and he'd been caught up in the hauntingly familiar dream of loving Catherine. And that time he'd not held back. He'd thought it was Isabella. Now he wasn't sure. Catherine hadn't mentioned what had happened. And he couldn't ask.

He'd been such a fool.

In the past three days they'd come close to dying, could still die, and he was worrying about honor. Honor had demanded that he send Catherine home until he could come to her with his name cleared and his monies restored. Now all that was in jeopardy.

Up to now, there'd been only him. He could take chances if he wanted to and nobody would be affected by the outcome except him and the willing men who followed him. And he had taken chances, putting himself in constant danger, battling those who stood in his way, taking from those who'd tried to take from him.

And he'd been untouchable. He couldn't bring himself to tell Catherine that was the way he'd risen in the ranks on the ship he'd stowed away on, or later when he'd been captured by pirates and convinced the bearded sea baron to let him pledge allegiance to a more profitable way of life.

Patrick's risk-taking increased. His reputation and his status had grown proportionately. Over and over, he'd looked the devil in the eye and spit in his face. Until one day the captain of his ship had fallen in battle and Patrick had taken command. A few years later, his purse full, his need for excitement took second place to his need to find a place for himself in the world of normal people.

Luck had followed. Everything that Patrick touched had prospered. And luck, or fate, or perhaps a vision, had led him to Petersburg and Catherine.

Catherine, wearing her Indian dress and moccasins, was now only an arm's length away. And she was sighing in her sleep.

A terrible sadness filled his mind as he thought about the cause of that sigh. Until he'd met Catherine, Patrick had never loved anybody, except the memory of his mother. He'd never allowed himself to be close to anyone. That way the only pain he'd feel was his own, and he'd pushed that so deep inside that it was not there at all.

Except it wasn't dead. It was very much alive, and ever since he'd fallen in love with Catherine it had begun to creep out of the cracks she'd made in the shell around his heart. For the first time in his life, Patrick had allowed himself to need someone, even if the need could only be temporary.

And temporary was all it could be. They had to survive and that depended on their trusting each other, working together, sharing. Out here, in the wilderness, he wasn't certain he could stay away from Catherine. He wasn't sure she'd let him.

He wasn't even certain he'd try.

For the length of time it took them to know their fate, they'd be together. He couldn't change that, just as he couldn't change her falling in love with him, or her coming after him. Moria was right about one thing; what was to be would be. There was no other way now. For out here, in this blackness, there were no little people, no rainbow and no pot of gold.

For now, they were all each other had. Patrick and Catherine, fighting their enemies together. But she was at one end of the boat and he was at the other. There was still Lopaz and Simicco to deal with, the long night ahead, hazards they could neither anticipate, nor defend against. But for now they were together. For now Patrick loved Catherine and he would protect her with his life.

Behind them, danger slid through the night. Evil holding on to its threat like a whisper, gaining in intensity with every labored breath of the bearer.

Chapter Twelve

Lopaz, his hand pressed against the wound in his side, forced his eyes to search the burning village. The ceremonial ground was dotted with bodies and shrouded with smoke like the crepe on a widow's bonnet. "Where is Stone?"

The guide, the only Indian still alive in the clearing, stood wide-eyed and trembling. "He and the woman, they ran toward the river."

"And the wild one, the one who shot me?"

"I don't know, Excellency."

"Forget him, for now. We have to stop Stone." Lopaz felt the blood drip between his fingers. He wasn't going to die, not out here, not after all he'd gone through, not without killing Stone. No, not Stone—McLendon.

Patrick McLendon, the Irishman he'd thought he killed, was escaping, heading back to civilization, toward the governor. When the governor heard McLendon's charges, he would send Lopaz to the farthest post in the Spanish empire. The captain would never see New Orleans again—unless he stopped McLendon.

He glanced at the mound on which the two throne chairs were placed. For a moment he considered climbing the steps for a good look at the village. But the effort hardly seemed worthwhile. Instead he turned back to the guide.

"Find him, you heathen, if you expect to be paid. Find him and kill him!"

But the man who'd led Lopaz to the Green Mounds of Earth for money didn't have a chance to betray his people any further. He died where he stood, from an arrow that sailed from the darkness.

And the resounding cry that accompanied the deed was something not quite human nor animal.

Lopaz bit back a cry of pain and motioned for his men to retreat. With fear etched on their faces, they stepped over the bodies of the Indians they'd killed, made their way back to the boats and pushed off into the brackish water. The swamp was suddenly more acceptable than the foreboding sense of evil they were leaving behind.

They had gone only a few hundred yards when the boats began to fill with water. By the time they sank, the men were terrified. Death was imminent, either by drowning, snakebite, gators or the unseen enemy they could hear following them along the shore.

Lopaz was the last to die and the most vocal. His cries stirred the swamp animals into a frenzy. Until finally there was only silence and the land of moving water swallowed the evidence of the intruders, as it always had.

Patrick lost all sense of direction as he poled the boat through the night. His shoulders ached. The bleeding seemed to have stopped, but his ankle continued to swell until he found himself using the pole as much for a support as to move the boat forward. Finally he was forced to rest his knee on one of the kegs in the boat. The only thing that kept him going was the need to get Catherine to safety.

Catherine slept. Time blurred. The night went from black to a dull gray, and he wasn't certain whether it was because daylight was coming or because his vision was clouded from pain and lack of sleep.

There was a dreamlike haze about what he was seeing, almost as if it weren't real. Only the sound of the night animals calling out to one another broke the silence, that and the plop of the pole in the water. Wisps of fog shimmered eerily, just above the black surface. Mist rose, disintegrated and reformed, floating upward like an errant cloud that had fallen to earth and been snared by an unseen hand below.

Then suddenly the fog was gone, and they were out of the swamp and into a moonlit clearing. A crude shack hugged the bank, like an old man hunched against the cold. From the block of shadows a platform extended out over the creek where it had widened into a small pond.

"Catherine?"

Catherine came instantly awake. The sky was growing lighter, a wavy smear of shadows that began to take shape behind Patrick.

"Patrick, why did you let me fall asleep?" she cried out in dismay. Then she remembered where they were and whispered, "What's wrong?"

"Nothing, yet. Look ahead. Is that a cabin?"

A cabin? Shelter? She blinked her eyes, forcing the sleep away. Her head was pounding so that she could scarcely focus on the dwelling. "Yes. Do you think it's safe?"

"I don't know, but I don't think I can go any farther. We need rest. If we're to be attacked, we'll know it soon enough."

Using the last of his strength, Patrick poled the pirogue up to the dock and caught hold of the wooden piling supporting it. Trying to stand alone was futile. The application of only a slight pressure to his ankle resulted in a groan he couldn't hold back.

Catherine cast an anxious eye around the shoreline, then turned back to Patrick. She didn't know how he'd come this far on that ankle.

"Can you turn around and sit on the dock?" Catherine asked. "If you can pull yourself up, I'll secure the boat."

With the boat rocking dangerously, he managed to lift his backside onto the platform. Catherine looped a vine rope attached to the dock through an iron circle that appeared to have been fashioned for that purpose at the front of the pirogue.

By the fading light of the moon she could see that Patrick's entire lower leg was swollen. It might even be broken. She didn't think he'd be able to walk on that leg now as he had when she helped him to flee to the boat. She eyed the cabin warily, ever conscious of the grimness which seemed permanently chiseled in his face.

Following Patrick's example she lifted her bottom to the dock and pulled herself up beside him. "Can you stand if I help you?"

"I'll stand," he said. "I was told that I never crawled as a babe and I won't start now."

He got first to his knees, then up on one leg, this time without a sound. But Catherine could tell from his tightly drawn expression and the weight of his body leaning on her that every step was sheer torture for him.

"Hello, the house!" Patrick called out. He waited and added, "We come as friends."

But there was no response and they started forward. The distance from the shore seemed to stretch out interminably. Patrick stumbled once, only once, this time not from pain but from almost three days without sleep. He nearly knocked Catherine down before he straightened and stepped onto the porch.

"We made it," Catherine whispered. "Are you all right, Patrick?"

This time he didn't attempt an answer.

The hint of a breeze ruffled the giant tree limbs behind the hut like a warning. Catherine shivered. "Well, it looks deserted. Let's see if the door is locked."

It wasn't. Catherine pushed it open and heard the scurrying of some creature inside. She hesitated. Whatever waited might be cornered. At least, outside, there was space to run. But Patrick needed to lie down. She stepped through the doorway, hoping that whatever occupied the hut had decided to vacate the premises.

Through a hole in the roof, the dying moonlight played across the shadowy interior, illuminating the shape of a crude bed, its head fastened to the wall.

With the last of their strength they crossed the creaking floor to the bed, where Patrick collapsed heavily, his good leg on the bed, the other resting on the floor. Carefully she placed one hand behind his knee, cradling his heel with the other.

"Does it hurt bad?"

"I've hurt worse," he growled, stone-faced and silent as he lifted his leg from her hands and settled it onto the straw mattress. The only sound was that of Patrick's breath hissing between his teeth.

"I'll see if I can find something to make a fire so that I can treat your leg."

"No, not until morning. We don't want to signal our presence." Patrick lay back on the crude bed, unmindful of snakes, Indians or any other presence. Total exhaustion was claiming him. He could go no farther.

"But you're hurt."

"My leg isn't going anywhere, and neither are we. It's nearly morning. We'll rest for a while."

"What about that Indian, Simicco?"

"If he's out there we can't change it. We have to trust that Jillico found a way to slow him down. If not, I don't think I can fight him off anyway. Let us rest, Catherine. Please, come lie down with me."

Moments later they were encased in each other's arms, peacefully, blissfully together. Catherine arranged herself carefully, taking care not to touch his injured leg. Patrick was asleep almost instantly. She could imagine how tired he was. She lay for a long time, her cheek pressed against his bare chest, feeling every breath he took and every beat of his heart.

Outside the hut the day broke.

Deep inside the swamp behind them, creatures went about their daily lives. The strong conquered the weak. The cunning outwitted the less crafty. On silent feet the night fled, leaving behind those who live in the light. Mother Earth met the sun once more.

When Catherine awoke, the sun was straight overhead, casting a circle of light to the floor from the hole in the roof. For a moment Catherine thought it to be a ceremonial fire in the centre of the room.

She shifted her position, felt Patrick's arm still clasped loosely around her and smiled. Throughout the night he'd held her, bonded the two of them together as if he'd been afraid they'd become separated. And neither had moved.

The cabin, made of logs chinked with mud, was crude, but it offered protection. In the corner was a rock fireplace with a table before it. The remains of the cooking fire suggested that it had been some time since it had been used. Catherine's stomach growled, reminding her how long it had been since they'd eaten.

They needed food and water. Carefully she extricated herself from Patrick's arms and came to her feet. In the light she could see his leg and the damage.

The lower leg was badly swollen. Blood was crusted along the side of his calf just below his knee. It had dripped down and dried in rivulets of red. A deep rough cut through the surface of the skin. No wonder he'd fallen. He'd twisted his ankle, yes, but more, he'd been wounded. Either a knife, or a ball from one of the Spanish guns had sliced a chunk from his lower leg and buckled it under him. Patrick had been beaten, stabbed and wounded, all because of her.

And the wound had been left to fester. Catherine let out a most unladylike oath. They'd traveled all night without so much as even cleaning his injury, leaving it open to dirt, insects, God knew what. There was a tightness about his mouth that suggested he was in pain, even as he slept, but he was too exhausted to know. She risked touching his face.

Patrick didn't react.

A quick glance around the small cabin did little to reassure Catherine. She found a tin dipper and a lantern half-filled with oil on a bench beside the rickety table. But there was no food or medicine.

For a moment she wished for Moria, the medicine woman. But Moria was wounded. Jillico had stayed behind to care for her. Patrick's treatment was up to her. And the only thing she knew about doctoring was watching her mother wash wounds with wine and apply hot compresses to loosen phlegm in the chest.

She cast a worried glance through the open door. Beyond the porch she could see the small inlet of water surrounded by tall grass. There was something strange about the color of the water; it looked pink. She moved out the door and onto the dock, trying to understand what she was seeing.

Water lilies. Hundreds of pink water lilies.

The pond was edged with satiny green leaves and large pink blossoms. Beyond, great green trees lined the clearing, their branches bent gracefully like arms reaching out to clasp one another. She had the absurd feeling that they were sentries, holding out the world, protecting this place.

Dark blue dragonflies darted about while fish jumped out of the water then fell back, leaving widening circles on the surface. The flatboat was still bobbing against the small dock.

With a silent thank-you to whoever had found this lovely spot and built the hut, Catherine hurried to the boat. In the darkness she hadn't been able to discern what she'd been leaning on. Now, in the daylight she peeled back the blankets and let out a cry of dismay. What she'd hoped were barrels of foodstuffs were in fact gunpowder, pistols, bags of lead balls and knives. The only edible substances in the pirogue were a cask of coffee, a sack of dried beans, and a jug of ale.

She took the food and one of the knives back to the cabin. At least she'd found ale. It wasn't the wine that her mother used, but it ought to work. And food, if they could survive until the hard beans were cooked. There was plenty of water and from the look of the pond, fish.

First a fire. She'd boil some water and wash Patrick's leg and examine his wound.

A more careful search of the hut produced an iron pot, two tin cups and a flat tin pan, all of which she washed in the pond.

The fire took some thought. Without matches or hot coals she had to improvise. She picked dry grass and fashioned a mound over which she placed a scattering of small twigs. Two flat rocks had been left on the hearth by the cabin's previous occupants. She couldn't be certain, but she thought that one of them was flint. Hoping that she wasn't about to burn down their shelter, she struck one stone against the other, eliciting a spark that quickly caught the dry grass and blazed up. Moments later the pot, filled with water, was hanging over her fire.

Keeping a constant watch on Patrick, she considered what she would do as the fire heated up and the water began to simmer. The loincloth barely covered his male parts, and it took great concentration to keep her attention on her preparations. He'd been so exhausted that he'd slept through all her moving about the cabin. Catherine used a small amount of the hot water to wash any remaining touch of the Spaniards from the knife. They'd already harmed Patrick enough. There was no ball in Patrick's leg, but she'd have the knife ready if the flesh needed searing.

Emptying the pouch in which the lead balls had been stored, she dropped it into the boiling water. Once it had boiled long enough to be clean, she used the tip of the knife to fish the steaming cloth from the water.

Perspiration matted her hair and ran down her face. Already the humidity of the day had soaked into the very air she was trying to breathe. Hurry! Hurry! She took the steaming cloth, dropping it and chartising herself for her tender flesh. Once more she pulled the canvas bag from the water and let it drip until she could take it in her hand and clean the wound.

Patrick's eyes opened. He flinched but made no sound. Once the wound was clean, she poured the ale into its angry flesh. This time, Patrick swore. "What the bloody—?"

"You've been wounded," she answered, mopping the perspiration from her forehead with her lower arm.

"I know, it isn't the first time. What do you think you're doing?"

"I'm trying to kill the poison."

"And me along with it. What's this?" He grabbed the cask from her hand.

"It's ale. I'm using it as medicine."

"Well, you're putting it in the wrong place," he said, rising on one elbow and taking a long swallow.

Catherine would have reprimanded him for wasting the ale, but she was so glad to see the light back in his eyes that she swallowed her protest.

Patrick didn't swallow his. "What happened to my clothes?" He was looking down at his half-nude body in disbelief.

"That's what you wore to Simicco's little welcome party. Don't you remember?"

With a groan, Patrick fell back to the bed, Catherine catching the jug just as it slipped out of his fingers. "I thought—I hoped it was another of those hallucinations. It's that damned drink they fed us. I can't seem to clear my mind of it."

"Not a hallucination, Patrick. It was real. You're just suffering from lack of sleep and whatever they gave us. Don't you remember Captain Lopaz's men attacking the Indians?"

Lopaz. It was all coming back to him. The sound of guns firing, the fire, the smoke. Then came the memory of their flight. "Where are we?"

"A little deserted cabin. I don't know how you found it, but you did."

His lips quivered as if he were trying to smile. "Not me, darling, it was the little people who showed us the way. Watch out for the rainbow," he said, but the levity was short-lived, the last part of his words slurring as his head fell back wearily.

"I'm still so tired. It was a hallucination, wasn't it, Catherine? That night, in Isabella's bed?"

"What do you want it to be?"

He'd asked the question, but she wasn't certain he heard her answer. Either that, or he feigned sleep once more to avoid the truth.

A second trip to the pirogue and Catherine brought the beans and coffee back to the cabin. Cooking had never been her responsibility at home but she knew enough to heat fresh water and start the beans to boiling. Fishing was totally foreign, but she had watched the slaves fish, and other than taking the creatures from the hooks, it didn't look too hard.

A more thorough examination of the exterior of the hut revealed no fishing traps. A length of cord hanging from the rafters would make a fishing line. But a hook proved to be a bigger problem. If only she had a pin from her hair or— She glanced down at the garment she was wearing. It had been decorated with beads and shells of all shapes and sizes. They were attached to the cloth with tiny lengths of animal hide through holes painstakingly made in the tops of the shells.

Quickly she examined the shells until she found one with a natural curved shape. With the striking rock from the hearth she managed to hone the tip of the shell to a reasonably sharp point.

From a moist loamy spot beneath a rock she pulled a fat wiggly worm. She apologized to the worm, took a deep breath and impaled it on her makeshift hook. From the platform she dropped the hook in the water and waited, her mind racked with concern for Patrick, who was still sleeping inside.

The pond lay still in the midday sunshine, sending up shimmering wisps of heat. She wondered who had built the cabin. Had some man and woman thought to make a home here? Why had it been abandoned?

If it weren't for Patrick's injury this would be a beautiful place to be together. She sighed, knelt and wiggled her fingers in the water to rinse off the grains of black dirt.

She hadn't known what to expect when a fish swallowed her hook, but the jerk threatened to topple her into the lake or pull the cord from her grasp.

"Oh, no, you don't," she shouted and jerked, slinging the line over her head. The protesting fish shot through the air and landed against the side of the hut with a resounding thud.

The laughter that followed reached out and grabbed her heart. It was a welcome sound, as was the sight of the figure leaning against the doorframe.

"Patrick, you're up."

"First it was pigs. Now it's flying fish. Ah, Catherine darlin', what am I going to do with you?"

Chapter Thirteen

Patrick cleaned the fish while the beans cooked. A second iron pot was unearthed, scoured and filled with water for coffee. A green branch laid across the rocks at either end of the fireplace became a spit for the fish Catherine had caught.

By the time the fish was done, she'd managed to scrub the rickety table clean enough for them to eat on. She sat on the bench while Patrick sat on the bed with his foot propped up on the bed frame. They ate with their fingers from the shared tin plate.

"That song you're humming," he said, "what is it?"

"Song?" She hadn't realized she was making a sound, but the merry tune came immediately to mind. "It's called 'A Frog Went A Courting.' I sang it for Isabella's guests."

She waited for him to say something about her singing for Isabella's guests, but he didn't.

"I like it," he said instead. "I like watching you bustle around. You always look so pleased with what you're doing."

"I guess I am, here. Always before, Amanda was in charge. I didn't mind then. I was still a child and Cadenhill was still home."

"And it isn't home any longer?"

"First Amanda married, and then Mama. Suddenly I didn't belong anywhere."

"And not belonging bothered you?"

"No, not really." She cut an eye at him and grinned. "By then I knew that I was waiting for you. So I managed."

"And I let you down."

"You couldn't help that. And besides, we're together now."

"But this cabin isn't what I promised you."

"I don't care. I like being with you. It doesn't matter where. Is this what it will be like when we're married?"

Patrick slowed his chewing. He had refused to allow himself the luxury of thinking about what marriage to Catherine would be like.

Socializing with people like the Cadens was fine, on a temporary basis, but becoming a planter and living as one of them had always been a faraway dream. Until Catherine set her sights on him. Watching her around the cabin made him want to believe it could be true. But the fact remained that he was a wanted man. And until he cleared his name of murder charges, he couldn't think about marriage.

No matter what Catherine said, she deserved a fine house, satin dresses and pert little bonnets with plumes and bows. Not some crude cabin with a dirt floor in the wilderness. Not canvas dresses with fringe and seashell trim. Not feathers in her hair.

Yet she was smiling and happy. She'd treated his wound and caught a fish for their dinner. And Catherine Caden, the daughter of a man who'd advised those who drew up the Declaration of Independence, was eating with her fingers and licking them as if she'd never held proper eating utensils.

He liked watching her, with her hair flying free about her face, her shapely legs tucked around the end of the bench, her beaded dress hitting her thighs about midway. There was a spot on her chin and she didn't seem to care. The beans were only half-done and the fish was charred on the outside, but he'd never enjoyed a meal so much.

Catherine caught a fragment of fish with her tongue and, with mischief continuing to light her eyes, looked up from beneath a fringe of sooty-brown lashes. The smile that followed was so provocative that he felt himself smile in return. Both stopped their eating as they gazed at each other.

"Why are you grinning?" she asked.

"No reason. I just like looking at you."

"And I like looking at you, too," she said, widening her grin. "But I do think we're going to have to do something about your clothes. You're going to look a little odd returning to Natchez wearing a loincloth."

Patrick followed the line of her vision and shook his head. His garment consisted of two squares of skin, one in front and one in the rear, hanging from a cord around his waist. In the village he hadn't thought much about what he was wearing, but now—

"I see what you mean."

"So do I, and a lot more."

"Does it bother you?"

"Looking at your body? Back in Petersburg, Patrick, I tried for weeks to look at your body and you wouldn't let me. Now I have you at my mercy. I can look all I like, and there's not a thing you can do about it."

"Hardly seems fair," Patrick observed, giving a doleful look at Catherine's fringed dress.

Catherine swallowed the last of her fish, licked her lips and stood. "I think a person should always be fair." She caught the bottom of her dress and lifted it over her head, revealing her nude body beneath.

Patrick couldn't speak. His throat closed off as he struggled to fill his lungs with a last greedy gasp of air.

"Now I'm at your mercy, Patrick. Close your mouth and touch me."

"It was you in my bed that night, wasn't it?" he asked tightly.

"Of course it was."

"Why, why would you come to my bed?"

"Because I love you, Patrick McLendon, and I have no intention of letting you refuse me, ever again."

He'd known Catherine was beautiful, but he hadn't expected perfection. Her breasts were small and pert, the nipples like delicate pearls caught by a ray of pink light.

"Somehow I knew, but I wouldn't let myself believe. If I thought you were Isabella, it would be all right for me to want to love you."

She dropped the tunic and waited, her chin jutted forward with a slightly downward tilt that said I dare you.

"I knew what I was doing, Patrick. I always knew. And now that you know, do you, still?"

His mouth was dry, his heart pounding. "Do I what?"

"Want to love me?"

She ran her fingers through her hair, drawing it forward across the tops of her breasts and waited.

But the time to wait was past. The words were gone, leaving only the connection between them, the unseen glow that heated the air and wrapped them in a cocoon of rapture.

Catherine pushed the table away and knelt on the floor beside the wooden bed.

"I think that the Indians were very wise about some things," she said as she moved the panel of deerskin away and allowed his male part to spring free.

"Catherine."

"You are very beautiful, Patrick," she whispered.

"I think that I'm supposed to say that."

"Don't talk, Patrick," she said, rising from the floor and lying down beside him. "Just stay there and let me do the things I've dreamed of."

"The things we've dreamed of," he said in a low tight voice.

She supported herself on her elbow, gazing down at him with starry eyes and lips that seemed permanently crinkled in a smile.

In the sweltering heat of a July afternoon, in a crude cabin perched on the banks of a lake pink with water flowers, Patrick McLendon and Catherine Caden loved each other. How fragile the moment seemed when their lips met. How timeless. How perfect.

Neither pulled away. Neither held back. Mouths met and opened, allowing tongues to taste, to slide away to find new points of heat outside the honeyed sweetness they were just beginning to know.

Perspiration trickled from her face and fell to his chest. With her tongue she traced the scars across his body, gently as if she were healing the hurts that had left them. In fact she was. Catherine was making Patrick whole, and she was learning that without him she'd never been complete.

"Where did they come from, these terrible scars?"

"Captain Lopaz. He thought he'd killed me. He meant to kill me."

"That's what I was told, but I knew you weren't dead."

She kissed his cheeks, following the line of his strong jaw until she'd traveled back to her starting place.

"How could you know I still lived?"

"Because," she answered, as she slid one leg over his thighs and rested her knee against that part of him that was hard, "because my heart still beats in response to yours. It never would have, if you'd died. I would have known."

"Ah, Catherine." He felt her breasts pressed against his chest, her hair feathering his shoulders, her woman's scent tantalizing his nose. "Were you always so sure?"

"No," she admitted honestly, pulling back so that she could look down into his blue eyes. "There were times when I doubted. I'm sorry."

Patrick felt a great surge of protective instinct sweep over him. What was there about this woman that made him feel invincible? How petite she was. How precious. He wanted to care for her, to make her life safe. Instead, he'd brought her into the swamp, exposed her to dangers that even he couldn't control.

Other than his mother, he'd never thought much about giving to a woman, or trying to bring her joy. But now he wanted, more than anything, to give Catherine pleasure. His thumb was absently rubbing the spot beneath her breast, while his lips were planting light kisses on her hair.

"I'm sorry I left you, Catherine. And I'm even more sorry that you followed me. You've linked yourself to Stone and that isn't safe."

"Why did you leave me?"

She moved over, was sliding herself up and down his body, catching his manhood between them as she grazed his stomach, her hair mingling with his, her perspiration becoming his, her desire feeding his. A sudden tightness squeezed his chest as he tried to explain, and found no words that spoke the truth.

Fear. He'd left Catherine behind in Petersburg because he didn't believe he could have her. He was afraid that she'd come to harm because of him, like his mother. He loved Catherine and he wanted her to be safe.

Love. It had hovered there, nudging him with the truth of its power, with the intensity of its desire, with the power of its control. He wanted her, not just for now, not for this moment in this enchanted place, but for always—because he loved her.

And for the first time, Patrick couldn't control what and when that always was.

But for now, it didn't matter. "Cat!" His hard mouth captured hers as his body sought and found the place of softness where his hardness belonged. "Catherine," he whispered over and over again, branding her with his voice and his touch.

He didn't feel the pain in his leg. He closed out the little voice that kept saying, "No." He had to touch her, to hold on tight, to prove that this was real.

He knew that he was hurting her, that the hard strength of his hands holding and pressing against her bottom caught and held her. So in tune was he to her response that he could feel it when the deep coil of heat inside her began to erupt. She cried out and began to tremble. And then his own feeling took over, selfish and rough and indescribably potent.

Together they soared through the hours of the afternoon, closing out what had been and what was to be, until at last Catherine fell back to his side, exhausted, sated, languishing in the aftermath of what they'd shared. Later, as Patrick held her, he felt tears gather in his eyes. He should never have let himself give in to loving her.

How would he survive when she was gone?

How could he bear to send her back?

How could he keep from loving her again?

He moved his leg and groaned. It wasn't healed enough yet for travel, and so long as they were here he'd be fooling himself if he thought he could stay away from this woman who was such a part of his heart.

They slept that night, together, bodies slick with perspiration and smeared with the root of the plant that kept the biting insects away. The moon shone through the hole in the roof, casting a glow of silver across their bodies, anointing them with beauty and peace.

In the woods beyond, the animals went about their regular nightly pursuits. They were not disturbed by the presence of their enemies, nor did they call out overloud to wake the lovers.

Morning brought a new acceptance. No longer did either worry about clothing. Cool air kissed their bare skins, giving a new touch of freedom. Breakfast consisted of coffee and berries. Catherine washed Patrick's wound in water so hot that it practically burned. Then she sloshed more ale into the area that was beginning to lose its angry color.

Cleansing and soaking the ankle was causing the swelling to diminish, and by midday, Patrick was able to hobble about with less pain.

"I think I'll shoot us some meat for dinner," he said, loading the pistol with lead and powder.

"I don't think you need to go into the woods without clothes, Patrick. What about the blankets? We can fashion some kind of garment for you. We'll cut a hole in the center and you can drape it over your head."

Quickly she used Patrick's knife to chop a circle out of the middle of the blanket. She draped it over his body and, using the cord from the loincloth, tied it around his waist. "There. Perfect!"

"Just like a shepherd. All I need is my staff and sheep."

"You need a staff, all right. You can barely walk, Patrick. Let me have the pistol. I can kill something for our supper."

"Have you ever shot a gun before?"

"No, but I couldn't sing, either, until I tried."

"Catherine, darlin', to those men back in Heaven, it wouldn't have mattered whether you could carry a tune or not. To kill a bird does take skill."

"All right, then, I'll go with you."

"No, you'll stay here. Let me find a green limb with a fork in its branches. I'll do fine."

Patrick managed to get out the door and to the edge of the woods. He couldn't talk. He hurt too badly. The wound was healing, but there was still great pain in his ankle, pain that rolled around his head and took his words away.

"No, you won't. At least let me help you find something to lean on." Catherine slipped her arm around his waist and was rewarded with his weight against her.

Together they found a young sapling with two limbs exactly opposite each other. Patrick chopped the extraneous limbs away and was left with a crutch. Using the cloth cut from the center of the blanket, Catherine padded the limbs, tying the fabric to the crutch with strips of blanket cloth.

In the end Patrick settled for sitting on a dead log and allowing Catherine to walk along the shore, flushing the birds feeding in a stand of wild rice. He killed two birds. The noise of the shots scared a rabbit from the end of the log on which Patrick was sitting. He got that, too.

"Now we can eat," Patrick said, his voice tight with pain. "Let's get back to the cabin and you call tell me about Cadenhill."

"Cadenhill?" Catherine questioned. "What about Cadenhill?"

"What happened after I left? Did Rush get his cotton planted along the river?"

"Yes, and Amanda planted more tobacco."

"And your mother? Is she well?"

They were making their way awkwardly back to the pond, filling the moments between steps with questions meant to distract.

"Mother married Judge Taliferro and moved to his plantation with the girls."

"And Cadenhill?"

"Is prospering. Rush and Amanda have a baby."

"And you, Catherine? How did you fill the time, when they told you I wouldn't be back for you?"

There was something different in Patrick's question.

"I don't know what you mean?" But she did. She'd allowed a man to court her, a man who'd asked her to marry him. She'd forgotten all about that, it had been so unimportant. She had to tell Patrick about Charles.

"Captain Lopaz. He said he'd found Stone and the missing bride. Whose bride, Catherine?"

They'd reached the cabin. And they'd reached the moment of truth.

"He came to Petersburg after we received word that you were dead. He was on his way to New Orleans as President Washington's emissary."

"Yes, I'd heard about an American who was to deal with the tariff problem the Americans were having. Do you love him?"

Catherine cast a disbelieving eye on Patrick. "Do you love Isabella?"

"Of course not. She was just kind to me at a time I needed help."

"So was the man—"

"But you didn't—"

"No, Patrick. You are the only man who ever made love to me. You're the only man I ever loved or ever will love. Promising to marry a government official was the only way I could send someone to New Orleans to find out the truth about you.''

''Did he?''

''I don't know. When nobody had heard of Patrick McLendon I gave up and let him know I was with the Weatherbys. I hoped that when he came he'd have word of you. But he didn't. We were to be married, but I couldn't go through with it.''

''So you ran away from him.''

''No, I ran to you.''

They reached the cabin and Patrick sank wearily to the floor. He took Catherine's hand and held it, looking into her eyes.

''And what you found is a pirate, a murderer, a man with a price on his head. And no matter how much I want it to be different, I don't know that I can ever change that, my love.''

''Of course you can. We'll force Captain Lopaz to tell the truth. And Charles—Charles will help us clear your name. I'm certain of it.''

''Perhaps,'' Patrick said softly, allowing himself to cling to that hope for one more brief moment. ''Perhaps.''

The next afternoon when he woke from the nap Catherine insisted he take, she was not in the cabin. He sat up in panic, listening to the sound of movement in the water beyond the cabin.

Someone was coming.

He came to his feet, took the pistol beneath the mattress and slipped quickly to the door so that he could see the dock. At first he saw nothing except the ripples of water rocking the water lilies like fairy boats. Then he saw her, rising from beneath the water like some water sprite, lifting her hands in supplication to the gods.

She laughed and whirled around.

"Catherine! What are you doing?" He limped toward the pond, concern masking the pain of walking with his full weight on his leg.

"I'm bathing, Patrick. Come and join me."

"But there are snakes, alligators. I insist you get out at once." He knew he was practically growling at her, but fear pushed all logical thought away.

"Nonsense, Irishman. Don't worry. This is a magic place." She swirled around again, her fair skin shimmering in the water, her hair spread out around her like a circle of fire.

"Catherine, please, come out of the water. I can't protect you if—" He couldn't finish the thought.

"But you don't have to, I'm already protected—by your little people. Don't you see them?"

She was the magic, the enchantment. The little pond filled with pink water lilies was her throne, and if there were no little people there, there should have been. All his life Patrick had blithely referred to the power of the leprechauns, but he'd never believed in their power. For the first time, in the middle of a swamp, he was suddenly caught up in the bewitchment.

She was right. There should have been snakes. They hadn't seen any. There should have been alligators. There'd been none. Someone should have come for them. No one had. They'd been swept up in a fantasy and he was powerless to stop what was about to happen.

She suddenly disappeared beneath the water, surfacing at the end of the dock where he stood, and held out her hand. When he took it in his he knew that he was caught in her spell.

She was nude. Water streamed down her body, across her breasts and down her legs. Patrick could only stand completely bemused as he followed the course of the rivulets. Her breasts were even more beautiful, pert, announcing her arousal with the tightly beaded little pink nipples. Between her legs the thatch of strawberry-colored hair caught the sun and glistened with droplets of water.

"Catherine, I—"

"You're going to love me, Patrick, now and forever."

"Not here," he said hoarsely, "someone might come."

"No one will come, Patrick. We're being watched over."

She loosened the ties of his loincloth and let it fall to the dock. Then she drew him down beside her, her heart shining in her eyes and her love warming the fingertips that began a slow exploration of his face.

"My Irishman with the laughing eyes needs to learn to laugh again."

"I'm afraid that man is gone forever."

"No, he's had an evil spell cast over him. My love will free him. My love will be his anchor and his shining star, just as those laughing eyes have been mine."

No power on earth could have stopped Patrick from loving Catherine.

Her lips touched his lips, slyly moving across his cheeks, and pulling back. Then she looked at him, her breath caught in the wonder of the moment. He placed his hands on both sides of her face and pulled her lips down to meet his, gently parting them, joining them in such sweet torment.

This time he laid her on her back, coming to his elbows over her. Her hands were exploring his head, the back of his neck, his shoulder blades. He could feel her heart racing, like some wild thing caught up inside her chest, frantically trying to free itself to touch his own fluttering captive.

As her hands continued their quest, Patrick felt as though he'd been sketched with lines of heat. As the lily pads had rocked beneath the ripples of waves set off by her cavorting in the water, she was pressing herself against him, fanning the flame dangerously high, until there was no longer a space where he ended and she began. They were one perfect entity, moving together.

A thread of guilt moved fleetingly through his conscience, then disappeared into the wonder of what they were building together.

Her little pants had changed into deep moans of pleasure that held nothing back. Whatever Catherine felt, she expressed. Whatever she wanted, she took. And the shattering of that sensation burst into a ball of fire that seemed to meld two bodies into one jolt of lightning.

It sliced through them, setting off waves of such joy that Patrick couldn't hold back a roar of appreciation. He knew that he was laughing once more, that his life was, for this moment, complete.

He was no longer the bastard, the outcast, the pirate. He was Catherine's love and that was enough.

Chapter Fourteen

Patrick loaded the pistols and placed the gunpowder in strategic spots around the cabin. The longer they stayed, the more likely it was that someone would find them, and he intended to be ready.

But he soon learned that any unexpected movement, no matter how carefully made, frightened the coveys of birds that fed by the bayou into frantic flight. Patrick and Catherine had their own lookouts, ready to notify them of intruders. Thus reassured, he found himself relaxing.

At first he felt great guilt over having made love to her, and determined not to allow it to happen again. He pleaded pain from his wound. Fine, she'd responded, she'd make love to him. He reminded her that her mother wouldn't approve of her forwardness. She reminded him that her mother had never approved of her forwardness and that hadn't stopped her before. He warned her that they might conceive a child. She simply began to glow and he was lost in the warmth of that joy.

Three days passed, three days of quiet, three days of happiness such as he'd never known, three days of loving Catherine, without regrets, without restraint.

And nobody came looking for them.

At night he slept, fitfully, in snatches that seemed designed to drive him wild when he'd wake and find Catherine in his arms, holding him, her hair spread across his chest. He was aware as he'd never been of her softness, her trust, the way she came to life at the slightest touch of his hands on her body.

And touching her was part of the happiness he'd never allowed himself. He stopped asking himself what he could give her, how he could justify their being together. Questions wouldn't change anything and they'd come too late. He was intoxicated with Catherine, drunk with feelings that bubbled and fermented inside his mind and body.

And although he refused to think that far ahead, the aftereffects would likely be just as gut wrenching.

For Catherine there was nothing wrong about being together. To her, they were already married and there could be nothing sinful about the wonder of their lovemaking.

For Patrick it was so natural, so right, that he allowed himself to be lulled into the same kind of dreamlike state of insanity. While they were here, they could forget what lay behind and what was waiting ahead of them.

He'd worried about using the pistols for hunting, but the sound of his shot hadn't brought anyone to their secret place, and they had to eat. Along with birds and one plump rabbit he shot, they caught fish and picked wild berries. One afternoon they discovered a vine of tomatoes that must have grown from where the occupants of the cabin had thrown the seed. That night, with the wild onions from the forest, Catherine managed a fine stew.

Patrick, in his loincloth, had turned into some wild-looking heathen, his hair falling across his shoulders like one of his Celtic ancestors. The leg was healing; each day supporting his weight came more easily. And gradually he began to come back to full strength.

Patrick knew it was time for them to go. They were becoming too close. The longer they stayed the harder it would be to go. But for once in his life he found himself delaying. He justified that delay by saying he didn't know exactly where they were or what they might walk into, but in the back of his mind was the fear they might not be able to get out. That, and the admission that he didn't want to go.

Still, it was time he checked out, in the daylight, the bayou on which their cabin was built. Before he allowed Catherine to leave their safe haven, he wanted to examine their route. There were thousands of miles of waterways crisscrossing one another, intersecting and joining and peeling off again. He knew they could travel for days and never be very far from where they'd started.

He wasn't certain what he was looking for, but he couldn't start back to Rainbow's End without making certain that he knew the general direction. Having left the village in the dark, and in pain, he wasn't certain that he knew where they were.

As he'd anticipated, he left Catherine pouting because he refused to take her with him.

"If something happens to you, what will I do?"

"I'm only going back to the point where this stream intersects with another. I have to make plans to get us back, and I don't have any idea where we are."

"Then I'll come, too. If you get lost, we'll get lost together. I don't want to be apart from you, Patrick, ever again."

But it was more than checking the bayou that drove Patrick. He needed to pole the pirogue. He needed to test his strength. He needed to be alone, away from Catherine so that he could focus on what they were going to do.

"No, Catherine. Stay here. I'll be back by noon. I promise."

And he'd left her, standing in the doorway with her eyes targeted on his back with such force that her gaze seemed to burn little spots on his skin as he poled the pirogue through the water lilies and away.

As always the bayou seemed alive in the silence. Birds sang, water creatures skated across the surface, and the trees along the bank seemed to absorb the sound, closing out the world beyond the cabin. From the position of the sun he could tell that he was going north. The tributary he was following eventually joined a larger body of water that, by checking the sun, he guessed was running east and west.

He poled the boat west for a time, checking for signs of the Indian village, some point of reference from which to start. But time was passing, and in order not to leave Catherine unprotected, he turned back. Even knowing where he'd come from, he almost missed the waterway that led to the cabin.

As their refuge came into sight, so did the figure cavorting in the water, frivolously cavorting, he thought, remembering her earlier angry charge. Disregarding his cautions about snakes and gators, Catherine continued to bathe in the pond. She firmly believed that it was a magic pool, protected by his leprechauns, and nothing he could say would dissuade her.

She had no soap, but the sensual expression on her face told of the pure delight she felt in letting the water flow through her strawberry-colored hair. So intent was she in her frolicking that she didn't know Patrick was watching until he spoke.

"A creature from the sea," he said softly. "The sailors always talked about the mermaids, but I never thought to see one."

"Patrick, join me. I wish you would join me."

He looked at the water with anticipation. Up to now, he'd stayed away because of the wound on his leg, but it was almost healed, and a real bath was appealing.

"All right, let me tie up the boat." He fastened the pirogue and lifted himself to the dock, where he unfastened his loincloth and stood looking down at her with eyes of love.

"I do say, Mr. McLendon, you are a fine figure of a man."

"I'm glad you approve." He slid into the water, holding on to the pole holding up the dock.

"Oh, I'm not certain I approve. I think I'd better check you out."

She paddled over toward him, her hair pooling out around her, her sun-kissed face beaming with joy. An aching tingle began in him even before she touched him. An anticipation of what was to come. Would it always be like that, only a touch and they'd be together?

Catherine was nineteen now. He was thirty-three. How many years would they share? Then, as she planted her legs around his hips and took him inside her, he pushed away the thought of parting.

"I can't touch bottom here, Catherine."

"But you're so big," she said breathlessly, "and I'm so tiny."

That thought took his breath away and for a moment they both sank beneath the water. She was tiny, and tight. He managed to touch the muddy bottom and push off, directing them back until he could hold to the log on which the dock was built.

"Catherine, this was supposed to be a bath."

"Then let me wash you," she said, and proceeded to slosh water over him as she planted her kisses across his face and down his neck.

"Catherine, stop it. You're going to drown us. If you don't stop right now, I'm going to—"

He did, and so did she. And for that moment, drowning didn't seem like a bad way to die. And then she flung back her head and laughed.

"But I don't want you to die, Patrick. I've gone through too much to find you."

She tore herself away and pulled herself to the dock. "Finish your bath and join me." This time it was Catherine who stood, dripping in the sunlight, stunning the big man with her beauty.

Patrick ran his fingers over his body, leaned his head back and lifted it, slinging the water away as he followed her onto the dock.

"You're so beautiful, Catherine," he said, catching his fingers in her hair, already drying in the hot sun and curling softly around his rough hand, like the feathers on angel's wings.

"No," she said. "My sister was beautiful. I'm just—just—"

"What makes me happy," he said, finishing her sentence, wondering how she could not know how lovely she was. Her body, colored by the sun to a golden shade so perfect as to be worshiped, her lips begged to be tasted, her perfection demanded that he pay homage to it for one last moment.

Patrick surprised her by lifting her in his arms and walking away from the cabin into the woods.

"Your leg," she said.

"My leg says for you not to worry. It's a very happy leg. My entire body is very happy. Can't you see it smiling?"

"It's sending a message, all right, I can feel it writing messages on my bottom. Where are we going?"

"Just away from the clearing. Don't want to upset the fish any more than we already have. They might get carried away and overpopulate the pond."

He hadn't noticed the feeling of apprehension when they were making love on the dock, but suddenly it was there. He glanced around. Nothing. The birds were quiet, the water still. But it was clear that every hour they remained here increased the risk of discovery. He didn't know what to think about Lopaz, but he would have expected the captain to go back for reinforcements and return.

Allowing Patrick to remain free was a threat to the Spaniard, and Lopaz wasn't a man to leave himself open to criminal investigation. Granted, the bayous were a maze, but there would be someone who would take on the job of guiding the Spaniard. And sooner or later, Patrick and Lopaz would have to face each other again.

For now, as if she knew what he was thinking, there was a little worry line creasing Catherine's forehead.

Her lips were pursed in concern, and she clung to him as if she were afraid that she might fall.

Then they were inside the forest, beneath the moss-hung trees, in a private bower of green, shielded from the outside world by gossamer hangings of gray. And he kissed her, wiping away her worries. As always, he felt her eternal sweetness catch fire at his touch.

"You know this is wrong, Catherine Caden."

After a moment, Catherine pulled back and smiled, her finger touching the crinkles at the corners of his eyes. "You're full of blarney, Patrick McLendon, but I love you anyhow."

"The test of a true Irishman," he said with a laugh.

Pressing her face against his chest, she let out a painful sigh. "Oh, Patrick, I love you so. Let's never leave here."

He laid her down on the carpet of pine needles. "One day, I'm going to cover you with lilies from the pond and diamonds from the sun," he said, his voice husky with desire.

She lowered her lashes, allowing her gaze to wander down his chest, lower, lower. "I'd like that, but could we talk about what you're going to do later, later?"

He moved over her, kissing her face, committing every part of her to memory, as if he knew he might never see her again. Her hands moved across his shoulders, down his back, catching his bottom and pulling him closer.

"Ah, Catherine," he whispered. "I wish we could stay here. But even Adam and Eve couldn't remain in the Garden of Eden forever."

"Maybe they didn't know what they had."

"Maybe they didn't."

And they closed out the world again, loving each other without fear. He wasn't sure he wanted this to be the Garden of Eden, Patrick thought, for the Garden of Eden had a snake.

But snakes didn't walk on two feet, and they didn't carry pistols. And if Patrick hadn't allowed himself the luxury of closing out everything so completely he would have heard the straw break beneath the step behind him.

For a few precious moments Patrick had dropped his guard and focused on loving this woman who had made herself his so completely. He'd begun to believe in the magic.

By the time he heard the flight of the birds, it was too late. He should have remembered the snake!

"Hello?"

Patrick would have reached for a cover to protect Catherine, except there was none. The best he could do was grab his loincloth and meet the intruder.

"Señor Patrick?"

"Jillico?" Patrick stepped out of the woods and let out a sigh of relief. "Are you alone?"

"I am alone. I will wait by the cabin."

Patrick whispered to Catherine to stay in the woods until he signaled for her to return.

With stiff, cautious movements, he followed the Indian with whom he'd shared so much, while tying his loincloth and about his waist. "How did you find us?"

"With great difficulty. I've been searching for days. Then it came to me that the Great Spirits would protect the White Woman, just as you were protected. I remembered the cabin. The Great Spirits led you here."

"And Moria?"

There was a long pause. "Moria is dead."

Patrick wanted to offer his sympathy, but something about Jillico's stern posture warned him to wait for the man, who in most cultures would still be a boy, to speak. He was still wearing his native costume. Carrying his bow and arrow over his back and a Spanish pistol in his hand, he looked fierce, yet vulnerable.

"And the Sun King?" Patrick asked softly.

"I do not know. After the battle, I buried my sister. He was not there, and he did not return."

"I'm sorry. If it hadn't been for me, none of this would have happened."

"Do not blame yourself. Moria saw her own death. She tried to change what was meant to be. I have come here to protect the White Woman, as she bade me do before she died."

"Protect me?" Catherine had disregarded Patrick's instructions, reclaimed her tunic from the bank and now stood beside Patrick. "Why?"

"I do not know. I only follow her dying wish. Protect the White Woman, she said, for the child she will bear must live."

"But I—" Catherine stopped. She had little knowledge of such things, but enough time had passed without her monthly flow to make his words true. She could be carrying a child, Patrick's child. A laughing blue-eyed boy like him, or perhaps a little girl with golden curls. She was caught by the possibility and the future a child promised.

But if she admitted to that possibility, Patrick would certainly send her back to Petersburg, for the protection of the baby. "I—I'm not carrying a child," she said with false conviction.

"Perhaps not, but one day you will," Jillico said just as firmly.

Patrick was eyeing her curiously. "Can you lead us back to Rainbow's End, Jillico? I'm worried about Lopaz. He won't rest until I'm dead, for I'm the only one who can prove he is a thief."

"Yes, I will take you. But we must go now, for if the spirits have revealed this place to me, perhaps others will come. You may no longer be safe."

Catherine began to gather up their things. She didn't want to go, but everything had changed. Their beautiful, private world had been penetrated. There was a catch in her stomach as they gathered their things and loaded them on the boat Jillico had brought. With a sad heart she watched the cabin until it was out of sight, the pink lilies winking sweetly through the tree limbs.

Jillico had brought the outside world into their private garden and it would never be the same again.

They'd been gone from the plantation only a week, and Patrick hadn't known what to expect. But the former slaves were busily at work. The house hadn't been destroyed; rather, the progress was amazing. The walls were up, the roof complete and the floors were finished. Wrapping the upper level was a large porch that circled the house like a collar. The veranda below was larger, reaching out in welcome to those who came to call.

Catherine, who hadn't seen it when she arrived during the fire, was transfixed. "Oh, Patrick, our house. It is our house, isn't it?"

"No! It's just the plantation house." He couldn't say that it was their house. No matter what they'd allowed themselves to believe back at the cabin, that was a fantasy. This was real, and reality was that Patrick wouldn't marry Catherine until he was no longer a wanted man.

Now more than ever he was resolved to send her back to Petersburg where she'd be safe. From him. From their desire. From their love.

"Of course it is," Catherine said. She let out a soft sigh and threw her arms around his neck. "It's ours. You were building it for me, weren't you?"

"I guess I was." Patrick unclasped her arms and stepped away. "But we can't live in it until my name is cleared."

Just her touch erased his resolve and he couldn't let that happen. She would never be able to restrain herself from showing how she felt. Her spontaneous gestures made their relationship much too obvious. That couldn't be allowed to happen. Not when he'd made up his mind that she was going back. And Patrick didn't delude himself; once he'd given in to her, he'd be powerless to refuse.

Catherine didn't argue. In her mind it *was* settled, but there was no point in arguing with Patrick about their situation before the workers. Instead, she took his hand and walked around the house, examining every detail.

At the rear was the completed cook house with a fire already burning in the fireplace. To one side, between the house and the bayou, were the burned indigo fields. Already green shoots were visible between the brown grass, and the sound of workers' voices echoed down the bayou.

And beyond the patch of sugarcane were workers moving up and down the rows with homemade hoes. They were singing as they worked.

"What are they doing, Patrick?"

"I'm not sure, but I think they're hoeing the cotton."

"Oh, Patrick, cotton. That's what you wanted. But are all these men your slaves?"

"No, ma'am. Dey's Mr. Patrick's workers, free men," a familiar voice said as Pharaoh came from around the cook shed.

"Pharaoh!" Catherine ran toward the old man and hugged him. She'd missed him, and the thought that he was here, waiting for them, made her feel as if she were really coming home. "Oh, Pharaoh, I'm so glad to see you. Are you all right? What about Isabella and Sally? Did Captain Lopaz close Heaven?"

"No, ma'am. Ain't nobody seen the captain since he took off after Mr. Patrick. We wuz 'fraid he was still chasing you."

Patrick turned a questioning eye on Jillico. "And you didn't see him anywhere?"

"No. He and his men left the village, headed back toward Natchez-under-the-Hill. I thought they were coming here. There was one boat blocking the waterway near the village, but it had a hole in the bottom of it, as if it had been deliberately sunk."

"Simicco!" Catherine said. "He's responsible. That's the only answer."

Patrick considered her comment. If she was right, and there was a good possibility she was, what was the

Indian up to now? His plans to reunite the Natchez had suffered an almost fatal blow, which meant he'd lost his hold over them. He'd tried to punish Lopaz in the village. A growing conviction told Patrick that he'd succeeded. If that were the case, Patrick's hope of clearing his name was gone forever.

For Simicco, to escape his lot as a slave and return to his royal status must have seemed like a miracle. Now he'd lost the power and glory—and—Catherine. Patrick was beginning to realize that he and Catherine had gotten away from one enemy only to become the prey of another. Now, more than ever, Patrick was determined to get Catherine away. But how, and to where?

"You may be right, Catherine. I think I will go and see Isabella. She must know what's happened at the fort, and downriver as well." Patrick didn't say so, but he wanted to know more about this Charles, who thought he was going to marry Catherine.

"Oh, good. Is there some way I can get cleaned up and find some other clothes? I don't think it would be too smart to walk up the dock in an Indian dress."

"You won't be going!"

"Why not? If I'm not safe, neither are you. Besides, Isabella won't turn us in."

"Maybe not, but somebody did, and somebody led Lopaz to the village. Natchez is a den of thieves, Catherine, and thieves only care about themselves. You stay here. Pharaoh, don't we have a couple of trunks of women's clothes we've—acquired?"

"Dey's in the house. You come with me, Miss Catherine. I'll have the women prepare you a good bath and comb your hair."

"Not Catherine," she snapped. "My name is Cat. Cat O'Conner, and Cat O'Conner is respected under the hill."

Patrick smiled. Proud and stubborn, to the last, that was his Catherine—no, he corrected, his Cat.

"Well, Jillico, let's move off." Patrick started back to the pirogue, considering his next move, when Catherine's words stopped him.

"Patrick, aren't you going to kiss me goodbye?"

No! He had no intention of kissing her. He didn't even trust himself to touch her. But there she was, in his arms, standing on tiptoes with her eyes closed.

If a pig came out of the woods he'd give it all up.

He didn't need the pig. His lips were touching hers and he hadn't known he was moving. Just that quick moment and he knew he'd lost again. The woman was able to curl him around her little finger, even when he knew what she was doing.

"Pharaoh, look after her. Set guards!" He growled and marched off with his teeth and lips pressed tightly together. A lot of good that would do now. He'd already been taken advantage of by Catherine's simple gesture.

He'd better get to Heaven before he started seeing rainbows, before he was completely caught up in Catherine's fantasy that they'd live in the big house like a real family. Patrick knew that could never happen.

Isabella laid down her hairbrush and turned away from her mirror.

"You can't take her to New Orleans now, Stone. There's sickness there. The commandant at the fort has even set up a quarantine. We're having to check out the gents when they come in the door. Any sign of fever or yellow skin and they're turned away."

"Sickness?"

"Yes, Patrick, the fever death."

Patrick balled up his fist and slammed it into his palm. "God's blood. Is even the Almighty conspiring with Catherine?"

"She's got you, hasn't she, Stone?. This little thing has you wrapped as tight as a Christmas goose and you can't do a thing about it."

"I'll bring her here," he said, striding back and forth across the Persian rug that had hidden his escape tunnel from the Spanish.

"I don't think that would be wise either, Stone. Too many people are fleeing the city and many of them have come here. We haven't had a death yet, but we will. We always do. No, she's safer with you."

He was defeated. He might as well accept his fate. Catherine would be in his bed and in his arms before sunrise of the first night he returned to Rainbow's End. Even the thought of her started his heart racing and blotted out the important things he needed to learn.

"Why is this such a problem, Stone? It's obvious that she's crazy about you. Marry the wench."

"I can't, Isabella. Not until my name is cleared."

"Why in heaven's name not? Along the Mississippi people don't care what you were. All they want to know is what you are now and that you're not going to do them harm."

"I care. I'm a bastard, Isabella. Oh, I have a name, but it isn't that of my father. The man who gave me to my mother never knew, and the man who got saddled with raising me, punished me every minute of my life until I finally ran away. I'll never wish that kind of pain on anyone."

"Your child will have a name, Stone. And you don't have a wife. Or do you?"

"Certainly not. And Catherine isn't having a child, either."

But that statement sobered him. Moria had been overly concerned about Catherine bearing a child. Patrick had assumed that she was worried about Simicco's mating with her, but suppose she'd seen something else in her vision. Suppose Catherine was already carrying a child?

"I've got to go, Isabella. I'll send someone to find out when the sickness is over. If you learn of anyone going to the coast overland, send me word."

"If you're determined. But the sickness won't slow down for another two months, not until fall. Summer is always the worst."

Two months. Isabella had to be wrong about that. Patrick reviewed his options. He could move into the cook shed and give Catherine the crude little house the Spanish don had built for himself and his wife. He had enough money for them to live for a while. But the payment on his land was due, overdue, and there would be no paying that unless he returned to the river.

By the time he got back to Rainbow's End he'd resigned himself to the fact that Isabella wasn't wrong, and neither was he.

"Miss Catherine waiting for you in the parlor, suh," Pharaoh said. "I'll bring your supper."

"Never mind that now, Pharaoh. Is everything here all right?"

"Ain't seen no sign of nary a human, but there's some kind of creature prowling around the woods. It's done killed one of the pigs and a couple of chickens."

Patrick nodded and walked down the large open hallway to the room Pharaoh was calling the parlor. It was that, and the dining area, and the room in which all other daytime activities took place.

Catherine was waiting there for him, wearing a wrapper of fine, gauzy material that only enhanced the soft warm color of her skin. She had a fire going, even in the late July heat. Standing before it, her body was outlined perfectly, making it obvious that she was wearing nothing else. Pert little nipples announced her interest in him the moment he stepped into the room.

This woman wasn't the lady from Cadenhill, this was Cat O'Conner, straight from Heaven, and he could no more have turned away from her than he could stop breathing.

"Catherine, what the hell are you doing? First you try to drown us and now you're trying to burn us alive?"

"You mean the fire? That's Pharaoh's idea. He says it keeps the sickness away. But we don't need a fire to burn, do we, Patrick?"

They never did eat. And later that night, as Patrick felt her soft breathing feather his chest, he pondered on the truth of her words. They were like lightning. All they had to do was look at each other and they ignited a fire that couldn't be quenched. And that would continue as long as they were together.

The answer became clear.

If he couldn't send her away, he'd have to leave.

He'd go to the place by the river where he kept his horse and his flatboats. It was crude, but it was close enough to Catherine to keep an eye on her, yet far enough away so that he could not lie with her. From there, Stone could carry on with his piracy until he'd taken enough money to pay the note.

Since he concentrated only on the Spanish vessels that had completed their trading missions he considered that he was only reclaiming what they'd taken from him when they stole his ship. He'd refurbish his coffers and deal.

Then, he'd take Catherine back to Petersburg, across country, himself. He didn't know how he'd face her family, or what they'd say. But he'd do whatever they considered the proper thing—once they learned the truth.

When Catherine awakened the next morning, Stone was gone. And she hadn't even told him about the child she was carrying. She stretched and made a happy little mewing sound. That was all right. She'd tell him soon. For now she could just lie there and enjoy her thoughts.

She wondered if she was supposed to feel guilty. She wondered what Patrick thought about her wantonness and decided it didn't matter. As long as she could wake up in his bed every morning, the rest of the world could, as Settie used to say, "go to grass and eat mullet."

They were supposed to be together and she defied anyone to say otherwise.

Patrick had been wrong about there being a snake in the Garden of Eden. Patrick had created a beautiful rainbow for her, with a pot of gold at the end.

Chapter Fifteen

Catherine was growing angrier by the minute. Patrick had been gone for days and nobody would tell her where, only that she was to wait.

Waiting patiently was not Catherine's style, but this time even Pharaoh refused to help her. She'd already learned how untamed the area around Patrick's plantation was. And she couldn't find a single worker who would agree to take her out, no matter where she told them she wanted to go. This time she didn't have any choice except to follow his orders.

If she had to wait, she'd find something to occupy her time. She started out by moving herself into the plantation house. She could oversee its progress better if she were living in the building. But she soon saw that her presence only slowed down the work, so she took to walking along the bayou where she enjoyed the beauty of the area.

Wildflowers bloomed abundantly in the areas touched by sunlight. Beautiful vines climbed the huge old trees, filling their branches with clusters of fragrant purple blossoms. She watched the heavy bees lumber through the air from flower to flower as if they had nowhere to go and all the time in the world to get there.

Nowhere to go, like her. She was trapped, alone. Being held prisoner at the end of a rainbow without Patrick wasn't her idea of happiness. Besides, there were times, in the early morning and sometimes late at night, when she felt positively ill. Having a baby was no fun without Patrick. In fact it was downright irritating.

Here he was, off doing who knew what, without even knowing that he was going to be a father. What if he got himself killed? What if he were making arrangements to send her home as he'd threatened? She could imagine herself walking into Judge Taliferro's parlor and announcing that she was with child and without a husband.

Growing more and more short-tempered, she finally pulled on a sun hat and took to the fields, working alongside the runaway slaves who'd taken advantage of Patrick's protection.

Resolutely, she refused to admit either to Pharaoh or to the woman who attended her that she was carrying a child. This was Patrick's baby, and Patrick would be the first to know—if he ever came back.

One hot day rolled into another. The cotton bloomed and made bolls, and the sugarcane, now shoulder high, was turning a deep purple color. Catherine, a familiar sight in the fields, turned as honey-colored as the mulatto girl who suddenly appeared at her door one morning with her needle and thread.

"Pharaoh sent me, lady. I will alter your clothes," the bright-eyed girl said.

"My clothes are just fine," Catherine snapped, trying to draw the waist of her skirt together.

"Of course, lady," the girl agreed, clipping the threads to allow Catherine's expanding waistline room to breath.

"What's your name?"

"I'm called Consuelo."

A Spanish name. English spoken with a Spanish accent, like many of the girls back at Isabella's. "Where did you come from anyway?"

"The captain found me, on the ship of my Spanish master. He thought I would suit for you."

"The captain? You mean Stone?"

"*Si!* He is making ready for your journey home."

Though she'd imagined all sorts of reasons for him to stay away, underneath her brave resolutions she'd really feared that he was back in Heaven with Isabella. Of course he still might be. All she knew for certain was that he had turned to piracy again.

"That rogue, that lying, rotten outlaw. He's out robbing the Spanish, risking his life while I'm left here alone."

Catherine, in a rare display of temper, threw the girl's sewing basket through the window and sent her scurrying out the door.

"He'll be killed, or caught, or—"

"Miz Cat!" Pharaoh poked his head in the door cautiously. "What you doing, throwing things out the window?"

"I'm practicing, Pharaoh. If Patrick McLendon ever sticks *his* head in that door, I'm going to bash it in."

Pharaoh backed out and closed the door. He allowed himself a smile. Miss Catherine was a fine lady, a real firecracker, just what Mr. Patrick needed. Word had come, just this morning, by the man who'd brought Consuelo, that Stone would be making the payment on his land and returning to Rainbow's End by the next week.

He'd be pleased when he learned about the child. And they'd be together just like Miss Catherine wanted.

Pharaoh allowed himself a sentimental sigh of contentment.

There was nothing sentimental about the tears streaming down Catherine's face. They were tears of frustration and anger, mixed with fear.

Making ready for your journey home!

Stone had no intention of coming back. He was doing just what he'd said he would, making arrangements to send her back to Petersburg. Nothing that had happened between them had changed his mind. The anger inside her swelled, choking her, slowly squeezing her heart like a giant hand.

What was she going to do?

How could she make him see that this was where she belonged, where they both belonged? Like her, the cotton was splitting the seams of its cover. Patrick would have a fine crop. A slave who'd escaped the sugar plantation on the Caribbean island was busy overseeing the construction of a shack where the cane juice could be turned into sugar crystals. He'd done it there, and he was convinced that it could be done here, if not with this crop, then with the next.

In this lush new country, life was taking on form and order. Were it not for Patrick's refusal to marry her, their lives would be perfect.

The morning passed as Catherine paced the tiny room where she'd spent too many long sleepless nights considering the problem. Through her window she watched Pharaoh oversee the unloading of the supplies that had just arrived by flatboat. On the return trip the boat would carry pelts and the portion of the indigo crop that they'd managed to salvage after the fire.

As she watched the workers loading the indigo she was suddenly struck with the answer. This boat was going to New Orleans. Charles was in New Orleans. If anybody could help Patrick clear his name, it was Charles. She'd suggested that to Patrick before, but he'd refused to go to Charles, even if he was President Washington's representative.

But Catherine could go. And she would. She'd explain to Charles that Simicco had killed the planter. Charles would meet with the governor and have the charges dismissed. Then there would be no barrier to Catherine and Patrick's marriage.

Quickly she plowed through the trunks of clothing that Patrick stored in the sleeping loft. She'd disguised herself as a man before. She could do it again. Then she'd hide herself somewhere on the boat until they reached New Orleans. Once there, she'd find Charles's office. It couldn't be too difficult. If she'd got from Petersburg to the Mississippi, she could get to New Orleans.

First, Catherine tied her disguise inside a sheet of muslin and dropped it out the window, watching it fall harmlessly to the ground by the back of the house. After her throwing the sewing basket out the window several days ago, the workers would dismiss this as her latest fit of fury.

Telling Pharaoh that she was going for a walk, Catherine then left the house by the front door, circled around to the side and claimed her bundle. Moments later, her feminine clothing left behind, she was dressed once more in men's shirt and trousers, with an old felt hat pulled down over her hair and obscuring her face.

Boarding the flatboat was less difficult than she'd expected. She simply lifted a keg, shielding her face, and followed the deckhand ahead of her. Once she'd deposited the keg, she found a tiny space between the drums and crouched down. She hadn't counted on being so hot, nor on the delay being so long. But finally the boat moved away from shore and left Rainbow's End behind.

The shadowy figure watching from the swamp frowned. He'd been watching for days, trying to find an opportunity to get to the fire-haired woman. But there was always someone around, either that old black man or a number of younger ones who seemed always to be busy somewhere nearby.

But now the fates had smiled on him. She'd left the protection of the blacks, fled into the swamp, and if he were any judge, nobody knew she was gone.

But he knew. The Sun King knew. The White Woman had put herself within his reach. And more, he could tell that she was with child.

With a smile of satisfaction he slipped away, reaching his boat and sliding it into the water. The medicine woman was dead. He regretted that, for her magic had been powerful and she warmed his loins, but more than that, she'd brought the White Woman. And until he'd made certain that she delivered her child, he couldn't rest.

His father had used black magic to impress Simicco with his duty. The planter who released the boy to be

trained as one of the island entertainers had used force
to keep him in line. Between the two, the Natchez had
become half man and half god, held controlled
through fear. There had been times, as he'd watched
the woman who called herself Catherine walking in the
woods, that he'd lost touch with who he really was.

Legend and mysticism had carried him to this land
of his people and given him a heavy burden to carry.
His first attempt at rule had ended in disaster. He'd
lost Moria, and only now that she was gone, did he
understand how much he'd come to rely on her judgment and her comfort.

Resolutely now, he put those thoughts behind him,
chastising himself for the weakness that made him lust
after this woman. She was not the important one. The
legend had foretold her coming, and it had shown the
child with bursting fire behind, with the sky lit by light
and the ripple of colors in the wind. This child was his
immortality. This child was the key to the future.

"What do you mean she's gone?"

Patrick held on to his rage by a thread. He'd worked
the river for weeks, making certain that there'd been
no report of Lopaz, adding to his purse until the sickness was over and he had enough money to make the
payment on his debt for the plantation. He'd sent Jillico to New Orleans with the payment and was making ready to return to Rainbow's End and accompany
Catherine back to Petersburg.

Then the messenger had caught up with him. Catherine had disappeared. She'd been missing one day
then. This made two days she'd been gone.

"I thought you had people watching her. Where did
she go, Pharaoh?"

The old man answered, his voice laced with guilt. "She said she was going for a walk, like she often does of late. There was men about. She couldn't have wandered off without passing one of them."

"But she did."

"When she didn't return, I sent out a search party. They found her clothes in the forest."

"Clothes? Were they torn? Was it some wild animal?"

"No, suh. Dey folded up nice, like she always do."

"A swim. Maybe she went for a swim."

"Yes, suh, but she walked down the bayou where the crocs lie in the sun. And she knew dat boat was gonna be leaving and pass right where she was. I don't think she would've done that, cause they'd have seen her."

"What boat?"

"The flatboat what brought the supplies. It loaded up with skins and de indigo and it headed to New Orleans."

"And Catherine went with them." Patrick knew it. Catherine had no fear. She'd already stolen a boat and come in search of him. She'd have no compunction about taking off downriver on a trading boat. But why? He'd thought she was happy, here on the plantation.

Then he remembered.

President Washington's representative. She'd gone to New Orleans, to him, to ask for help, and she had a two-day head start.

"Pharaoh, I'm going to New Orleans. When Jillico returns, tell him to come after me."

Arming himself with both money and weapons, Patrick poled his one-man pirogue back to the Mississippi where he traded it for a flatboat and a crew. He didn't want to take any chance of capsizing this trip, and he needed the safety of numbers.

By the next afternoon he was again poling a pirogue down a bayou that joined the Mississippi just beyond the check point outside New Orleans where the flatboat would be boarded by Spanish officials and assessed a tariff. He couldn't take a chance on being discovered. Instead, he'd cross the river in the pirogue and travel the rest of the way on foot. It shouldn't be too hard to find President Washington's representative. He only hoped that Catherine hadn't found him first.

Catherine got off the flatboat the same way she'd gotten on, by unloading one of the kegs. The levee was remarkable. It seemed to stretch forever, a broad, flat plain piled high with cargo, left in the sun. The warehouses were yards away, across an open area of new silt being washed down the waterway.

She'd understood enough of the conversation on the way downriver that if she were asked, she'd say her destination was the French Market. But no one asked. On reaching the first warehouse, she managed to mingle with others inside and disappear into the bustle of the commerce taking place in the street beyond.

Once out of the warehouse she started toward the congested area of businesses. It made sense to her that Charles would have an office in town. Around her, a cacophony of sounds assaulted her ears. Street vendors and hawkers called out their wares on the street corner.

"Ah got ba-na-na, lay-dee!" was the melodious cry from one coffee-colored man, who carried a stalk of bananas over one shoulder.

A mule-drawn cart carried vegetables down the muddy street, its driver singing the praises of his goods in an odd dialect that Catherine couldn't understand.

Catherine passed one black woman, whose head was tied in a colorful bandanna. She was selling rice cakes. Food. Catherine thought about how long it had been since she'd eaten and wished she had coins to buy something. But she'd had no money of her own since hers had sunk in the Mississippi.

She passed a print shop with a newspaper tacked to the wall beside the open doorway. Catherine wished she'd paid more attention to the French lessons her father had provided for her so that she could read the composition.

All eyes and ears, Catherine came to a stop before a building that proclaimed itself to be a theater. The advertisement posted suggested a musical review. In fact she heard the sound of drum music inside. Sooner or later she'd have to ask someone for directions. Perhaps one of the entertainers spoke English.

Inside the building was a stage, lined with candles to be lit for the production. Now two men and a woman were dancing. For a moment Catherine was caught up in the rhythm. She'd heard it before. They were dancing in that same sensual way that the Sun King has danced that night in the clearing.

The Sun King!

For a moment she was back in the bayou, in the village called Green Mounds of Earth, reliving that horrible moment when the Spanish had invaded the clearing. No, that couldn't be. The sound of the drums was doing it to her.

The man she was watching was tall, very tall, with the same commanding bearing as Simicco. His back was to her, but she couldn't shake the feeling that he knew she was there, or that as she was watching the dancers, someone was watching her.

Her heart began to pound. Imagined or otherwise, she had to get out of there—now. Whirling around, she fled into the midday sun, jostling a well-dressed businessman who'd just crossed the street and stopped to clean the caked mud from the bottom of his boots. Their impact was such that she knocked him back into the mud, bottom first.

"Oh, my goodness! I'm so sorry. Here, let me help you."

"Mon Dieu!" He stood up, took a good look at Catherine and frowned. *"J'ai été agressé par un gamin."*

"Sorry, I don't understand you. I'm looking for Charles Forrest. Mr. Charles Forrest."

Her victim finally realized that she was a woman and began eyeing her curiously. *"Oui, Monsieur Forrest!"*

He knew Charles. He would take her to him. At least that was what she thought until he pointed to his ruined trousers and caught her by the neck of her jacket. From then on, as she scrambled to keep up with his rapid pace, Catherine was just as glad that she didn't speak the language.

She'd been dragged like a rag doll just about as far as she intended to go when he stopped at a red brick building that opened directly onto the walkway beside the street. The Frenchman knocked rapidly on the outer door.

Almost immediately it opened, admitting them to a foyer that was a part of, yet not open to, the house. After a brief exchange between the man whose pants she'd ruined and the black woman who'd answered the door they were directed to go back to the street and come to the rear of the house. When the back gate was opened they stepped into a beautiful little courtyard and garden. Catherine was relieved.

Until she heard the voice.

Charles's voice.

"What is the meaning of this, sir? What makes you think I owe you a new pair of trousers?"

Catherine would have explained, but the Frenchman let go of a torrent of words and gestures that blocked out her voice, all while he was still holding on to her. Finally, just as Charles was ordering him ejected by a tall black man who was coming from what appeared to be a stable, she managed to interrupt.

"Charles, tell this man to let go of me or he'll need a new pair of legs to fit into those trousers!"

Charles hushed, his eyes opening wide in disbelief. "Catherine?"

"Yes, it's me and I'm very tired and very hungry. Please pay this man and send him away."

Charles slapped a coin in the man's hand and dismissed him, taking Catherine by the arm. "Why are you dressed like that and where in bloody hell have you been?"

"I'm dressed like this so no one would recognize me and I've been in the bayou. Can we please go inside? I really am very hungry."

"A bath wouldn't hurt, either," Charles observed, confusion evident in his manner. "Are you alone?"

"Of course I'm alone. Who would I have with me?"

"Catherine, I have no idea who or what you might have waiting beyond the wall. Come inside and I'll have Topsy clean you up."

The inside of Charles's house was cool and dark. The black woman who had opened the gate was standing openmouthed as she watched Catherine peel off her hat and shake out her hair.

Charles snapped orders, directing Topsy to prepare a bath and find Catherine something decent to wear. He stood at the bottom of the stairs and watched as Catherine followed Topsy up. He was both disturbed and elated. He hadn't understood her flight, nor her disappearance. But he'd been willing to give her the benefit of the doubt.

Had Captain Lopaz brought her back he would have announced his displeasure, but he would not have canceled the marriage. He'd planned on marrying Catherine Caden. Most of what he'd done was based on that presumption. Had he found her betrothed he might have stepped back, but to be replaced by a pirate was a discourtesy he would not accept.

Catherine, already planning the plea she'd make to Charles failed to notice his grim expression.

After her bath, her hair was combed and pulled on top of her head where it was secured with a set of combs.

Once clean, she'd thought that she'd feel better. She didn't. There was a sense of unreality to what was happening. Charles's house was lovely, expensive even, but she kept remembering her house in the swamp, and the bayou with its wild profusion of lush, untamed beauty.

The garment Topsy produced was little more than a wrapper, but ample enough so that the changes in Catherine's figure would not be obvious. Catherine fastened it and wondered briefly about its purpose. An undergarment of loosely woven fabric, almost like a nightrail, was covered with an equally light wrapper. It seemed a strange choice of dress for a slave, but then perhaps it didn't belong to a house servant, but rather to a guest—one of Charles's houseguests.

So, Charles had lady friends. Somehow that thought amused her. He was worried about her having been with Stone, but he'd not been alone.

Catherine allowed herself an impish smile as she trailed down the staircase in search of the source of delicious odors she was smelling. "Charles?"

"In here—" He stopped abruptly as she entered the dining area. "Come in, Catherine. You look—lovely. Welcome."

He went to great pains to seat her, ordering the first course of a meal to be served. Topsy brought soup, which Catherine ate without stopping for conversation. By the time she'd completed the main dish of fish and rice she was ready to talk. Laying down her napkin, she leaned back and smiled at Charles.

"Your cook is very good."

"Thank you."

"Your house is lovely, too."

"Yes, it was furnished for you," he said simply. As if he'd been waiting, Charles put down his napkin and asked, "You have been with that pirate, haven't you, Catherine?"

"Yes, of course."

"Of your own free will?"

"Not exactly," she answered, remembering her forced imprisonment while Patrick returned to the river.

"I sent the Spanish army to find you, but they never returned."

"I know. Captain Lopaz and his men chased us but by then we were at the Green Mounds of Earth. They attacked the Indians. But then Captain Lopaz was wounded and fled. I think the alligators probably got them, but nobody knows for certain."

"But—but you got away. How did you escape?"

For now a shortened version of her escape might be better. "I hid on a flatboat bringing trading goods downriver."

"Then he, Stone, doesn't know where you are?"

"Not yet, but he'll figure it out, and come after me."

Charles groaned. During the time Catherine had been bathing he'd considered the situation carefully, trying to decide how to use her arrival to his best advantage. Originally he had told the governor that he would produce Stone in return for certain trade arrangements for the Americans. The governor had been most enthusiastic. But when the plan failed, Charles had not been able to gain further audiences.

In fact, none of President Washington's hopes to establish diplomatic relations with the Spanish had been realized. The Spanish officials simply ignored Charles as if he weren't there at all.

Every day Charles had expected to receive orders from President Washington that he was being replaced. Every day he'd grown more desperate. He held

Catherine totally responsible for the sorry state of his affairs. Now she'd returned and this time he intended to make certain that he fulfilled his promise to Governor Carondelet.

"So you expect Stone to come for you."

"Not Stone, Charles, Patrick. Patrick and the pirate, Stone, are one and the same. You couldn't find any trace of Patrick because that Captain Lopaz had put him in prison."

Quickly, Catherine explained how Patrick had been beaten and his ship stolen; how Patrick had been falsely blamed for the plantation owner's death. "And that's why I've come to you. You are the only one who can go to the governor and have him clear Patrick's name. Patrick never killed anybody. Simicco, the Indian slave, did."

"And you expect me to act in Patrick's behalf?"

"Of course."

"Why?"

"Because—because, I intend to marry him, Charles. I always did. Patrick and I belong together at Rainbow's End."

"What about me, Catherine. What about your promise to marry me?"

"I'm so sorry, Charles. I never meant to hurt you. When you came to Petersburg I'd been told that Patrick was dead. I thought we suited well enough, and I couldn't go on mourning forever. Then when you came to the Weatherbys I knew that it would be wrong. I should have faced you with it, but I feared that you'd send me back to Cadenhill."

"You're such a child, Catherine. Everyone warned me about your stubbornness, but I refused to listen."

"You're right. And I'm pigheaded and unthinking and, oh, Charles, I am sorry."

"You should have married me, Catherine. I came here and built this house for you. I told everyone that you were to be my wife. How do you think I felt when the governor found out that you'd run off after that pirate?"

He was right; she'd gone after what she wanted. She'd have used the devil if he could have gotten her to Patrick, but the hurt had never been intentional. Charles had led her to Patrick, and for that reason alone, she'd always be grateful.

"Please, Charles, forgive me. I know that what I did was wrong, and you have every right to be angry. But you're a good man—and I'm asking your help for Patrick. He isn't a pirate. He only robs the Spanish of their own money to replace what they took from him. He's been wronged and I've come to ask for your help."

"And what will you do in return, Catherine, if I save your pirate from hanging?"

"What will I do?" Catherine was puzzled. "I'll be very grateful."

"I'm afraid that your gratitude won't be enough."

He was going to turn her down. She could tell from the strange intensity of his reply. His hurt went deeper than she'd thought. The one hope she'd had to save the man she loved was drowning in the stern displeasure of the man she'd once thought to marry.

Desperately she searched for a way to bargain. "Help Patrick and I'll do whatever you want."

Charles looked directly at her. Here, away from the Mississippi, he was a different man. Gone was the gentle, understanding person who'd promised to find out about Patrick. Instead she was facing the smartly dressed man she'd watched walk up the path from the river at the trading post.

She'd finally come to him, albeit unwillingly, and he intended to hold her to her rash promise.

"You are very beautiful, Catherine Caden. But you really must temper your actions. The wife of a man in power cannot be so aggressive."

What was Charles talking about? Patrick wasn't in power and he would never love a woman who tempered her actions.

"I don't understand."

"Of course you do, my dear. I'll help Patrick. You will send for him, and I'll petition the governor on behalf of President Washington."

"Oh, Charles! I knew I could count on you. I'll go back for Patrick right away."

"No, I'm afraid I can't allow that. Your family would be most displeased if I let you go. I've already sent word that you've been found and that we will be married as soon as it can be arranged."

"You did what?"

"I did the proper thing, Catherine, as you will soon do, if you want to save this criminal. In the meantime, I'll leave you to get some rest."

He stood, walked the length of the table and held out his hand to assist her from her chair. She was startled when he pressed his lips to hers, and alarmed. There was something intense about Charles, a hard edge that she'd never seen before.

"You expect me to marry you, after what I've said?"

"Of course. Remember what you said, that you'd do whatever I asked. And marriage is my price to clear Patrick McLendon's name. Otherwise, I'm afraid that he's a dead man. Good night, Catherine, sleep well."

Chapter Sixteen

There were guards, Patrick could see them. He'd hugged the shadows of the surrounding building for most of the night until he determined where Catherine was. Why had she left Rainbow's End? There she was safe. This fool American couldn't know about Simicco and the danger for Catherine.

From what Patrick had learned, the American had not made a good impression in New Orleans. He'd been carried away with his own importance, more concerned about appearances than representing his government. Instead of accepting him with open arms as he'd anticipated, society had ignored him, as they did all Americans.

Patrick weighed the possibilities of calling on the man directly and decided he didn't trust him any more than he trusted the Spanish governor. Discretion would be his wisest move. In fact he intended to be so discreet that the best way he could protect the woman he loved was by stealing her away.

Having made up his mind, he scaled the live oak tree by the brick wall outside the American's residence and dropped soundlessly into the tiny courtyard. He skirted the enclosure and made his way back to the servants' stairs leading to the balcony. Quietly Patrick climbed, his heart hammering louder with every step. At the top, he stopped and listened. The night was quiet, too quiet.

As always, Catherine's nearness distracted him, making it impossible for Patrick to determine whether his sense of unease was coming from Catherine, or from some unknown danger.

The windows, which also served as doors on the upper level, were closed against the damp December air. He counted until he came to the room where he'd seen Catherine earlier, took a deep breath and slid the panel open, stepping inside.

With any luck he could reach Catherine, signal her to silence and get her away before anyone knew he was around. He didn't know what kind of servants the American employed, but Patrick concluded that they paid as little attention to their employer as the governor did.

Moments later, he learned they were neither sloppy nor unaware of his presence. And it wasn't servants he need fear, it was armed guards.

"Well, now, Mr. McLendon, or is it the pirate, Stone?"

Patrick had heard that voice before, beneath his window that night in Natchez-under-the-Hill. He was the man who'd sent Lopaz after him. Patrick was stunned.

Catherine had come directly to the man from whom they'd been escaping. Patrick could make no sense of what was happening. His best action was escape. It took four guards to subdue Patrick, but in a matter of minutes he was shackled, chained, pushed down to a stool and surrounded by guards.

A lamp was lit as well as the candles in the holders along the wall, revealing the American sitting in a large chair in the corner.

"You have me at a disadvantage, sir," Patrick said. "I don't believe we've met."

"I don't really think we need an introduction, Mr. McLendon. You knew where you were coming and why. You know who I am and that Catherine is here."

A noise down the corridor heralded the approach of the woman in question. "Charles? What is it?" She was fastening her wrapper as she stepped into the room.

"Hello, Cat," Patrick said, giving her an appreciative, involuntary grin. "Looks like I've run afoul of the law again. It's back to the dungeon for me."

"Not this time!" she exclaimed, running to his side and dropping to her knees on the floor. "Unfasten him, Charles. This is Patrick."

"I know, my dear. I've been waiting for him. We wouldn't want to marry without having your pirate as a guest, would we?"

"I can't do that, Charles. I don't understand all this."

"Oh, but you do. You promised that you'd do whatever I wanted, if I would arrange to clear Patrick's name. And I told you that what I wanted was for you to become Mrs. Charles Forrest, just as we'd planned."

"But—but you can't be serious. I'm in love with Patrick. You know that. I always have been."

"Love? What does that signify?"

Catherine felt Patrick's muscles tighten beneath her hand resting on his thigh. She hadn't believed Charles was serious when he'd left her earlier. He didn't understand how she felt about Patrick. She'd planned to explain her feelings when he returned. But it was obvious that he had no intention of listening.

How could she have been such a fool? Why hadn't she listened to Patrick? Because of her, Patrick had been lured to New Orleans, where Charles intended to hand him over to the governor for execution as the pirate, Stone.

Finally, shoulders bowed in defeat, she stood. "If I marry you, you'll release Patrick?"

"Don't believe him, Catherine. He's lying to you. He set you up, knowing I'd come for you."

"Of course," Charles agreed, ignoring Patrick. "Take him away." He directed the men who were standing at the four corners of Patrick's stool. At their nudging, he uncoiled his well-honed body and stood proudly, undaunted by the danger of the moment.

Catherine thought of the child she was carrying and weighed the consequences of her rash actions while Patrick moved toward the door. As he came even with her, he smiled, lifted his eyebrow and gave her a devilish wink as if to say, take heart. Then he moved on and she wondered if she'd imagined his carefree boldness.

No, this was Patrick, her Patrick, and he'd never give in to defeat. He was telling her to be patient and he'd think of a way out. But this time the way out might get him killed and she couldn't let that happen.

"You tricked me, Charles," she said as she turned to face this man she'd once thought to marry. "And I suppose that's only fair after what I did to you. But Patrick doesn't deserve this. He never did anything to harm you."

"Doesn't matter," Charles admitted. "Patrick is my leverage. As long as I have him, I have your cooperation."

"I can't think why you'd want a woman who doesn't love you."

"It's very simple. I intend to make a name for myself in government service. But, I'm afraid that Governor Carondelet isn't as cooperative as he should be. Your father was a prominent man in the revolution and I need the prestige of the Caden name, and your dowry. And now I have the means to get both."

Catherine let out a gasp. "My dowry? I'm afraid you're in for a surprise, Charles. There is no dowry."

"But of course there is. Your mother's new husband, Judge Taliferro, is supplying it. We settled the terms before I left Petersburg."

"You went to the judge and asked for my dowry?"

"Or course, why else do you think I went to him except to offer to take you off their hands? You'll find that I always do what is proper, Catherine, and expect the proper response in return."

"You never loved me, did you, Charles?"

"No more than you loved me, Catherine. We were both the means to an end. But don't worry, I will be good to you and in return you will enjoy a fine life and give me children."

Catherine didn't mean to laugh. She knew as quickly as her laugh spilled out that she'd angered Charles at a time when she needed to maintain some kind of reasonable relationship between them. She'd never given in to hysterics, not even when she'd been told that Patrick was dead. But suddenly she couldn't stop herself from retaliating.

"Children?"

"You find it amusing that I expect children, Catherine?"

"No—no." She struggled to control her emotions. "At the moment, I find it impossible."

"Impossible? Why, are you barren?"

"No, Charles. Quite the contrary. I'm already carrying a child, Patrick's child. Any children I give you will have to wait."

"He took you?"

"No, Charles, I gave myself to him, not once, but many times."

Charles had never thought himself to be a violent man. He would have said he was not. He honestly didn't know he'd moved, until he slapped her. Even as he pulled his hand back, acknowledging the sting, he attributed his rage to the uncivilized city to which he'd been sent, not jealousy.

A post in Paris or London was what Charles had requested. He'd been bitterly disappointed when he'd been sent instead to the Louisiana Territory, and he'd intended to quickly accomplish his goal and apply for a post in the new capital. He hadn't expected the Spanish governor to refuse to discuss the negotiation of favorable trade agreements with the Americans. Nor had he expected the defiant look in Catherine's eyes.

Even now, with the red print of his hand staining her face, she glared at him. No trembling, no fear. He felt a swell of repulsion sweep over him. His Catherine was carrying another man's child. The body that was to be his had been defiled by Stone.

Stone.

Well, this time Charles held the upper hand. He wouldn't be beaten. The child didn't matter; it only took away his desire for Catherine's body temporarily. The wedding would still take place. Let her have Stone's brat, then she'd have to learn what was expected of a proper wife. They'd still be married right away.

But first he had to deal with that pirate. Tonight Catherine could wait.

Three days later Catherine was still waiting. She'd been confined to her room. Only Topsy was allowed to go inside, to bring food and bathwater. Charles didn't send for her and he refused to respond to her summons. She'd paced the balcony nightly, searching in vain for a way to distract her guards in the courtyard below.

Then one night a figure slipped through the window and put his hand over Catherine's mouth, signaling her to silence.

"Jillico! Where is Patrick"

"Shhh. He's in jail."

"In jail? Then the governor refuses to pardon him?"

"Stone is to be executed tomorrow night. Señor Forrest delivered him to the governor himself. In return, the governor has agreed to grant free trade."

"Prison! That liar! Get me a knife. If they hurt one hair on Patrick's head, I'll kill Charles myself!"

"There is more. Your wedding is to take place the same night. I have not found a way to rescue Stone, though Pharaoh is trying to find a way to reach you through Topsy."

"Topsy?"

"Yes, she was on the ship with the others who came from the island. She knows that Patrick didn't kill anybody, but she's afraid of the Sun King's black magic. He is a very powerful man. And they say that he's dangerous as well."

"I wish we had some of his black magic right now. There has to be a way to get into that jail and rescue Patrick. Even a dying man deserves—wait, that's it! A confession. I will visit Stone as the priest who goes to hear his last confession, Jillico."

"You can't mean to go to the jail yourself. What will that accomplish?"

"I'm not certain yet. I'm thinking."

"I will go."

"You cannot go, Jillico. Suppose they notice that you're an Indian. There are no Indian priests."

"And I don't suppose they'd notice you're a woman?"

"Of course they wouldn't. They'll accept what they see. If I look like a priest, they'll believe I'm a priest. Get me a priest's robe, Jillico, and...yes, I will take Patrick food, and a jug of wine that you will have drugged. The guards will take the wine and drink it. Later, when they sleep, Patrick can be set free."

"And what about you and Mr. Forrest?"

"I don't know," she answered in a tight whisper. "I'm working on that."

Charles caught himself just before he slammed the door to the governor's office. He'd planned to hold the marriage ceremony first to make sure that Catherine didn't have a chance to change her mind. But he'd been thwarted at every step of the way. The dress wouldn't be ready until tonight and the minister was not free until the next day, unless he would accept an evening hour.

After reasoning that Catherine wouldn't know when the execution was to take place, he'd agreed to a ten o'clock ceremony. That way he'd view the execution at nine and by the time his bride found out what had happened, it would be too late.

At least one thing had gone right—he'd collected the reward for Stone's capture, and he'd made an appointment with a banker who knew a potential buyer for his house. Staying in New Orleans held no appeal for Charles now; he and Catherine would leave on the next ship. He checked his pocket watch. Just enough time to arrange passage on the ship and meet with the house buyer. Then he'd be off to the jail.

As he stepped into the street he heard the frightened cry of a horse barreling down the narrow street, forcing him to jump back into an alleyway adjacent to the French Market.

"Hold up, governor!" Two masked men stepped out of the shadows and pushed him against the wall.

"Don't move," the tall slim one said. "Hand over your purse, or die!"

Another man might have recognized the melodramatic flair and the affected voice of the robber, but Charles was so frightened that he didn't even turn around. Instead he thrust his purse containing the reward behind him and held his breath, expecting to be stabbed at any moment.

He wasn't. He was hit on the head, and after being checked to make certain that he wasn't hurt badly, left abandoned in the alley. After a time he came to, rubbed his pounding head and pulled himself to his feet. He was alone. The robbers had taken the reward money and disappeared into the night. After a quick check of the time he hurried toward the bank. He was late. He'd already lost a considerable sum of money, he couldn't afford to lose more.

"I feel like the grim reaper," Catherine said, adjusting the length of the priest's robe she was wearing by tightening the ties.

Jillico didn't answer. Already dressed as a servant accompanying the holy man, he was placing the jugs of wine over his shoulder, suspending them by a thong tied between.

"You are certain that Señor Forrest will not return tonight before the wedding?"

"Certain. He finally honored me with a visit to explain. He is buying my wedding gown and arranging for our departure. First he has to sell the house to pay for our passage. And he won't leave until he's collected the reward for Patrick's capture. Then he returns with the priest to conduct our wedding."

Jillico grinned. "It would be too bad if the American official collected the reward and was robbed on the way home, wouldn't it?"

"No, Jillico. Stone must cease to exist. We don't want any more robberies blamed on that river pirate. Come, let us go. You have the wine?"

"Yes, *Señorita,* forgive, I should remember not to call you Miss Catherine."

"You should remember to call me Father. I just hope the prison guards are not going to wonder why an American who isn't even Catholic is pretending to be a priest."

"Yes, Father," he said with a grin, and followed Catherine out into the corridor. The house seemed empty. Nobody but Pharaoh and his old friend Topsy knew that Charles's guards, having tested their first bottle of drugged wine, were sleeping off the results in the storage room.

It was only five o'clock in the afternoon, but December darkness had already fallen. The gloom of the day was made even worse by a heavy fog, which had emptied the streets. When they arrived at the prison at the dinner hour, the food and drink they were carrying would lend credibility to their pretended mission, so that the guards would accept their story that they'd come to hear the confession of the pirate Stone before his scheduled execution.

Catherine hoped what she was doing was right. Patrick was in prison because of her foolhardiness, because she'd disregarded his wishes and gone to Charles for help. She'd never expected Charles to turn Patrick in. Nor had she seen anything in his quiet demeanor back in Petersburg to suggest the cruel streak of ambition that drove him.

Down the foggy streets they hurried, heads bowed, conversation hushed. A rosary circled Catherine's neck, from which a crucifix was hanging. Now she clutched it, praying silently that she wasn't making another foolish move.

Inside his jail cell Patrick was also praying. This time there were no cellmates, no broken manacles with which to dig his way clear and no bird signals from beyond the barred window over his head.

His execution was scheduled for nine o'clock. Charles had bragged that his marriage to Catherine would take place an hour before. There was nothing Patrick could do to stop the wedding. She wouldn't run away this time, for she believed that only by her wedding Charles would Patrick be freed.

Dear Catherine, who always believed in the goodness of man, had not learned that some men couldn't be trusted. There'd been no petition to the governor for clemency. Charles had never had any intention of carrying out his part of the bargain.

Patrick rubbed his eyes. He'd faced death before, and faced it without fear. But now there was Catherine. Because of him she'd be married to a cold, calculating man who would never appreciate the gift he'd been given.

No, Catherine would do something. He didn't know how, but he knew that she'd make some last-minute desperate attempt to get away. She always did.

How had his life come to this? If only they'd never left their cabin in the swamp. She'd been safe there; they'd been safe there. He could still see her swimming among the lily pads, surrounded by pink blossoms, all satiny in the sunlight.

Sunshine and satin. That was how he'd remember her, for as long as he had time to remember.

He still couldn't explain the feelings that rushed through him when she touched him. He'd thought that hurt and pain had shriveled his heart long ago. But she'd brought it back to life again, and made it long for the promise of love. She never held back or pretended. Catherine was what she was and she never hid her feelings.

Not like him.

He'd hidden his, shoved them so deep inside that he'd never allowed them the freedom to be spoken. He was going to die without ever having told her that he loved her. He regretted that, almost more than dying.

He'd had nothing to offer her. But she'd wanted nothing. He'd given her even less, for he'd held back the one thing she wanted, his declaration of love.

His body shuddered and he slammed his fist against the wall, reveling in the pain that took away his thoughts. If only Charles had been what Catherine had thought him to be. Patrick wouldn't mind dying so much if he knew that Charles really loved Catherine. But he didn't. He never had. He'd bragged to Patrick about marrying the Caden name and using Catherine's dowry to secure himself in a society where a man was judged on his financial worth.

Catherine had simply been from the right family, with the right connections to help his career, and he'd caught her at a time when she was vulnerable and ready to get away from the pitying platitudes of her friends.

God's blood, Patrick thought, he couldn't die and leave Catherine to a man who planned to use the reward for Patrick's capture to take Catherine on a wedding trip.

Patrick swore again and closed his eyes. No point in looking for rainbows or leprechauns this time. He'd used up all his wishes and all his luck. This time there wouldn't even be a pig.

At the practically new theater on St. Peter Street, the group of slave actors gathered around the candle and listened to their leader. Months ago, along with the planters, they'd boarded Patrick's ship to escape the uprising. Patrick hadn't known that they were not plantation slaves. Once in New Orleans, they'd fled the ship and used their occupation as stage actors to cover the darker practice of black magic. They'd brought their power to this land from which their forefathers had come. Already they were becoming known for their secret powers.

"The time is soon," the leader said. "The White Woman is here. She must be protected."

"But Simicco," one Indian asked, "how can this be accomplished?"

"We will watch her as we have done before. The American plans to take her from the city tonight. This cannot be allowed."

"I don't know," the same Indian argued. "Perhaps we should give up on this woman. We thought our tribe would be mighty. Instead our people, the Natchez, are gone from this land along the mighty Mississippi. Those who have not been killed have joined with the other tribes. Moria is dead and Jillico has joined with Stone."

"No! Cease this talk. We have been returned to the land of our fathers. We have been provided with a purpose and we have this theater in which to work to bide our time."

"But acting on the stage is all we know how to do, Simicco," the lone woman in the group said. "I have no wish to live in the village of the Green Mounds of Earth. That life is no more."

"You have grown soft, all of you. The lesser slaves worked the fields, grew the cane and forgot the old ways. But we were the chosen ones. We learned to read and recite. We have the ways of our people and the voodoo of those on the islands."

Simicco stood and walked about the table, studying the small band of Indians he'd trained and prepared for this moment. They'd enjoyed their places of

power on the island, but here, they were losing their
conviction. He couldn't allow that to happen.

"The white man believes that we are entertaining
him, but in reality, he is following where we lead. We
will survive and claim our place as rulers once more,
for we are the children of the Sun. And we will soon
claim the glory that is ours. It has been seen in all our
dreams for all our lives. Is this not so?"

Reluctantly they murmured their agreement.

And then he announced his final argument.

"The White Woman of Moria's vision is carrying a
child."

It was the smell of Topsy's fish stew that overcame
any reservations the prison jailers might have had, that
and the jailer's noticing the jugs of wine the priest's
servant carried.

"Confession from the prisoner?" he said, nodding
his head. "Then the last meal. That seems reasonable, even for a murderer. Why don't we hold the food
and wine until you've finished, Father?"

Jillico slid the jugs from his shoulder and handed
them to the Spanish official, who also took the con-
tainer of food Catherine was holding. Jillico made the
sign of the cross and waited by the door with his head
bowed.

The jailer motioned to the guard, who took the ring
of keys from a peg by the desk and opened the iron
door. "This way. You have ten minutes, no more."

With the same key, the guard unlocked the cell door
and waited until the two robed figures were inside.
Then the door slammed closed behind them.

Patrick pushed himself to his feet. "What the hell?
I didn't send for you."

"When did that ever stop me?" Catherine said and flung herself into Patrick's arms, drawing him to the floor.

"Catherine?"

"Oh, Patrick, I'm so sorry. I thought Charles would help us. Now look what's happened."

"Hush, Catherine." He drew her close and kissed her hungrily. They had only a few minutes. Minutes that would be all he'd ever have. "I don't blame you. I don't even blame Forrest. Hell, I'd probably have done the same thing myself."

Tears rolled unashamedly down Catherine's face. If she'd done what Patrick had asked her to do they'd still be at Rainbow's End and he wouldn't be about to die.

"I've placed everything in your name," Patrick was saying. "You'll have the land, and the men will follow you."

"Stone! Listen!" Jillico interrupted. "We have a plan, listen to—the Father." He went to stand watch by the door.

"Pretend to be praying." Catherine directed and dropped to her knees. Patrick assumed the same position, head bowed, his hands clasping hers in the shadows.

"How'd you two get in here? No, don't tell me. Just tell me that you have a way to get out."

"Of course. We've brought you food and wine, which, with any luck, the guards are already enjoying. They're both drugged. Later, we'll return and free you."

"Not *we*. It's too dangerous. You go back to Forrest's house and wait. You'll be safe, because he'll be coming here for the hanging. After I'm out of here I'll come for you. There is a little something that President Washington's representative has to know."

"What?"

"Don't worry. Just wait there."

"But what if—something happens?"

"Nothing will."

"The guard is coming back," Jillico said and knelt on the floor beside them.

The door opened. Jillico and Catherine rose, making the sign of the cross one last time. They walked slowly out of the cell and past the jailer's desk.

The man hadn't even waited for them to leave before diving into Patrick's last meal. He nodded to them as they passed and raised his glass of wine in salute.

On the street, Catherine let go of the the breath she'd been holding since they'd left Patrick's cell. Her knees were shaking so that she could hardly stand.

"Hurry now," Jillico said. "You must be there if Señor Forrest returns, and I have much to do."

"I'm not going back there," she said.

"And suppose Charles returns and finds you gone. Pharaoh and Topsy will be blamed, and he'll come immediately to the jail, before the time he's expected."

Jillico was right. Only by returning could she make certain that nobody else suffered because of her actions, or that Charles wasn't alerted to the escape. She turned and hurried back along the street. Through the open windows she could see people at prayers. The Holy Season of Christmas was approaching and the city would celebrate.

A brisk wind swirled in from the river, blowing the fog away and cooling the air. By the time Catherine reached Charles's house she was chilled. She slipped into the courtyard and hurried to the kitchen, shedding her priest's robe as she went. Pharaoh and Topsy were waiting by the fire as she nodded and hurried up the stairs.

Soon the guards would awaken. With any luck each would assume he was the only one to have fallen asleep, and her absence would have gone unnoticed. She began pacing once more, praying that the wine taken to the prison worked as well.

It was after supper on Rue Royal, less than five blocks from the house where Catherine was being held, and four children were playing in the hay barn. They were rolling leaves of tobacco that the oldest boy had swiped from the dock.

"Are you gonna do it, Pierre? I dare you."

"Course I'm gonna do it. Just get me one of them dry sticks from the hearth."

The younger boy scurried to the cook house and played around the hearth where the cook was banking the fire for the morning meal, until he could grab a stick and run away without being seen.

"Got it."

"You better not do that," the little girl said, watching balefully from her place near the door. "Papa will punish you."

"You're just a babe, Adalaine. Even I'm old enough to smoke," the runner with the stick bragged. "Let me have a leaf, Pierre."

But Pierre was having his own difficulties. The wind swept through the open door to the hayloft, lifting the sparks from the burning branch and slinging them into the dry hay. Moments later the entire loft seemed to burst into flames.

"Fire," Adalaine screamed. "I'm gonna tell Mama." She took off in a run, the fire like a snake slithering through the straw behind her.

The boys tried to beat out the fire with mats, but they only succeeded in flinging the embers across the room. The two horses screamed in terror, bucking down their stall doors and fleeing into the night.

The slaves, alerted by the little girl, instantly began a bucket brigade using the water collected in the cistern behind the house. But it was already too late. And like the disastrous fire six years earlier, the flames leaped across the city, eating buildings like some flame-blowing monster loose in the night.

The wind became more and more brisk. In the business district, Charles walked with his head down, his mind so focused on his night's program that he didn't notice the smell of smoke. Charles had sent a messenger to deliver Catherine's wedding gown and instruct her to dress and be ready for the ceremony at ten instead of nine. He would arrive with the minister who would perform the ceremony.

Catherine couldn't be still. Dressed in her chemise and petticoat she finally lay down on the bed and closed her eyes. She didn't know what the night would bring and she remembered other nights when she hadn't been able to stay awake to help watch for their enemies.

In the kitchen below, Topsy finished her duties. She didn't understand the American, or his cruelty to the woman he was holding prisoner. She sampled the wine that the guards had left, reasoning that a wee nap wouldn't hurt her, either. If she was asleep she couldn't be accused of knowing what was about to happen.

One by one, in the courtyard beyond, the sleeping guards Charles had left were carried away by Simicco's voodoo priests. Having accomplished their tasks, the entertainers melted away into the night in order to reach the theater in time to perform. Only the Sun King was left.

Across the Vieux Carré, when Pharaoh reached the jail, the guards were sound asleep. It was easier than he'd believed possible to steal into the facility and open the cell. Or it would have been, if the other prisoners hadn't realized what was happening and clamored to be freed.

"Unlock one cell and give them the keys," Patrick directed and slipped out into the streets of New Orleans. He stopped and sniffed the air. Smoke. There was a fire. A sudden fear fell over him and he began to run.

Catherine. He had to get to Catherine.

The smell of fire woke Catherine. A thick black curl of smoke crept under her balcony door. She knew instantly what it was; she'd been through this before when the barn at Cadenhill had burned. By the time Catherine made it to the window, she could see the flames curling around the buildings toward the river on Bourbon Street and behind the house on Bienville as well.

"Topsy," she called out, "the city is burning. We have to get out."

But there was no answer. She knew that Pharaoh had gone with Jillico to rescue Patrick. The guards outside the house surely must be awake now. Charles wouldn't want her to die. She began to pound on the door and scream. But the door was locked. Finally she was able to break through the shutter onto the balcony. But waiting in the courtyard below was the one figure she had not expected to see.

"Simicco!"

"Come with me, White Woman. I will take you away and keep you safe."

"No. I won't leave until I know that Patrick is free." She ran back inside and pushed a chest in front of the window behind her. Charles was the enemy she knew. Simicco was the unknown.

Embers were flying through the night air, falling harmlessly on the tin roofs and turning into black soot, bursting into flames on the thatch roofs, and spreading to the dry rose vines along the porch and catching fire. Flames were shimmying up the walls with such heat that the bricks were exploding.

Church bells were ringing frantically. Horses were charging along the muddy streets, miring the wheels of carriages as frightened citizens fought to get away from the blaze. It seemed to Catherine as if the entire city was burning. She saw Simicco climbing the servants' stairs. But the balcony was in flames between her room and the stairway. Behind her the heat from the fire was making the door to her room warm.

Catherine covered her nose with the tail of her petticoat and crouched in the corner. If she stayed in her room she would die. Her baby would die. And Patrick would never know that she was carrying his child. She should have told him. She should have insisted that they stay in the swamp, in their little cabin by the pond covered with pink water lilies.

And then she heard someone calling her. "Catherine! Catherine!" It was Charles, in the corridor beyond her door. "Open the door, Catherine!"

She tried, but she couldn't. "I can't. It's locked."

Charles kicked the door, again and again, until finally it flew open and he dashed inside. Great strings of fire were coming from the roof, falling on the bed and bursting into flames.

"Quick, out on the balcony!"

"No, Simicco is out there."

"God in heaven, Catherine! Who is Simicco?"

"The Sun King. He'll kill you and take me away."

Charles stamped out a blaze on his coat sleeve and kicked open the balcony door. "We have to get away, Catherine. We're going to be married. We have to get out."

"You're right, Charles. We can't change what is going to happen. Help me!" Catherine started shoving the trunk away from the shutters leading to the balcony. At that moment there was an explosion on the lower level, hurling new flames toward the ceiling above the open stairwell.

"No, that was gunpowder. We're being fired at!" Charles screamed, suddenly seeing the flames on all sides. "We're doomed. We're going to die right here." He started to sink to the floor.

Catherine caught sight of Patrick slipping through the gate. He stopped in the courtyard where he could see Charles tugging at Catherine's arm.

"Forrest!" Patrick yelled. "Let her go!"

Then he realized that it wasn't Charles who was holding Catherine so much as it was Catherine pulling Charles. She was trying to save the fool, who'd panicked in the flames.

Patrick started toward the balcony, when a figure slammed into his lower legs, knocking him to the ground. It was an Indian, a very tall Indian, wearing war paint on his body and a tall plumed headdress.

"Simicco! Bloody hell!"

Patrick and the Indian rolled across the courtyard, Simicco's war cries loud enough to be heard over the confusion in the street beyond. Charles was still whimpering inside the room as Catherine grabbed a rug and tried to beat out the fire on the balcony so they could get to the steps. She'd almost succeeded when the roof caved in, closing off their way to safety. Now the fire was all around them.

"Oh, God, Charles. We have to jump!" Catherine looked down into the courtyard and searched for the best spot. Where were Jillico and Pharaoh? Patrick had escaped death at the prison and now he was going to die at the hands of a madman.

"I can't do it, Catherine. We're going to die!" Charles moaned.

Simicco had the physical advantage over Patrick this time. He was pressing his thumbs into Patrick's throat, closing off the airway, squeezing out the life that Pharaoh and Jillico had saved only minutes before.

Dimly, Patrick could hear Charles yelling and Catherine giving orders. "We'll try to get down the inside steps."

Just as Patrick slid into total blackness he gave one last mighty heave. At that moment, Simicco was caught by a heavy blow to the head and fell forward across Patrick's half-numb body.

Jillico pulled Simicco off, and Pharaoh helped Patrick to his feet. A strangled cry from Catherine

brought Patrick to his senses enough to plunge into the
house to get to Catherine. The inner walls were burning. The rooms were so filled with smoke that he
couldn't breathe. The staircase began to fall away as
he climbed it, he reached the upper floor just as the
stairs collapsed. He could hear Catherine's voice.

"Holy hell, Charles. Stop yowling and get over
here."

"First two thieves stole my reward money for that
pirate, and now my house is burning up. It's all your
fault, Catherine. We're all going to die!" Charles
screamed.

"The reward money doesn't matter, Charles. You're
still alive, or you will be if you'll get up and help me."

"Catherine!" Patrick yelled. "Where are you?"

"Patrick! I'm in here. In the middle of the room.
My bloody petticoat's on fire."

And then he found her, lifted her in his arms and
held her close to him, beating out the fire with his
hands. "I love you, Catherine Caden," he said. "I
want you to know that before we die."

"We aren't going to die, Patrick. We have to get out
of here on our own. I don't see any leprechauns
around to help us."

He started toward the balcony, stumbled and fell
across the prostrate figure of Charles Forrest, who was
curled into a little ball near the window.

"Get up, Forrest. I don't want you to die before I
kill you," Patrick said, letting Catherine down while
he dragged Charles to his feet. He thrust both Charles
and Catherine onto the balcony.

"Wait, Simicco is out there," Catherine said.

"Yes, I know, he and I just discussed the future of the city. We had a difference of opinion on living in town and in the swamp."

They had almost made it to safety when a tree came crashing down, falling across the end of the balcony that was still standing, bringing the roof down to meet it, slicing the wooden frame like a knife.

"Help me, Charles. I'll jump and catch Catherine, then you," Patrick said, propping up the roof with a collapsed beam. "We can still get away."

Charles seemed to pull himself together for a moment and leaned his shoulder into the post. Catherine crawled through, with Patrick following. "Come on, Forrest, I'll hold it from here."

But Charles only looked at Patrick and shook his head. "No, I can't jump. Take care of Catherine, McLendon."

"Damn it, Charles, get over here!"

"McLendon, there are no murder charges against *you*. There never were. Lopaz thought you'd die and nobody would ever know. It was only Stone the pirate who was wanted—for piracy. I'm sorry, Catherine."

The flooring began to creak. Patrick knew that they had only moments. He turned to Catherine as the last of the balcony gave way and they plunged to the courtyard, the fallen tree shielding them from the burning structure. Patrick tried, but there was no way to reach Charles.

Moments later they were in the street, caught up by the masses hurrying toward the river. Patrick had sent Pharaoh to secure their boat. He only hoped that Jillico had made it to safety. He'd lost contact with the Indian when he entered the house. Patrick pulled

Catherine close. If they could reach the Mississippi, they'd be safe from the fire.

There was confusion and terror among the frightened people gathered at the river. Slaves, carrying pitiful little boxes, stood next to the very wealthy, many of whom had escaped only in their night clothes.

"How will we ever find Jillico and Pharaoh?" Catherine asked, hanging on to Patrick as if she expected him to vanish at any moment.

"We'll let them find us."

"Us. I like that. Tell me again."

"Tell you what?"

"That you love me."

"I love you, Catherine Caden. Now, let's go."

"Where will we go now, Patrick?"

"I think the only safe thing for us to do is go to Heaven."

"Heaven. Yes, and we'll see Isabella?"

"That, too, my love."

Behind them, in the burning city, Charles Forrest sucked in his last hot breath and felt his lungs scream with pain. He'd never meant to hurt anybody. He'd had such dreams. But that outrageous Irishman had spoiled everything.

Catherine hadn't understood. Charles had loved her. The dowry hadn't made any difference. Nothing had made any difference, except rejection. He couldn't take that. He never would. Leaving New Orleans as a failure was beyond his capabilities.

He'd captured Stone, and even that hadn't been enough. Charles had already lost his position. The word had come today that he was being replaced. Then Catherine had helped that pirate escape.

But in that last moment he realized that he hadn't been a total failure; he'd saved Catherine. And nobody could take that away from him.

Not ever.

Chapter Seventeen

Simply reaching the upper end of the levee was an exhausting ordeal, Catherine found. Fleeing people were knocked down and trodden upon. The heat was unbearable, and the air filled with thick smoke that clogged her lungs and made her eyes sting.

The worst of the criminal element quickly discovered that the people escaping the fire had brought along whatever gold and jewels they could get their hands on in their haste. And they began to search for those people who looked most vulnerable.

Catherine feared for their lives, for the life of their unborn babe. It wasn't fair. Now that she and Patrick were free of their other problems they were about to die because of a fire. She'd braved the disapproval of her family, the elements, Indians and the Spanish government, but now she felt a rising surge of panic.

"Patrick, I'm afraid." Her voice rose, her heart felt as if it were strangling in her throat. She was in a horrible childhood nightmare where her feet were moving and moving and she was still standing in one spot. "Can't we get away from all these people?"

"Hush, we'll get away," he said, shoving one man away and clearing a path for Catherine to follow.

Slowly they made progress. They were almost out of the worst of the melee when it happened. A warehouse exploded, sending its walls outward, pushing the crowd toward the water. This time the press of people carried Catherine and Patrick with it. There were new cries as people at the outer edge of the levee were shoved into the river, further fanning the citizens into a frenzy.

Patrick, already exhausted, reached inward and used the last of his strength to resist the push of those trying to get away from new dangers. Briefly, he considered throwing himself and Catherine into the river to be carried downstream away from the fire. But there were too many people already in the water who had panicked. Suppose they got caught by a person trying to save himself from drowning. No, this way was safer. Besides, his pirogue was upriver, and they needed the dugout to get home.

Behind him Patrick heard the shouts of policemen, who were trying to make order among the conflagration and resulting chaos. But they were too few to control this crowd, as well as try to prevent the spread of the fire.

By now, Patrick was practically dragging Catherine. He didn't have time to stop and reassure her. He knew that only luck had kept the riffraff from realizing they had the good citizens completely at their mercy. Sooner or later the criminal element would turn to more than theft and looting. Catherine wouldn't be safe until they were well out of New Orleans.

"Stay with me, Cat, darlin'. You can do it. We'll get out of here."

Patrick put his arm around Catherine and hugged her close, trying to shield her strawberry-colored hair from the view of an unruly group of men just ahead. It was obvious that the looters had taken advantage of the burning warehouse and helped themselves to kegs of strong spirits.

Patrick wiped his forehead, smearing soot across his face. That gave him an idea. Moments later Catherine's face was black and her hair was covered with a turban made from a section of one of her petticoats.

Finally he reached the end of the levee and the safety of the trees. They were away from the fire and the crowd, yes, but traveling in the darkness, through the liquid landscape ahead was a danger of a different kind. Though Patrick would willingly have taken on an English army, the Louisiana swamp was an enemy that didn't always play fair.

Catherine tried to hurry, but she was exhausted, as was he. She hoped that he could find a place where they could rest, or they'd perish because their fatigue would make them overlook some danger they'd normally have seen.

There was her child to think about. Patrick still didn't know about the baby. She should have told him back at the house, when he'd told her that he loved her. But she'd been so filled with joy at his words that she hadn't been able to speak. Then the fire had kept her from sharing their wonderful news. She'd tell him once they reached safety.

"Wait here, Catherine," he said finally. "I need to find us a dry spot to spend the night. Traveling through the swamp by darkness isn't safe."

"No," she said desperately, "I'll go with you. I can't let you leave me again, ever again."

Catherine clung to him. She was right, he knew. They were together, whatever happened.

Behind them the city of New Orleans blazed like an inferno in the night sky. Explosions marked the warehouses where gunpowder was stored. The conflagration would have been an awesome spectacle if they had not realized the tragic destruction.

By now, Patrick was almost carrying Catherine. She simply put one foot in front of the other, trusting that there would be solid ground beneath it. Sometimes there wasn't, and she stumbled into the inky water. Both she and Patrick were cold and wet.

The moon cast a watery light on them. Filtered by the smoke, it was a fool's light that turned the landscape into an eerie, unreal place where earth and sky came alive with slithery things that brushed Catherine's bare arms and slid over her feet and legs.

They circled a massive live oak, climbing the roots that had been left exposed by the last flood. The scream of a wild animal suddenly broke through the night, cutting through Catherine like the cry of a pig she'd heard being slaughtered when she was a child.

Catherine stumbled and fell. "I can't go any farther, Patrick. Can't we rest?"

"We're almost there, Catherine, where I left my boat. I'll carry you."

He lifted her and held her close, feeling the tremors rack her body and wishing he could take away the awful things she'd been forced to face this night. "Just a few feet more," he said, and was rewarded by her straightening her shoulders and nodding agreement.

He wasn't surprised. Catherine had always astounded him with her strength of purpose. She never wavered from what she'd set her mind to do. There had been no subterfuge, no false pretense before, and there would be none now. He had asked her to keep going and she would.

It was Patrick who had played games, who had refused to open his heart and his soul, to admit his desperate need to love and be loved. Even when he'd been with Catherine in their hut on the bayou, he'd refused to accept what she was offering. They were lovers, yes. She loved him and he let her, because he knew that it was safe. He wasn't good enough for her. His name would always be tainted. He ought to do the right thing—he'd send her home to her family. But—

He needed Catherine. He wanted Catherine. They belonged together. Tonight had taught him how precious life was. But that was the selfish way to justify his actions. Being with Patrick might be what Catherine wanted, too, but it wasn't the best thing for her.

Even Charles, in the end, had made his own sacrifice for Catherine. As badly as he'd behaved, he'd redeemed himself by saving Catherine.

In his mind's eye, Patrick could still see the flames licking at the balcony, threatening to engulf Catherine any second. But they'd saved each other, and now it was up to Patrick to save them one last time.

Because he loved Catherine. Because she demanded that he give to her as much as she was giving to him. She'd put her life, her heart and her soul in his hands, and it was up to him to accept her gift or throw it away. Tonight, until he got her to safety, he'd have these last few precious hours with the woman he loved. Then he'd send her back to Cadenhill.

They reached the place where he'd left the pirogue. After checking it for snakes, he helped Catherine inside and crawled in with her. He wasn't comfortable with traveling the bayou at night, but at least the boat was dry enough to lie in.

"We'll rest for a few hours, then start upriver."

"Yes," was all Catherine could manage as they collapsed in each other's arms.

Patrick folded his arms around her because he knew how badly she needed protection. Catherine, who'd never backed down to anybody or anything, was being asked to be strong again, and she was trusting him to keep her safe.

He cursed under his breath and swore he'd spend the rest of his life doing just that. He held her for a long time, waiting until he felt her breathing slow.

They slept.

The next morning Catherine opened her eyes to a smoky overcast sky with dirty gray clouds that obscured the sun. But the fire had warmed the air and dried her soot-stained petticoat. For a moment an errant ray cut through the mist and touched her skin. It brought a feeling of hope with its brightness.

They were crossing the Mississippi, Patrick's strong arms poling the flat boat first one way, then another to make use of the current.

Sometime during the night he'd removed his shirt. She was wearing it now. She was sore and stiff. Their trek through the wilderness had taken its toll of their strength. But they'd survived the December night and all the perils they'd faced. There were just the two of them and that was fine.

Catherine found great pleasure in watching the ripple of his muscles as he worked. She knew now that the scars on his body had come from being beaten by Captain Lopaz and she winced. Just remembering brought back the picture of the Spaniard who'd caused Patrick so much grief. But that was over now, too. By all accounts Lopaz was gone, perished in the bayou near the Indian village.

And she and Patrick had escaped. They'd come through so much, the two of them. And now, finally, they were free to be together. For now she didn't want to think about what had happened. She wanted to simply lie here and watch him, watch his beautiful stern face and steady blue eyes. Unconsciously she laid her hand across her stomach, connecting with the child in reassurance.

She'd been watching Patrick for a long time before his gaze dropped to meet hers and the blue eyes began to crinkle at the corners.

"Good morning, darlin'"

"Oh, yes, and it is a good morning."

That was when her stomach growled. She caught her lower lip between her teeth as she realized that Patrick had heard it as well.

"You're hungry."

"Yes, and I'm dirty, and I'm probably the worst looking thing since my little sister fell into the fireplace and came out smeared with soot and ashes."

"I think you're beautiful, ashes and all."

A seabird flew overhead, letting out a raucous cry as it dipped to the water in front of them and picked up a small fish.

Even the birds eat. Catherine swallowed hard and tried to find something other than food on which to focus her attention.

"How are you going to get this boat upriver? I don't think your pole is long enough to reach the bottom, is it?"

"In some places. But you're right. We're going up the bayou. That's easier than traveling against the current."

"How long will it take us to get back to Heaven?"

That stopped him for a moment. He could have told her that since he'd awakened with her in his arms, he thought they were already there. "We'll be at Isabella's place tomorrow, providing I can find the man I'm looking for."

"Man? What man?"

"He's a Frenchman, one of the Acadians who lives out here in the bayou. He knows this country better than I do. He's going to get us back."

"How do you know him?"

"We've done a spot of business now and again."

"Does he have food?"

"Oh, yes. He has about anything anybody needs."

His name was Louis and he had a real house and real food, or at least he was getting food ready when they arrived.

"'Allo, Stone, *mon ami*. You bring the black-faced *pichouette* with you?"

"Black-faced?" Patrick looked at Catherine and laughed. "Yes she does seem to have a dirty face, and an empty stomach. What are the chances of some soap and a little food?"

"Good! Come inside, we will make a feast."

The big dark-skinned man was holding a trap, filled with dark-colored moving creatures. Catherine, wiping her face on her petticoat, followed the two men onto the porch where she caught sight of her reflection in a piece of broken mirror hanging on the log wall.

She'd been more right than she knew when she compared herself to her little sister. Her face was black and her hair tied with a white kerchief, like one of the New Orleans street vendors. She began to laugh.

"Oh, Patrick, I can't eat like this. Where is that soap and water?"

Moments later Catherine was using the square of fabric from her head, first as a washcloth and finally as a towel. At least now her face was clean, though the rest of her was pretty sad looking. She thought back to how proud she'd been in her new dress when she attended her first ball with Patrick.

And she thought of how little that mattered now. She'd been only a child playing at being a woman. Now she was a woman.

Louis gave her a big smile and pulled out the iron pot hanging over the fireplace by the long arm on which it was hooked. He opened his wooden trap and held it over the pot, allowing the contents to fall into the boiling water.

"What are those things?" Catherine asked.

"Crawfish. The delicacy of the bayou. First we boil them, then we add them to the stew and eat them."

"I don't think I want to know any more," Catherine said, turning her backside to the fire. "I'm hungry enough to eat almost anything, but I don't want to know the details."

By the time the sun was straight overhead they'd filled their stomachs with the highly seasoned stew and beans and all three of them were climbing into the pirogue.

Patrick was right, Catherine thought. It was better to have a guide who knew where they were going. Louis kept up a steady commentary in that strange way he had of talking, all the while cutting across waterways, heading up one and down the other until they were completely enclosed in a world of cypress trees and moss.

"You are Stone's lady?" Louis asked.

"I am Stone's lady," she agreed. "We're going to be married."

"Ah, yes, it's good to have a woman. My woman, she died. I have not found another so good."

"He's too scared to look," Patrick explained, avoiding a response to Catherine's comment on marriage. "Louis is a good catch. He owns all the land between New Orleans and Necktie Bend on the west side of the river. He grows vegetables, tobacco and oysters."

"Oysters?"

"*Oui, chérie,* but I don't grow them, I just harvest them and remove the pearls from their shells. They thank me an' the ladies in New Orleans thank me."

"Pearls? Here in the swamp?"

"*Oui,* here in Louis's oysters."

Catherine took another look at their host. He appeared fierce because of his size, but it was obvious that he had a great deal to offer a woman who wanted her own home and—

"Patrick! Sally!"

"What about Sally?"

"Oh, I was just thinking that she'd be just about perfect for Louis, don't you think?"

"Who is this Sally?" Louis asked with a scowl. "I don't care much for the Spanish ladies. And those society women, they wear my pearls, but they have no wish to share my bed."

"Sally is an angel, Louis, a real angel with golden hair, a heart of gold and a strong wish to have her own home with her own bed."

Maybe it was the sense of well-being that came from knowing that Patrick wasn't wanted for murder. He was still wanted for being a pirate, but she'd worry about that later. Or, perhaps she wouldn't. Patrick was her world. If it took being a pirate's wife, so be it.

She thought about Sally, waiting for a man of her own to love. Maybe it was a lingering sense of guilt over what happened to Charles. Maybe it was escaping from Simicco and his plans for her future, but Catherine took comfort in thinking about Sally and this big, happy Frenchman.

By the next afternoon they were crossing the river to get back to the levee at Natchez-under-the-Hill.

Heaven was lit up like some celestial crown. Everything about it was light and bright and joyous.

The travelers looked like gypsies. Patrick's beard and hair still smelled of smoke from the fire, and his clothes reflected their trek through the swamp. He stopped, looked at Catherine and grinned. Catherine pulled his shirt together across her chemise, glanced down at her tattered petticoat and laughed out loud.

"We're a fine-looking pair," she said as the three of them climbed up the street toward Isabella's house of pleasure. Past the stilts that held the building out over the water, and around to the front. Catherine realized that she'd never seen Isabella's house from the front.

"That we are, darlin'. I'm thinking you've got to stop traveling in your petticoat."

Patrick locked his arm around her waist, gave her a light kiss as he knocked.

Pharaoh opened the door and let out a yell. "Praise de Lord! You be here."

"Cat!" Sally raced down the hall and threw her arms around her friend. "You're safe."

"We're safe," Catherine said, and hugged the girl who'd been so good to her. "I've brought someone to meet you. Sally, this is Louis."

The large Frenchman came to stand before Sally. He looked her over, circled her carefully and came back to his starting point. "*Oui, très bien,* she is an angel. I will have to consider whether I will suit."

"What does he mean, Catherine?" Sally was backing away.

"I'll explain it all later," Catherine explained. "Louis was kind enough to bring us here and I promised him a good meal. Will you see that he's taken care of?"

Catherine watched as Sally cast a puzzled look at Catherine and back at Louis who was still staring at her as if she were a piece of sugar. Finally she agreed. The conversation between the big man and the blond girl seemed lively enough. Later, Catherine would explain her plan to Sally, if an explanation was needed. Something about Sally's soft laughter made Catherine think that the situation would take care of itself.

"Hello, Stone," Isabella said, as she reached the bottom of the stairs and stood beside Pharaoh. "And Cat. I see you survived the fire."

Patrick nodded. "News travels fast."

"Pharaoh told us the city was burning. He couldn't find you so he came here to wait."

"Jillico?"

There was an imperceptible shake of Pharaoh's head as he answered, "He safe, too."

Catherine let out a deep sigh and rested her head against Patrick's shoulder, gazing up at him with overflowing emotion.

"It was awful, Isabella," Catherine said, closing her eyes briefly as she remembered Charles and their narrow escape.

"Blocks of houses and businesses were burned," Patrick said. "People were driven to the levee. I don't know how any of the buildings survived. Most of the warehouses are gone."

"Yes, and that will bring more people here. But that is another problem. For now, you're safe and Pharaoh said that you'd be coming. Should we prepare for a wedding?"

"As soon as possible," Catherine agreed brightly.

Patrick's answer was less definite. "For now, we just need food and rest. Do you think you could provide a room for Catherine and me? We need to rest."

"Rest?" Isabella let out a mock gasp. "Miss Cat O'Conner is going to entertain a gent?"

"Only one, Isabella, only her future husband," Catherine said with a blush.

"And I suppose you want my bed, again?"

Catherine's blush deepened. "No, I think I'd rather have another room, one without a tunnel. I have no intention of giving Patrick a way to escape again."

Patrick smiled. All the rooms had escape hatches, but he had no wish to use one. When he and Catherine parted it wouldn't be done in secret, with matters left unsettled. And they did have to talk, but one look at the expression in her eyes and he knew it wouldn't be tonight.

Tomorrow he'd have to think about right and wrong and future plans. But tonight, Patrick had a few questions for Miss Catherine Caden, beginning with the name Cat O'Conner.

Chapter Eighteen

The room was prepared and waiting, softly lit, with the bed turned back. A very large copper tub filled with steaming water had been placed before the fire.

And Pharaoh.

"How'd you get out of New Orleans and back here first?" Patrick asked curiously.

"De Indian brought me."

"Jillico?"

"No, the other one, Simicco."

"Where is he now?"

"Gone. They both gone. Jillico say let the king go. He say de Natchez are no more and dat Simicco have to find a new life, in a place across the desert, a place of de sun, where other peoples build mounds."

"And Jillico?"

"He gone to see to the crops at Rainbow's End."

"The crops?" Patrick didn't know what to say. Jillico was seeing to the future, a future Patrick would live without Catherine. Jillico wouldn't know that, but he'd understand. He and Jillico had been together a long time. More than that, they were friends. True friendship was a thing Patrick had too seldom known.

"Jillico say you look after Miss Catherine. The Natchez are leaving this land to you. One day you and your children will—" he frowned as he tried to repeat the exact words "—will bring peace out of chaos, just lak in the vision."

Catherine felt a swell of sadness in her heart. She had never understood Moria's belief that Catherine was sent to save the Natchez people. But she did understand that Moria had had a mission—both Moria and Charles. They'd failed, and now they were gone. Only Simicco had escaped. It didn't seem fair. But maybe the Great Spirits had other purposes for his life. There were so many things she didn't understand.

She could only know about herself. The only person she'd come to save was Patrick and they were together once again.

"I feel sorry for Jillico," she said. "He lost his sister because of me."

"Don't worry 'bout dat boy. He'll find his own happiness." Pharaoh gave the room one last look and moved toward the door. "I hope you're not mad 'cause we let Simicco go."

"No," Patrick said, "perhaps it's better this way. At least it's ended." He closed the door and turned toward Catherine. They were alone and suddenly he felt awkward. They'd been together intimately, survived a fire and come back to safety.

Catherine was standing by the window, looking out into the night, remembering the first time she'd come to Heaven, to Patrick's bed. She turned back to him and gave him an impish grin. "About that bath, Patrick McLendon. I think we'd better get to it. If I'm as sooty as you are, we'll turn Heaven into Hell."

She began to remove her clothing, beginning with his shirt, dropping it from her shoulder and letting it slide down her arms to the floor.

Patrick caught his breath.

Next came the chemise, which she unlaced with wooden fingers, so stiff that the deliberate action became even slower. Then came the petticoat, singed around the bottom and muddy from their boat ride back to Natchez, and finally her pantalets.

"Now, Catherine, about Cat O'Conner. I'd like an explanation."

"Cat O'Conner is an entertainer. I don't have a harpischord, Patrick, darling, but would you like me to sing?"

She tilted her head and allowed the chemise to slide to the floor.

Outside the rain began to fall. A quick little breeze swept through the open shutters and blew out the candle, leaving only the light of the fire.

"The only kind of singing I want out of you," he growled, "is in response to me loving you." He made a move toward her, then turned toward the shutter to close it.

"No, leave it open," Catherine said. "I will always love storms. One brought us together again. I want you to love me, Patrick, while the rain falls, to take away all the pain and grief, to make me clean again. I need you so much."

"I need you, too, Catherine. I need you to bring peace and joy to my life. I wish it could be like this always."

"Then stop cavorting around," she snapped, "and take off your clothes."

Talking could wait just a little longer. They had this night together. He wouldn't spoil it yet.

Just as slowly, just as deliberately as she had done, Patrick removed his clothes, beginning with his boots. Next came the oversize shirt he'd borrowed from Louis, and finally his trousers. He stood before her, completely naked and ready to make the music of love.

But Catherine was never one to wait for the thing she wanted, and she didn't wait now. Instead she flung herself into his arms, burying her face against his chest.

Happiness bubbled up inside her until she thought she might explode with the sheer exhilaration of touching him, this man with the stern blue eyes and the once-golden hair.

"First, our bath, Sunshine," he said, and strode to the copper tub with her in his arms.

"No, first there is something I must know. You said you loved me, Patrick. Back there at the fire. Tell me again."

He couldn't lie to her.

"I love you, Catherine. No matter what happens I will always love you. You are everything good in my life. It will kill me to let you go."

"Then I won't let you," she said, wrapping her legs around his waist and tightening her arms about his neck.

He stepped into the tub and settled himself, still holding her astride his body, feeling his engorged manhood caught between them. The hot water covered them, lapping over the edge of the tub and spilling to the floor. Neither felt the small burned places on their skin. The fire of their kisses obliterated the pain and made more precious the miracle of their escape.

The emotion that surged up inside them was like a flower, opening to the sun, petal by petal.

His skin was salty as she brushed her lips across his chest, and along his neck. He tasted only sweetness, a full dizzying sweetness that overwhelmed and gentled his rough motions. His hands stroked her face and hair.

Her mewing little whispers urged him on. "I won't ever let you go again. Our child needs a father."

"Our child?"

"Yes, Patrick. We are to have a child in the spring."

Patrick's heart raced at such a pace that he couldn't speak. There was no breath in his lungs, no air in the room. "A child? You're carrying our child?"

"I am, and I expect you to make an honest woman of me immediately. I don't expect to bring a bastard into this world."

Bastard. His son a bastard? Patrick's heart felt as if it had come to a dead stop. "Never! But how?"

"I'd think that was rather obvious, my Irishman. The instrument is that magnificent part of you that is caught between us."

"Oh, Catherine, I almost lost you!" He lifted her so that his mouth could claim hers, fierce and possessively. She responded by opening her lips and taking his tongue inside, inviting him, telling him that she was his, totally and forever. All that she ever was, or hoped to be was his.

There was a breathlessness inside her, a quivering that centered in the spot that now cradled the male part of him. She remembered that first night, here in Isabella Angel's Heaven, when he didn't know it was she in his arms. He had been rough that night, for a time, then he'd stilled his movements and loved her so gently. He'd given her a child and tonight, he'd love her again.

She gasped as his hands closed over her breasts, cupping them as he rubbed his thumbs across her nipples, then took one nipple into his mouth. She flung her head back, offering herself to him without restraint.

Awareness dissolved into only the hazy sensation of touching and being touched. The inner warmth began to flame hotter and to move upward to her breasts and his mouth. His fingertips splayed across her ribs and down, exploring every plane of her body, every new sunburst of heat that erupted beneath his touch.

For Patrick, his need for her rose, like some spring bubbling to the surface. He felt his body tightening, holding back, and he forced himself to wait until that moment when she crossed over the line of restraint and went wild with wanting.

She cried out, pleading, begging as he lifted her, letting his manhood find that place where it was meant to be. Stilling himself for a moment he basked in the wonder of sensation that erupted as they joined. Then she leaned forward, savagely capturing his lips with her own as she began to move, riding him, imploring, asking and, at that ultimate moment of response, tearing her lips away in a cry of ecstasy.

The bathwater was cold long before they soaped each other and washed the soot and ashes from their hair. They ate before the fire, feeding each other tiny slivers of fish and sweet cakes of rice. Patrick's hair was golden again and his blue eyes laughed with merriment as she fed him fruit with her lips and took it back again.

Later, as she sat wrapped in a blanket, Patrick dried her hair, threading it with his fingertips and spreading it across her bare shoulders to dry.

"When are you going to marry me, Patrick?"

The time had come to face the thing he'd pushed to the back of his mind, the thing that made it all impossible.

"You know this isn't settled yet," he answered in an oblique way. "I may not be accused of murder, but I'm not a free man. There's still the matter of my piracy and my prison escape."

"I've been thinking about that," she said softly, resting her head against his chest. "Patrick McLendon is a planter who owns a cotton plantation. Stone isn't. Patrick McLendon isn't a pirate, Stone is. Patrick McLendon is getting married, not Stone."

"But Stone and Patrick are the same person."

"I know that. Charles knew that. But the world doesn't."

"And worst of all, Catherine, I know it. I've given you a child, but I can't give you my name with honor. I would never allow my son to be a bastard, but at this moment, I don't know what to do."

She turned around in his arms, lifting her face to the light. "What would happen if Stone found a way to pay back what he's stolen?"

"Stone is broke. He couldn't buy one of your pigs in a mudhole. Without being a thief there's no way he could find the money to pay back what he's stolen."

"Maybe everybody he owes isn't entitled to be repaid. I was thinking of another way."

"I'm afraid to ask, Catherine, but what were you thinking?"

"An orphanage, or a shelter for families. That's it! With the fire burning everything, people are going to have a hard time for a while."

"So Stone, the pirate, is going to build a shelter and buy the dismissal of charges against him? How?"

"Well, Charles told me something I didn't know. I have a dowry. The judge arranged it, quite a nice one, from what Charles said. We could use that for a start."

"I don't think that would be nearly enough."

"But, wait, there's more. You recall that reward that Charles collected for turning Stone in?"

"Yes, though I didn't know he collected it."

"He did. And then on the way to watch your hanging, he was robbed, by an Indian and a black man."

"Jillico and Pharaoh?"

"I think so. Would that be enough? I could contact the governor and ask."

"No. You will do nothing. I will think about what I—what we will do and then we'll decide. You must let me do this. Will you agree?"

"Perhaps," Catherine began, biting back her smile of amusement over Patrick's attempt to be stern. "I never want to be accused of trying to make decisions for you, Patrick, but it is very late. Perhaps we could...I mean I'd like to suggest that if you're agreeable, we go to bed and consider this further."

"To bed? To consider pirates?"

"Well, one particular pirate anyway."

"No, wait. There's another little matter I want to talk about first. Stand up."

Catherine complied, allowing the blanket to fall to the floor.

Patrick's eyes didn't blink as he looked at her. She was a vision; her body the color of honey, as translucent as a pearl and yes, round where once there was only slenderness.

He dropped to his knees, laying his cheek against her stomach for a long gentle moment. With a kind of wonder he drew back and spread his fingers across her stomach, planting little kisses over every part of her.

"Is it really true? Is there a child, my child?"

"Yes, there must be, for I find I can no longer eat pork, and I'm getting very plump, don't you think?"

He leaned back and looked at her. "No, you are very small, mayhap too small to carry my child. I've heard it said that can make a birth difficult."

"Patrick darling, what is to be, will be. Besides, you have the magic of the little people to help. Won't they help me now as well?"

She was right. She had been from the beginning. What would be, would be. All other options had been eliminated. This was now and there was no point in worrying her with his fears. He searched for a way to push away that familiar darkness that seemed to reform inside him.

He wanted to give her everything. He wanted her to have pearls, beautiful garments to wear and a fine house to live in. That was what he'd planned. And yet here they were, in a house of pleasure, in a foreign land where he'd become an outlaw. But for now, none of that mattered. Just this moment in time.

"Sure and begorra!" he said, sliding his hands around her waist as he smiled. "I can see it now. You are growing very plump. Soon the little people will have to transport you by horse and wagon, instead of sliding over the rainbow."

Catherine nodded her head, glad that he'd joined in the game. "That means there'll be no room for treasure when we find it."

"The treasure is here, darlin'," he said, growing quite serious once more as his hands played about her hips. "It's just that I am quite large, Catherine, for a wee one like you."

Catherine looked down at him and grinned. "You're right about that. I can see one part of you that is very large. And, my bonny Irishman, this small person has learned well how to take care of that." She reached down and touched him.

He groaned. "You have, have you?"

"Oh, Patrick, my love, do not fear. Come lie with me."

The second time they made love slowly. They listened to the sound of the rain falling on the window ledge and bouncing inside. There were slow, deep kisses, gentle movements that spoke of care and giving. Until finally they lay in each other's arms, spent and content.

Outside the storm died down, rolling past the hill and downriver to New Orleans, where the city was already planning to rebuild. Catherine and Patrick had cleansed themselves of doubt and pain as the rain washed away the grime of the fire. As with the indigo fields, new seeds were already sprouting, seeds of the future, all their futures.

"I still don't understand why we don't just jump over a broom and call ourselves married," Patrick grumbled as Catherine shoved him out the door of the room where they'd spent the night making love. "And don't you think it's a little late to tell me that I must sleep alone?''

"Absolutely not. You will not share my bed again until we're properly married by a preacher, Patrick McLendon. Either you find one, or our child will be born in sin."

Isabella, who'd just come into the hallway, laughed and hid the pain she felt every time she saw Patrick look at Catherine.

Patrick gave up, as Catherine knew he would, and made the concession to her wishes by sending for the preacher from the settlement at Weatherby's Trading Post.

Mavis Weatherby brought the wedding gown that had come from Petersburg with Catherine all those months ago. She didn't comment on the alterations they were forced to make for Catherine to wear it, nor on the cradle that Pharaoh and the slave girl called Consuelo brought as a gift.

The wedding of Catherine Elizabeth Caden and Patrick McLendon took place on the twenty-first of December, in the parlor of the place called Heaven, in the area known as Natchez-under-the-Hill.

Sally stood up with the bride and the big Frenchman called Louis with the groom. There was a moment of pain in Patrick's eyes when he thought of Jillico, who should have been by his side and wasn't, and in Catherine's when she thought about her family far away at Cadenhill.

But for all the residents and the guests of the establishment, along with the other members of Patrick's crew, a happy time was being had by all.

The parlor was glittering with candles. Green vines had been woven into an arbor and winter berries made bouquets across the greenery. One of the other local establishments loaned Isabella their musician, who played a lively selection of saloon music, interspersed now and then with soulful hymns.

By the time the bride came down the stairs, the house was humming with Christmas cheer, both liquid and emotional. Catherine reached the arbor and came to a stop beside Patrick, who was resplendent in an emerald-green frock coat and yellow vest. The pale canary color matched the ivory lace on Catherine's satin wedding gown and made them look as if they were wrapped in sunlight.

Sunlight and satin.

The minister, who'd taken one look at Heaven and refused to perform a wedding ceremony in such a place—until he was told about the coming child—stood before them, plainly uncomfortable.

Had the dress not been so tight, or the room so crowded as to make it too warm, or the minister so long-winded, Catherine would have been fine. At least that was what Patrick told her when she came to as he was wiping her face with a damp cloth.

"You mean we aren't married yet?" She sat up, saw the corners of the room move and lay back down.

"Only half-married, I fear. I still have to say my part."

"Get that preacher," she snapped. "I don't intend to lose you now."

And so it was that from her place on a pink velvet couch, in the parlor of Heaven, Catherine Elizabeth Caden became Mrs. Patrick McLendon.

The dancing and feasting took up the early part of the night, the loving capped the activities with solemn joy and the promise of forever.

The following morning Catherine and Patrick slept late, then dressed and left their room with genuine regret. No matter where they went from here, neither would ever forget Heaven and how they had found it in each other's arms.

They went in search of their hostess to thank her for her kindnesses. They found the preacher, who'd stayed the night, in the kitchen having breakfast with the girls. He'd apparently gotten over his reluctance to being in such a place. Isabella was in her office, staring out at the muddy waters of the big river.

"We're leaving, Isabella," Patrick said. "Will you visit us at Rainbow's End when the baby comes?"

"Of course. I wouldn't miss the birth of my godchild for anything. But don't you think you're going to have a hard time explaining all this to a child?"

"Any child of Catherine's will probably explain her conception to me," Patrick said with a laugh and kissed Isabella on the cheek.

With a tear in her eye, Catherine held Patrick's arm tightly as they said goodbye to their friends.

A last hug from Sally was accompanied with the whisper, "Do you know that he's promised to drape my body in pearls? Dare I believe him?"

"Does it matter if he doesn't?" Catherine asked.

"No, I don't think it does."

Along with the crew and the slaves, Patrick and Catherine left once more for Rainbow's End. This time Catherine paid close attention to their route. She had no intention of having to find her way in and out alone, but you never know.

On arriving at the dock, Patrick consulted briefly with one of his hands before reseating himself on the flatboat, and nodding to the crew, who pushed off again.

"Where are we going now?"

"Just be patient, Mrs. McLendon. And for once, don't ask questions."

She kept quiet. There were times that it behooved a woman to be obedient. And then she thought back to the night, when over his objections, she'd come to Patrick's bed. There were times that it didn't.

She saw the pink before the cabin came into view.

"Patrick, the lilies, they're still blooming!"

"If they hadn't been we'd have painted them pink," he answered, giving her a loving smile.

"And the cabin, it's been repaired and white-washed. Oh, Patrick, a little bench by the pond. It's beautiful. How did you do it?"

"I didn't."

"Who?"

"It's your wedding present." Jillico stepped through the cabin door and stood waiting on the porch. "Come in."

Catherine almost capsized the boat in her eagerness to get out. "Holy hell," she swore. "Get me a tunic, or some men's pants. These skirts are in my way."

Patrick helped her out and joined her on the dock. "I seem to recall that you liked it better with no clothes at all," he whispered in her ear.

That brought her movement to an abrupt stop. She looked up at Patrick and took in a quick shallow breath. "Always!"

"If you want to be alone," Jillico called out, "you'd better check out what I've done and see if it meets your approval."

For a moment neither Patrick nor Catherine moved.

"Of course, you managed without any comforts before. My guess is that you won't even notice." He stepped out onto the porch.

"No, wait." Catherine tore herself away from the moment and moved into the cabin. "Oh, Jillico." There was newly built furniture, proper pots and pans and fresh bedding piled on a new bed. "You did all this?"

"I did. That's why I didn't get back to the wedding."

"How did you know?"

"Patrick sent word to the plantation."

"Thank you. But what about the owner? What will he think when he returns."

"The owner isn't a he, it's a she," Patrick said and handed Catherine a paper. "It's yours. I bought it for you as a wedding gift."

Joy first, then disbelief swept across her face. "How, Patrick? We need all our money for the family shelter. You didn't go out and rob anyone?"

"I did not. And neither did Stone."

"Then how?"

"It seems my small indigo crop brought a good price and I invested it in land. Rainbow's End now runs from the Mississippi all the way to this cabin.

Whatever happens, you'll have something that's yours."

"I already have something that's mine, a husband I love dearly and a baby, and—" she looked up at Jillico with tears in her eyes "—dear, dear friends who understand me and love me just the way I am."

Epilogue

Elizabeth Isabella McLendon was a baby when Thomas Pinckney negotiated the treaty with the Spanish for free navigation of the Mississippi in 1795.

The flatboats floated downriver, giving the Orleanians their first real look at the Americans who would settle the West. They weren't impressed. They'd take their money, but not welcome them into society.

Spain gave Louisiana back to France but Napoleon made no attempt to send officials to govern. The Spanish officials continued to rule without direction from Spain or interference from the French, eventually closing the port of New Orleans to all trade in 1802. George Houston McLendon was a year old when Patrick had to find another way to ship his cotton and sugar.

Thomas Jefferson signed the papers for the American purchase of the territory of Louisiana in 1803, just three months after the birth of Caden Louis McLendon.

"I want to go to the ceremonies, Patrick," Catherine said as she adjusted the baby in her arms so that he could nurse the breast she'd exposed.

"I'm not certain how safe you'd be," Patrick argued, eyeing his son with pride, and if the truth were known, with a bit of envy. "Tempers are flying high there. There're likely to be riots. New Orleans may belong to the United States, but it's still more French than English."

"Oh, pooh! That poor man is coming here into a hostile environment. Our new governor needs to see a friendly face. We're invited to the dinner following the official services. Besides, when did danger ever stopped me—us?"

She was right. Safety had never meant much to Catherine. Even after they donated funds to provide shelter for the homeless after the fire, Stone's pardon hadn't been forthcoming. Stone was no longer hunted, but he wasn't officially forgiven, either. That had never stopped Mrs. Patrick McLendon from claiming her place among the planters' wives along the Mississippi.

Nine-year-old Beth came running into the room. "Papa, come quick, my pig has babies, lots of babies. I want you to come and tell Houston that he has to go away. He's worrying Eunice."

"Pigs!" Patrick rolled his eyes back in exasperation. "It's hereditary. Okay, *chérie,* let's go and look at your pigs and stop your brother from interfering. We'll talk about going to New Orleans later," he told Catherine as he left the room, firmly in tow by a nine-year-old with her lips pursed and her eyes filled with devilment.

"That's all right, Papa," Beth said. "Consuelo has already packed our things. I think we ought to go to see the changing of the flags. After all, we're a part of history and we ought to be there."

Already packed? That figured. Patrick grinned. He didn't know why Catherine bothered to consult him. If he refused she had her own way of changing his mind. He felt a tingle shimmy up his backbone as he thought about the night ahead and how she'd come up with some new means of convincing him. She didn't have to; he'd already made up his mind to go.

New Orleans was rife with merriment. The French tricolor flag had been flown for the past twenty days over the Cabildo, the government building on the Place d'Armes where Governor Laussat held office.

There were no hotels, for the citizens of New Orleans offered no welcome to those passing through. Every plantation owner who visited had friends or family with whom they stayed. The McLendons were to be the guests of Patrick's banker, along with Louis and Sally, who'd left their growing family at home.

The day of the ceremony, Patrick, Catherine, Sally and Louis left the house and, with hundreds of others, walked about the newly rebuilt city. Beth had thrown a temper fit because she wasn't allowed to come, even after a passionate plea that it was part of her future as well.

They had traveled no more than a block before Patrick, acting on a hunch, turned back to discover the disobedient child lurking behind them. After a stern discussion about children who disobey their parents, she was allowed to accompany them, provided she remained silent and obedient.

"No frivolous cavorting, Beth!"

"Of course not, Papa," she agreed. "I'll be very serious, I promise."

Patrick gave his wife a solemn wink, seen only by the woman who understood its significance.

"Everything changes, my friend," Louis remarked as he looked around the town. "Now even the Negroes have slaves. There are gamblers, thieves, people plotting against the Spanish, against the Americans.''

"I know, but today everything seems quiet enough," Sally said, determined to enjoy the proceedings. "Let's go to the French Market and buy a sweet."

"What makes you think I can afford spending all this money?" Louis asked, in his most serious voice.

"Now, Louis," Sally said, "between you and Patrick, you could probably buy and sell the entire city. You've made a fortune from the sale of pearls and tobacco, and Patrick is the biggest cotton producer in the territory."

"She's right, my friend. With that gin your friend back in Petersburg invented and your new sugar mill, Rainbow's End is a pot of gold. Let us go where the ladies want."

"Not just yet," Catherine said. "The first order of the day is a stop by the governor's office."

"Why, Catherine? The ceremony doesn't start until later."

Patrick didn't like the satisfied gleam in his wife's eye, but as always, if she wanted to go, they'd go.

Inside the famous structure where all the laws were enacted and carried out, they were shown to the Spanish governor's office, where he was expecting them.

"Ah, my friend, Patrick, and the beautiful Mrs. McLendon. I very much appreciate your coming. I have one last act I wish to perform before leaving office."

Patrick and Louis looked at each other curiously. Though Patrick and the governor had a working relationship, none of the other three had ever been inside the government building.

The governor cleared his throat. "Friends, citizens, this day, December thirtieth, 1803, I have signed this document of pardon for the infamous pirate, Stone. All crimes are forgiven and removed from public record. Stone is forever hereafter a free man." He leaned forward to blot the signature, folded the paper and handed it to Patrick.

"I trust you will see that Señor Stone receives this document?"

Patrick could only nod his head. He didn't trust himself to speak. Although he'd known that Catherine carried on a busy correspondence with the governor, he'd never expected this. But then when had Catherine ever done what he expected?

"Thank you, Governor," Catherine said quietly. "Will you join us for a walk around the square?"

"I'm afraid I have official duties that will keep me here, but I hope I'll see you at dinner this evening?"

"We'd be delighted," Catherine said. "Now, Patrick McLendon, I'm ready for some excitement. What about you?"

He was ready. Patrick was always ready for whatever new adventure Catherine planned. He was still speechless as they left the Cabildo and stepped outside into the Place d'Armes.

"Who was the pirate, Stone, Papa?" Beth asked, tugging on her father's arm.

"He was just a man I once knew," he answered.

"A very brave man," Catherine added, "who also liked pigs."

They passed a woman hawking flowers on one corner, and made their way to the French Market where they inspected wiggly crawfish, and eggs wrapped with Spanish moss. Sally stopped at that counter and questioned the freshness of the eggs, whereupon the seller broke one on his stand and let it slide to the street.

There were meat vendors, hunters with fowl and turtles. Chickens squawked and birds screamed. There were Germans, Indians, Frenchmen and blacks all together in one place, in harmonious confusion.

Everywhere there was laughter and music and people. Suddenly a very dark-skinned man stepped in front of Beth and threw something to the ground. It burst into blue and red flames. Beth stopped and stared into the flames, then turned and looked around in confusion.

"Oh, Papa!" she said.

"What's wrong, *chérie?*"

"Who was that man?"

"What man?"

"The tall Indian with the plumes on his head. He was right there, looking at me with dark evil eyes."

Catherine felt a shiver of cold wash over her. She, like Patrick, searched the crowd for any sign of a tall man with plumes, but they saw nothing.

"Don't be afraid, Beth. He was probably just one of the slaves, celebrating the occasion."

Nothing more was said and the child seemed to accept the explanation. But for the rest of the day Catherine found herself searching the crowd, looking for him, the tall dark Indian wearing plumes.

Simicco.

But there was no sign of him and eventually she put it out of her mind. That was in the past. This was the future.

The American troops moved toward the city gates, their band playing the music of France and the United States. The Spanish troops met them and escorted them inside the Cabildo on the Place d'Armes, where the American representatives presented their credentials to the governor.

The contents were read to the officials who'd been invited to listen, and the delivery of the province to the United States was proclaimed. The keys of the city were handed over to Governor William Charles Cole Claiborne, who welcomed the people as American citizens.

They then moved to the windows that looked down on the Place d'Armes, where six nationalities of new citizens mingled in the courtyard. The tricolor was lowered and the Stars and Stripes slowly raised until they met midway on the staff where they were saluted. The American flag was raised and the French flag brought down and delivered into the hands of the French officials.

Catherine felt her heart swell. Perhaps it was Beth's sighting a man with plumes that made her remember Simicco's prediction that her child would play a part in the future of a new land. He'd been right. She would. They all would.

Patrick slid his arm around Catherine's waist and squeezed her as tightly as he could. He was free now, his name finally and forever cleared. There would never be another Stone; there'd be no need. He and Catherine had found their heaven and their life was good.

* * * * *

Author's Note

Little is known about the Indian tribes called the Mississippians, or the Mound Builders who occupied the Mississippi Valley. Seventeenth-century French explorers provide some of the written information about one tribe known as the Natchez.

They were successful farmers, who lived in permanent villages with sharply drawn laws governing religion and society. They made friends with the early explorers and settlers. At the same time they were fierce warriors who, when treated unfairly, killed their enemies and placed their heads atop the poles that marked the corners of their ceremonial grounds.

Their history also includes the legend of the appearance of a messenger from the Great Spirit called the Great Sun.

In a time of much chaos and uncertainty, the Great Sun was proclaimed the absolute ruler of the Natchez. He was aided by a powerful female called the White Woman. Nothing is known of the origins of either ruler, only that they established a new structure of society, creating laws and customs by which the tribe was to live. It was believed that so long as the Sun King and the White Woman were honored, the Natchez would prevail. But the Sun King was captured by the French and sent to Hispaniola, or Saint Domingue, as the island was often called, to be a slave. There is no reference to the fate of the White Woman. In fact it is not known that she was white. The title may have referred to the way she painted her face. But the Natchez knew that chaos would remain until the Sun King and the White Woman returned.

There are references to both slaves and freed men fleeing the slave revolt on Santo Domingo to seek safe haven in New Orleans. It is known that these refugees set up the first theater in New Orleans. Some of the members of this group were said to have been slaves who were trained as entertainers on their native islands. For the purposes of this story, I have taken the liberty of expanding this segment of New Orleans history. If it didn't happen in exactly this way, it could have.

We do know that in 1729 the French governor of the Louisiana Territory ordered the Natchez to vacate their main village so that he could build a plantation for himself.

The Natchez complaints met with no success. Finally, in a desperate attempt to hold on to what was theirs, they attacked the French and killed more than two hundred people, including the governor.

The French retaliated by sending troops who, with the assistance of their Choctaw allies, overran the Natchez, and except for a few who escaped into the bayous, captured the entire tribe. The Indians who weren't burned at the stake included the ruler of the Natchez people, called the Sun King, and his coruler, known as the White Woman; they were shipped away to become slaves on the sugarcane plantations of Santo Domingo. With this act the tribe known as the Natchez, and much of the Mississippian culture, came to an end.

Harlequin® Historical

Nora O'Shea had fled to Arizona seeking freedom, but could she ever find love as a mail-order bride?

MARIANNE WILLMAN

From the author of THE CYGNET and ROSE RED, ROSE WHITE comes a haunting love story full of passion and power, set against the backdrop of the new frontier.

Coming in November 1993 from Harlequin

Don't miss it! Wherever Harlequin books are sold.

Relive the romance...
Harlequin and Silhouette
are proud to present

by Request™

A program of collections of three complete novels by the most-requested authors with the most-requested themes. Be sure to look for one volume each month with three complete novels by top-name authors.

In September: **BAD BOYS**
    Dixie Browning
    Ann Major
    Ginna Gray

No heart is safe when these hot-blooded hunks are in town!

In October: **DREAMSCAPE**
    Jayne Ann Krentz
    Anne Stuart
    Bobby Hutchinson

Something's happening! But is it love or magic?

In December: **SOLUTION: MARRIAGE**
    Debbie Macomber
    Annette Broadrick
    Heather Graham Pozzessere

Marriages in name only have a way of leading to love....

Available at your favorite retail outlet.

REQ-G2

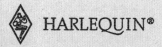

Harlequin® Historical

From *New York Times* bestselling author

The powerful story of two people as brave and free as the elusive wild mustang which both had sworn to capture.

A Harlequin Historicals Release
December 1993

1993 Keepsake

CHRISTMAS

Stories

Capture the spirit and romance of Christmas with KEEPSAKE CHRISTMAS STORIES, a collection of three stories by favorite historical authors. The perfect Christmas gift!

Don't miss these heartwarming stories, available in November wherever Harlequin books are sold:

ONCE UPON A CHRISTMAS by Curtiss Ann Matlock
A FAIRYTALE SEASON by Marianne Willman
TIDINGS OF JOY by Victoria Pade

ADD A TOUCH OF ROMANCE TO YOUR HOLIDAY SEASON WITH KEEPSAKE CHRISTMAS STORIES!

HX93

When the only time you have for yourself is...

STOLEN *moments* ™

Christmas is such a busy time—with shopping, decorating, writing
cards, trimming trees, wrapping gifts....

When you do have a few *stolen moments* to call your own, treat yourself
to a brand-new *short* novel. Relax with one of our Stocking Stuffers—
or with all six!

Each STOLEN MOMENTS title
is a complete and original contemporary romance that's the perfect
length for the busy woman of the nineties! Especially at Christmas...

And they make perfect **stocking stuffers**, too! (For your mother,
grandmother, daughters, friends, co-workers, neighbors, aunts,
cousins—all the other women in your life!)

Look for the STOLEN MOMENTS display in December

STOCKING STUFFERS:

HIS MISTRESS Carrie Alexander
DANIEL'S DECEPTION Marie DeWitt
SNOW ANGEL Isolde Evans
THE FAMILY MAN Danielle Kelly
THE LONE WOLF Ellen Rogers
MONTANA CHRISTMAS Lynn Russell

HSM2

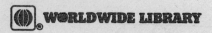 **WORLDWIDE LIBRARY**